T0046226

"*The Thorn Puller* should go down not just as one of the best Japanese novels in translation of this year, but of recent years. . . . Angles does an outstanding job recreating Ito's variety of inventive styles and approaches to language in fluid English. . . . Ito folds in the mythic with the mundane to connect the everyday types of suffering with the most divine kind of metamorphosis. This shape-shifting work flexes innovative literary devices while maintaining a Joycean directness in its approach to the crude banalities of life. The musical, playful language makes the story not only a joy to read but adds dense layers of spiritual, historical, and literary depth to one woman's tale." **ERIC MARGOLIS, *JAPAN TIMES***

"*The Thorn Puller* is a strong affirmation of life. . . . Working collaboratively with the author, Jeffrey Angles, a recognized poet in both English and Japanese, has done a wonderful job translating this work." **ERIK R. LOFGREN, *WORLD LITERATURE TODAY***

"Ito's chameleonic prose (each chapter ends with influences and inspirations) confronts mortality, cultural conflicts, religious comforts, and waning relationships, embellished with all manner of welcoming, unfiltered, surprisingly humorous honesty about the universally quotidian, from pimple-popping to good sex." **TERRY HONG, *BOOKLIST***

"Ito's work, which has long drawn us in, reaches a crescendo here, working off a base in fractured daily life: minefields of love and hate, frailty and death, identities and languages heard and unheard, a clash of cultures and religions in the context of the day by day. And all of this she sets against deep images of Japanese lore and literature, ancient and immediately modern, prose transformed into poetry: a contemporary master at the height of her many long-honed powers." **JEROME ROTHENBERG, EDITOR OF *TECHNICIANS OF THE SACRED***

"In Ito's literary vision, life unfolds more as a stream of language than a series of plot points. With each phase of life she records, Ito shows how language emerges from the rituals of social reproduction that mark the coming and going of generations, from childbirth to eldercare." **EVA ROSENFELD, *CHICAGO REVIEW***

The Thorn Puller

HIROMI ITO

Translated by Jeffrey Angles

Stone Bridge Press • Berkeley, California

Published by
Stone Bridge Press
P. O. Box 8208, Berkeley, CA 94707
TEL 510-524-8732 • sbp@stonebridge.com • www.stonebridge.com

This publication has received the William F. Sibley Memorial Subvention Award for Japanese Translation from the University of Chicago Center for East Asian Studies Committee on Japanese Studies.

The MONKEY imprint was established by Stone Bridge Press in partnership with MONKEY New Writing from Japan.

Cover design and original artwork by Hello Kirsten. Visit www.hellokirsten.com.

Originally published in Japan as *Toge-nuki Jizo: Shin Sugamo Jizo engi.*

First printing 2022; reprinted 2023.

Printed in the United States of America.

p-ISBN 978-1-7376253-0-8 (paperback)
p-ISBN 978-1-7376253-2-2 (casebound)
e-ISBN: 978-1-7376253-1-5 (ebook)

Contents

Translator's Introduction

HIROMI ITO IS ONE OF Japan's most prominent women writers—a fiercely independent poet, novelist, and essayist who has consistently explored issues of motherhood, childbirth, the female body, sexuality, and mythology in dramatic and powerfully vivid language. Following a divorce, she left Japan and settled in southern California in 1997, beginning a life of shuttling back and forth across the Pacific that eventually culminated in her taking permanent residency in the United States and citizenship in 2018. In the years since she first resided in America, she has moved beyond her earlier focus on the female body and started writing about migration, national identity, death and dying, and the cultural pressures placed upon women to be caregivers.

In 2006 and 2007, she serialized what would become one of her most ambitious books, the strikingly original and stylistically innovative *Thorn Puller: New Tales of the Sugamo Jizo* (*Toge-nuki Jizo: Shin Sugamo Jizo engi*). She routinely describes this work as a long poem rather than a novel. If anything, the text is a generic chimera; readers will find many places in the narrative, sometimes even midsentence, where she shifts from a prose-like style of writing into lineated verse, and then back again. However, even the sections that appear to be prose are filled with carefully embedded rhythms and creative flourishes that give it a playful, poetic sensibility. Yet the blurring does not end there—just as the book blurs the line between prose and poetry, the plot too blurs the lines between fiction and non-fiction, between realism and surrealism.

The book takes its name from a famous statue of the bodhisattva Jizo in Sugamo, a historically working-class part of north-central Tokyo, immediately adjacent to Iwanosaka, where Ito's grandparents lived. In Buddhism, many enlightened beings are worshipped like deities, and one of the most popular in Japan is Jizo (Ksitigarbha in Sanskrit), known for guiding lost souls, travelers, and children. He most often appears in art and religious tales in the form of a monk with shaven head and a walking stick to help him traverse vast distances to help people in distress. In Sugamo, however, there is a special form of the bodhisattva known as the "Thorn-Pulling Jizo" (Toge-nuki Jizo), believed to have the ability to remove the "thorns" of suffering that afflict worshippers. For this reason, Sugamo became an important pilgrimage site, especially among the elderly, and even now, centuries later, tens of thousands of worshippers pour each month into the streets around the temple on pilgrimage days to seek Jizo's divine help in healing whatever afflictions trouble them.

Ito wrote *The Thorn Puller* at a time when her own elderly parents were growing increasingly infirm, and so it is not surprising that in caring for them, Ito was reminded of the pilgrimages she took as a child to the temple with her mother and grandmother to ask the benevolent deity for help. In the passages describing the narrator's memories of these trips, one quickly realizes that for generations of working-class, largely uneducated women, visits to Jizo were one small way in which they might seek refuge and succor from their difficult and troubled lives, perhaps even gaining some small, temporary sense of agency. The book weaves stories of visits to the Thorn-Pulling Jizo in the busy streets of Sugamo into a larger narrative loosely based on Ito's own experiences racing back and forth between southern California and Kumamoto (the southern Japanese city where she maintains a second home) while caring for her ill and aging parents. In language that is often self-deprecating and funny, the narrator describes the endless absurdities of maintaining two households on opposite sides of the Pacific, each with their own distinctive and profoundly separate cultures.

Although the book is rich in its depiction of daily life, one of the major themes she explores in her humorous, brash style is the differing conceptions of family in the two countries, and for this reason, the book deserves to be recognized as a contemporary masterpiece of Asian-American literature. In Japan, where filial piety is an especially important value, the expectation is strong that children will dutifully care for their parents in their advanced age, but in the West, the bond between spouses comes before all else. The book's central conflict is the tension between the Japanese expectation that she spend time in Japan with her ailing parents and the American expectation that she prioritize her Californian family, caring for her elderly husband, whose health is also shaky, and her children, who are undergoing their own growing pains and emotional difficulties. The "husband" mentioned so often in this book is modeled after Ito's partner whom she never married, the British-born artist

Harold Cohen, famous for his experiments programming artificial intelligence to produce original works of art. He was twenty-eight years older than Ito and died in 2016 after an extended period of decline, part of which is described in the book. After his death, Ito returned to Japan, where she continues to spend her time teaching, writing, and mentoring a new generation of writers.

The novel is also important for how it reflects larger social concerns, particularly the demographic crisis currently afflicting Japan. There, in the nation with the world's longest life expectancy, the number of senior citizens is swelling to enormous proportions, leaving already aging children to become caregivers, even when they have their own families and problems waiting at home. One of the biggest reasons this book hit such a nerve in Japan was that Ito shares in it her frank thoughts and observations about the interrelated processes of aging, dying, and death—subjects rarely discussed honestly and openly—with a readership of peers facing similar situations in their own families. At the same time that she describes what it means to die, Ito beautifully illustrates what dying means for the caregiver, showing how caring for elderly parents prompts one to consider one's own position, career, legacy, ideals, and dedication to family at almost every step.

Ito weaves into this semi-autobiographical tale elements from folklore and classical Japanese literature, producing a wildly imaginative and sometimes even surreal tale. This novel can be enjoyed on many levels—for its detailed descriptions of the life of an immigrant who ends up shuttling back and forth between cultures; for the amusing and often absurd plot, which sometimes veers into the surreal and imbues scenes of everyday life with mythological grandeur; or for its clever use of literary devices, including its deployments of folklore, archetypes, and frequent literary references. Like Yoko Tawada and Haruki Murakami who frequently veer into a mythological, dream-like, and even surreal mode of storytelling when writing about contemporary society, Ito produces a tale of daily life that is enhanced and enriched by legends, stories, poems, memories, and the force of imagination. Certain passages, especially those that describe the narrator's walks in Tokyo, Kumamoto, and California, are reminiscent of James Joyce's *Ulysses* in the way the narrative abandons ordinary logical strictures and incorporates various points of view, literary styles, and modes of narration. Ito's novel is certainly funnier than Joyce's classic, but like her literary antecedent, she draws on different types of language, including profane and elevated registers of speech, onomatopoeias (some of which are unusual even for readers of the original Japanese), and little snippets of poetry and prose culled from all over.

Throughout the text, Ito includes passages, turns of phrase, and ideas borrowed from prominent writers, poets, novelists, lyricists, manga artists, singers, storytellers, and monks. Almost never does she use quotation marks, however, giving the impression that the literary language of Japan, as well as the language of her friends, fellow writers, and contemporaries, flows through her narrator, shaping her worldview and modes of expression. At the end of each chapter, Ito cites those whose voices she has "borrowed," but an astute, well-read Japanese reader might recognize a number of the references through the text alone. Partly owing to Ito's borrowing from so many sources, the language of the original Japanese is unusually rich, rapidly switching between various literary styles in amusing and entertaining ways, while deploying the spectacularly rich vocabulary and register of Japanese stylistics to its fullest. (Alas, in English there are often only one or two ways to say what in Japanese may have numerous possibilities of expression, each with its own specific sound, implication, and linguistic register. For example, the various forms of the copula *da, desu, degozaru, degozaimasu, dearu,* and *nari,* all of which Ito uses to produce various effects throughout the text, all simply turn into the verb "to be" in English.) It was partly because of the book's stylistic richness that it received the rare distinction of winning two of Japan's most important literary prizes—the Sakutaro Hagiwara Prize in 2007 and the Murasaki Shikibu Prize in 2008.

Most of the references from Japanese will not be familiar to English-language readers, and indeed, most of the texts she cites do not even have translations. However, her creative, sometimes silly, sometimes poignant redeployments of other people's turns of phrase reveal how Ito, an infinitely innovative, creative, and well-read author in her own right, is constantly drawing upon everything around her, absorbing, synthesizing, and transforming language to create a richly textured, polyvocal world that is, ultimately, entirely and uniquely her own.

Ito Returns to Japan and Finds Herself in a Real Pinch

MOM'S QUESTION CAME AT ME through the phone: When are you coming back to Japan?

Not this month, Mom. I've got too much going on.

Okay, I guess it's a good thing you're busy, she said.

But I'll come in August.

I call my parents every other day from the States, but sometimes I'll wait an extra day to get Mom to pick up the phone and call me. If I'm the only one who does the calling, I'm afraid she'll forget how to call me if there's an emergency.

When are you coming to Japan again? She asked me this question only two days after I'd told her I'd be going in August.

Remember, I told you. I won't be visiting this month, Mom. Too much work here.

Okay, I guess it's a good thing you're busy.

But I'll be back in August.

Then three days later: When are you coming home again?

August, I told her. Say, are you asking because there's something you want me to do? In April she'd done the same thing, asking me over and over when I'd be back. When I tried to figure out why, she admitted, well, it's no big deal really, but I'd like you to go to the post office for me. So when I went home a month later, I went to the post office.

This time too, she said, well, it's no big deal really, but I'd like you to go with me to the hospital. The other day I went to a surgeon to talk about my varicose veins, and he told me an operation would help. Next time you're home, I want you to go with me and hear what he's got to say. No hurry. Next time. He said it can wait until September.

I ARRIVED IN KUMAMOTO ON August 24. The heat was brutal.

This isn't so bad, people were saying, but I'd grown used to the dry air of southern California, and the humidity was sheer torture. I felt like I was being broiled alive, like I might melt away in a syrupy mess. I'd brought my daughter with me this time. She was sweating from head to toe, and her thin, soft hair stuck to her skin everywhere it touched. I was so annoyed at her sloppy appearance that I couldn't look at her. As the sweat poured off me, I blew up. Why don't you ever listen? You don't know what summer is like in Japan, but I do. Why don't you listen? I tell you to tie your hair up, off your neck, but you never pay attention.

The next day, my computer broke. It wouldn't boot up. I'd been thinking of getting a new one for a while, so I calmly went to the computer store and picked one up—tower, monitor, keyboard, software—the whole deal. When I sat down to use it, however, I realized I'd made a huge mistake. It had a new operating system, which made me feel like I'd left everything I knew behind for a brand-new life. I couldn't figure it out at all—nothing worked like I thought it should. What was the damn machine for if I couldn't use it to write? I couldn't figure out the most basic things, like how to send emails in Japanese. Just imagine! A poet who writes in Japanese, finally back in Japan, but only able to type in English! What was I to do? If all I could do was write "Ito Hiromi desu" (This is Hiromi Ito) and "gera OK desu" (The book galleys are OK) in English letters, the machine wouldn't do me any good at all. What a disaster.

Meanwhile, Mom had no idea anything had happened to my computer. It didn't even cross her mind that I might have another problem that was driving me nuts. As soon as she saw me, she'd start talking about her legs, and then she'd show them to me. Her wrinkled legs. Her poor wrinkled legs were dappled with dark spots from her knees to her ankles.

Here, look, she complained. This isn't how legs are supposed to look. They're all stripy. What do you think's going on? It's not urgent, but I'd like you to go with me and hear what the surgeon's got to say. He said an operation might help.

Could we do it in September? I asked. She had told me the doctor said it could wait until then. The next day, however, she repeated, here, look at my legs.

I'd come prepared to be frank with her. Mom, listen. Aiko's going to start school in September, so I'll have a lot more time then. Can't we wait?

Sure, she said. September will be fine.

Except for the problem of her legs (and the post office too, I suppose), Mom was able to live normally and have normal conversations, even though she was aging quickly.

She's depressed, Dad told me one day when she wasn't around.

After he'd undergone surgery for stomach cancer, his legs had grown weak and he spent whole days sitting, barely moving. He'd grown hard of hearing and didn't like talking anymore. Mom was left all alone trying to deal with him. She had to shout for him to hear, but he seemed to get by, floating from day to day, buoyed by her support and verbal abuse.

She's depressed, he said. She just wants to get the hell out of here.

EARLY THE NEXT MORNING, I got a call from Mom. The first words out of her mouth: Will you take me to the hospital today?

Didn't I tell you yesterday I'd be happy to take you in September?

I want to go today, she said. It doesn't matter if you come with me or not.

What do you mean, it doesn't matter? If I don't go, who will? Of course, I didn't say the last part out loud.

Of course, nothing would be nicer than if you'd come too.

Yesterday you said we could wait until September, but now you want to go today? What's going on?

I've been in pain since last night.

Once she admitted that, I knew we had to go. I pushed everything aside and took Mom to see the surgeon, dragging Aiko along too.

Hospitals and medical clinics are places of stagnation. The buildings are old, warped, and rotten—full of so many holes that if you had trouble walking, you'd get stuck and never find your way out. The surgical clinic we went to was no exception. Dozens of people with swollen legs, mostly around Mom's age, were waiting in the long hospital corridors. They were so old and motionless, it was like they were playing dead. They waited with such quiet, single-minded devotion that I wondered if they had forgotten who they were and what they were waiting for. As we waited, my mind wandered. Why doesn't the hospital take appointments? My god, I wanted to get the hell out of there. If I'd known how long this would take, I would've brought a book or some work, but honestly, I probably couldn't concentrate. Why am I so scatterbrained? Time inched slowly forward.

Aiko started whining, I'm bored, I'm bored. I gave her a book and told her to read it, but she refused. I've memorized it, every word, I've read it dozens of times since we got here from California. She'd brought the book from the States. She'd read it in the airport, in the airplane, then again after we got here. She'd read it over and over because it was the only thing she had to read—just a cheap American paperback, already falling apart. Please, Mommy, she whispered reproachfully. If I just had a Gameboy for times like this—a Gameboy like all my friends in California. They've all got one, Mom, all my friends.

Mom's legs and feet had even more dark purple spots now, from her knees down to the tips of her toes, and the swelling was terrible. One leg had developed ulcers and grown inflamed—she had holes in her flesh, and the skin around them was turning black. She wasn't registering a fever, but the ulcers burned like charcoal.

The surgeon supported Mom's leg, held some sort of machine to it, and listened. It's just like I told you the other day, he said. It isn't bad enough to warrant surgery. The veins are still working and the blood's getting through. If anything, I think your problems are more in the realm of dermatology. Go see a dermatologist. And with that, he wrote her a referral to a dermatology clinic.

As we were leaving the surgeon's office, Mom tripped. There

was nothing to trip over, but she still fell flat on the ground. A man ran over and tried to help me get her up. She squirmed as she rose unsteadily, trying to regain her balance. With an embarrassed smile, she said, my goodness, that was quite a tumble, wasn't it?

The next day, I took her to a dermatology clinic.

Dozens of people sat quietly in the waiting room, all with itches, rashes, and blisters. Aiko was mumbling, I'm bored, I'm bored, so I gave her some change and told her to go outside and buy some juice.

You think she'll be okay? Mom asked. She's just come to Japan, she doesn't know her left from her right, but you're sending her out on her own? Aiko darling, don't let anyone spirit you away, okay?

Aiko grumbled in English, she thinks I don't know anything. She thinks I'm helpless. Aiko left the room haughtily, only to rush back moments later, screeching, the machine ate it, it ate my money! I didn't get anything, I don't know what happened, what should I do?

Sure enough, as the expression goes, she didn't know her left from her right. I had to go to the store with the vending machine out front and ask the clerk for her money back.

There's a problem with her blood vessels, the dermatologist said. He opened a thick book and looked for a photograph. He showed us a picture of someone with festering legs. They looked badly burned—blistering and full of pus. Necrosis, he said. You're in real trouble if it gets this bad. I'll write you a referral to a doctor in the big hospital. He knows all about this sort of thing, okay?

Mom said, tomorrow's the day I get my medicine. I'll let my regular doctor know I'm going to have to go to the big hospital. And that was how it came to be that, on the very next day, I took Mom back to her usual doctor in the very same clinic where she goes every two weeks. And that was also the very same day Aiko was supposed to start school.

THE FIRST DAY OF SEPTEMBER. That's typhoon season when waves of blustery winds come blow in to bowl, bowl, bowl us over. And it was the first day of school. So this was my plan. I had come back to Japan for my parents anyway, so I thought I might as well stay a while and enroll Aiko in a Japanese elementary school for a semester. That way, her Japanese would improve. I'd bought her a school uniform and gym clothes. I'd even bought her a yellow umbrella and orange boots in case a typhoon did hit. Everyone was going on and on about how a big one was likely, so big there'd no doubt be blackouts, the sewers would back up, and lots of people—hundreds even—might be washed away. It might even get as big as one of those huge hurricanes in the States. The last time a hurricane hit the U.S., everyone in Kumamoto asked me, is it okay where you are? I had to explain over and over that the hurricanes they were talking about hit the East Coast, but I live on the West Coast, on the opposite side of the country. I had to keep repeating, hurricanes aren't what we worry about in California—the natural disasters that get us are the mountain wildfires, the wildfires, the wildfires, the wildfires. I talked about the damn wildfires so often I could hardly stand it.

So anyway, the first day of September arrived.

But there was no typhoon, no blustery winds to blow in and bowl, bowl, bowl us over. The typhoons stayed much further south in the Pacific. That morning, jet lag woke me around five-thirty.

Light was streaming into the building, which was already baking hot. The previous night, the heat was so ferocious I had no choice but to leave the air conditioner on in the bedroom—something Japanese people never do. Now the sky was clear and blue, except where big clouds were billowing on the horizon. The temperature was already climbing. Children poured out of alleyways and apartment buildings on their way to school, all carrying summer art projects and other rolls of paper in their hands. I led Aiko by the hand. She wasn't carrying anything. I was going with her because the school had asked the guardians of new transfer students to come to the ceremony marking the beginning of the new semester.

Not long before, about seven o'clock, just as we were preparing to set out, the telephone had rung. It was my neighbor in California—I say "neighbor," but we're more like family, since we stop by each other's houses so often. My husband in California was scheduled for a test that involved inserting a catheter into an artery to check his heart. He'd been talking about it for months. He was depressed and kept mumbling to himself, my heart's giving out, my heart's giving out. Honestly, all his gloominess got on my nerves. I assumed he was making a mountain out of a molehill. Yes, we might share lives and finances, but our bodies were another thing. I couldn't fret about him the same way I would about myself. We all have to take care of ourselves, right? I couldn't feel his pain, so maybe I didn't pay enough heed. Just before I left for Japan, however, he opened up and explained a little more to me. I looked up the word he kept using in the English-Japanese dictionary and discovered he was talking about angina. I didn't say anything, but I was ticked off inside. If he was suffering from angina, why didn't he tell me? (In fact, he had, but he said it in English, and I was the dummy who didn't understand.) Suddenly, I understood why we weren't having sex any longer and why he was always so out of breath.

You might assume this realization made me terribly worried. Well, not exactly. I worried his health would bring my world crashing down, but as terrible as that sounds, I knew it might be the next step life had in store for me. All living beings are destined to die—that's a fact, and no one can do anything about it.

Lo and behold, the day of his tests had arrived. I hadn't forgotten. I'd been planning to call him later to see how things were. I thought I'd call after going to the ceremony at Aiko's school and then taking Mom to the hospital.

My neighbor had bad news. The test results were much worse than expected. The doctor had decided to perform emergency surgery as quickly as possible—my husband had checked into the hospital, and in three days he was going to have bypass surgery. Not an uncommon operation, they said, but it was a big one. They'd open up his chest. My neighbor asked, what do you want to do?

School was starting that day—that very moment, in fact. I had all of Aiko's school supplies organized. I'd leased a car, I'd hooked up the phone and the computer and the internet, I'd finally put everything in place to stay for a while. Our return flight to California was four months away. Would I have to throw it all away, go back to San Diego, pace the floor while he underwent surgery and stare at his pale sleeping face as the anesthetic wore off?

My only living relatives were my parents in Kumamoto. My ex-husband had moved us there for work, and my parents had moved there from Tokyo to be with us. We were the only ones they had to rely on, but their daughter—in other words, me—got divorced, found someone else, moved to America, and left them to grow old all alone.

You don't have to decide right now, not right now, my neighbor told me. Let's see how it goes, then you can decide what to do. As I said before, my neighbor is a lot older, and I trusted her advice.

So I went to the school as planned. I exchanged a few words of greeting with her homeroom teacher and the principal. I stayed long enough to watch Aiko make a quick bow from the podium at the front of the room, then slipped out to pick up Mom to go to the doctor. She poked around for what seemed like ages, and it took forever to get her into the car. Then when we arrived, she started poking around again, and it took forever to get her out.

Something's wrong, she said. The day before yesterday I took a tumble, and now I seem to be having trouble walking.

The clinic was a peaceful place that specialized in geriatrics. Mom had been seeing a doctor there for years, and he listened patiently as usual. Then he began talking about Doctor So-and-So at the big hospital, saying, you know, he's really better equipped there, he even has the newest MRI machine, I know him well, he's just the right person for you. But when she stood up and he saw her start to walk, he reconsidered. His face was pale as he said, what do you think, why don't we give you an MRI right now? Our machine is old, but we might get a better picture of your condition. I'll admit you straight away. He almost made it sound like an invitation. Then he lowered his voice and whispered to me. Judging from the way she's walking, she might have had a stroke.

Before I knew it, she'd been admitted. When I called Dad to

tell him, I could tell how upset he was. Oh no, oh no, oh no, oh no, why, why, why? As I was filling out the admission forms, I kept obsessing about my daughter. It's Aiko's first day of school, she's not used to this awful Japanese heat, she's going to have to walk home from school, it'll take her twenty minutes, she's not used to this heat, she's going to have to walk home from school, it'll take her twenty minutes, she's not used to this awful Japanese heat—these thoughts ran through my head in a continuous loop. I imagined her trudging down the brilliantly illuminated street, her back, legs, and forehead dripping with sweat, her body shimmering and twisting like a mirage in the heat. I couldn't just stay there. I rushed through the paperwork and flew home as quickly as I could, but to my relief, she wasn't back yet. I was glad she hadn't rushed home, drenched in sweat, only to find the place empty. I phoned my husband in the hospital in California, and he picked up. He sounded the same as always.

He said, I'm just about to try napping, but it's never easy to fall asleep in hospitals. I gave him the quick version of the story about Mom being admitted. I told him my first inclination was to rush back home to him, but I couldn't since there was no one to take care of my parents. I said, you can handle the admissions paperwork yourself, and you have our neighbors and friends and relatives to help. Everyone'll pitch in. In American culture, everyone helps out. He said, I get it, I'll be okay, don't worry, I'll be sure to let you know if I need you.

As soon as he said that, I fired back: But I want you to make me a promise.

Sure, he said, whatever you want. What is it?

I asked, will you keep this promise, even if you live to be one or two hundred years old?

He repeated, even if I live to be one or two hundred years old.

As long as you and I are married?

As long as you and I are married.

No matter how much we argue and fight?

No matter how much we argue and fight.

And I'm sure we'll argue and fight.

I'm not so sure we'll argue and fight.

You promise.

I promise.

You'll never, ever criticize me for not being there right now with you during your operation.

I'll never, ever criticize you for not being here right now with me during my operation.

THE DOCTOR TOOK A LOOK at Mom and said, yes, it appears she's had a stroke. The MRI is almost as old as her, so maybe that's why nothing showed up. By that time, she had lost all movement in the big toe on her right foot. Two weeks later, her right hand was hanging from her wrist. Two more weeks, and she'd lost movement in the fingers of her left hand. The paralysis was spreading quickly. Even though the hospital specialized in geriatrics, there were limits to what they could do. The doctor wrote a report to take to a surgical clinic, then her family doctor gave us a referral to an orthopedic surgeon, and then the orthopedic surgeon wrote a referral to a neurologist in another hospital.

That was how our pilgrimage from hospital to hospital started.

I'd take her in her wheelchair from one hospital to another, and when we were done, I'd bring her back home. Each time, we had to wait for ages. We'd go in the morning, and when midday came, I'd buy some rice balls and eat them with her in a corner of the waiting room. Often, we'd still be there when it was time for Aiko to come home from school. On those days, I'd call the school anxiously and ask to speak to the homeroom teacher, then explain the situation and ask if they'd mind keeping Aiko at school a little while longer. Next, I'd have to call Dad and tell him to take a taxi to pick Aiko up. Or I'd call the neighbors and ask if they'd allow Aiko to stay with them until I got home. I'd apologize repeatedly and explain that she'd arrive around 4:30. Then I'd drive home—no, speed home—as fast as I could, ignoring all but the stoplights.

I'd even make right turns. They drive on the left side of the road in Japan, so making a right turn means turning across traffic. It might sound irrational, but turning against traffic totally terrifies me. I always avoid right turns on those overcrowded streets—there's nothing scarier in the world to me—but I was so desperate to get home for Aiko that I did it anyway. Yes, that's right. I turned right for her. Some of the roads in Kumamoto are so narrow, there's barely enough room for two cars to pass, but I managed to do it anyway.

People would honk at me. Yeah, at me. I didn't slow down, I just cursed under my breath. Don't be such a jackass. Don't blame me, I'm just a middle-aged woman in a little car. Give me a fucking break.

THE GAS AND ELECTRIC BILLS tended to pile up in my mailbox in Kumamoto. Other things piled up too, including reminders to renew my driver's license and books of poetry from people I'd never met. You can pay gas and electric bills in just about any convenience store, and I could easily ignore the books of poetry, but I couldn't ignore the reminders about my driver's license. I had to make a trip all the way across town to the office that handles such things. Ordinarily, I don't mind errands like that, but it was really, really far away at the foot of the mountains. I kept putting it off, and the expiration date kept getting closer and closer. Finally, early one Sunday, I set out with Aiko. I thought I'd take her to the big toy store in the mall afterward.

She'd said, I wish I had a Tamagotchi. I could use my time better if I had one, she insisted, I'd have more fun when we're waiting in hospitals and in airports and in planes.

She said, all the Japanese girls have one, every single one.

She said, I don't want to be different. I want to be like my friends, I was different from all the other girls in California.

The other girls in California have Caucasian faces and Caucasian hair—that's what she meant.

I said, there were lots of Mexican kids in your class, weren't there? She responded, yeah, lots, but the kids that weren't Mexican were American, there were lots of them, and they all look the same, they're all blond, I was the only one who was different. Well, only me and that girl (the one with the mother from the Philippines), no, wait, just me and that girl and that other boy (the one with the parents from India).

The numbers keep growing, I thought.

She responded, it doesn't make any difference, I'm still a minority. I don't want to stand out, I don't want to be different.

I got the picture. I decided to take her to the toy store in the mall after renewing my license.

Sold out! The new model had arrived just a few days earlier and had flown off the shelves. An employee told us they wouldn't be getting another shipment for two more weeks. Aiko was really, really disappointed—her already small body seemed to shrink to half its size. Was she trying to make me feel even worse? She was so dejected that after we left, I decided to make another stop, hoping to make her feel better. I stopped at a teeny-tiny place that sold rubber balls and other things. I made an excuse and told her I wanted a ball. I handed her some money and told her to run into the store to pick one up for me.

A few moments later she came dancing back, rubber ball in hand, speaking excitedly in Japanese. Mommy, I found one, I found one, I found one, I found one, they've got one! I asked her what she was talking about, and she shouted, Tamagotchis! You're kidding, I thought. The shop wasn't much more than the sort of makeshift stall you'd find selling cheap junk at festivals, but to my surprise, she was right. Tamagotchis. According to the young woman working there, they weren't the newest model, but even so, there were only two left.

It's okay, it'll be okay! Aiko screamed in Japanese, one girl at school's got one like this, another girl too. She reached for her Tamagotchi excitedly.

She could hardly wait until we got back home. She made it come alive, gave it a name (it was a boy), hung it around her neck, and hurried out to play with one of the neighborhood girls. From her, she learned how to make it hibernate. She played with it for the whole rest of the day. She fed it, let it defecate, and collected her points. Things went so far that I scolded her for not paying attention when I talked to her. In fact, I scolded her twice—no, three times—saying, you're not listening, all you're doing is playing with that darn thing. Even so, she didn't put her Tamagotchi to bed until she went to sleep. The instant she woke up the next morning, she woke it up and started playing with it again. Then she put it back to sleep and, reassured that everything was okay, went to school.

Or at least, that's what I'd like to think happened, and that's what I'd like you to think too. In reality, I was too busy to pay much attention. I was busy with Mom, busy with Dad, busy with myself, and then the cycle started all over again—busy with Mom, busy with Dad, and so on. During one of the rare twenty-minute stretches of free time in the middle of my crazy life, I was stalling, dreading going out again, when I happened to notice the Tamagotchi on Aiko's desk. It wasn't sleeping like it was supposed to—instead, the screen showed it had returned to its unhatched state. The date and time were completely wrong, and the screen was blinking. Perhaps the creature had died while Aiko was fiddling with it, or maybe it was taking its last breaths. I tried to give it emergency first aid, but as soon as I reset the time, the screen switched on and the thing came out and started hopping around. It was alive, strong, and healthy. I later found out that the blinking date and time meant it was hibernating, and by fiddling with it, I'd woken it up.

It was like I'd woken a sleeping child. Having slept so soundly, it was full of energy. It looked at me with its charming little face, a bit hesitant like it needed to pee. I stared at it helplessly, not knowing what to do when it began to go. Electronic pee splashed all over. Too late. I needed to put it to sleep. I tried pressing the different buttons, but I didn't know what I was doing.

There I was, busy as always, helping everyone—Mom, Dad, Aiko, my husband. I never have any time or money, I never have any freedom, so how could I possibly find time to mess around with her Tamagotchi? Still, if I set it aside, it would starve, freeze, get smeared in its own feces, and be dead as a doornail by the time Aiko got home. I didn't want to play with it, but I had no choice. As I was fiddling around, I had an idea. I pulled out my computer, went to the net, and searched "make Tamagotchi sleep." And with that, I learned how to put it to bed.

MOM WAS GETTING USED TO her wheelchair. In fact, it seemed like it had become part of her. It wasn't just the big toe on her right foot that was paralyzed now. Her right thumb, index finger, middle finger, ring finger, and little finger had become paralyzed too. All the fingers on her right hand were affected. Meanwhile, she was losing movement in more and more of her left side—both her fingers and toes. Only the ring finger and little finger on her left hand were working. I parked her wheelchair in a corner of the hospital dining hall and bought her a rice ball. She clutched it between her ring finger and little finger, carrying it to her mouth like an eagle clutching its prey in its talons. When I was little, she'd scolded me countless times for not eating my food properly—cut it out and eat right, she'd say. Now she was the one eating strangely. No one had said a thing, but I could hear her words echoing in my ears, and a mean-spirited part of me wished I could say, now who's eating funny?

She said, oh goodness, I need to go to the bathroom for a second. I took her to the wheelchair-accessible restroom. She spoke out loud to herself, saying *yotto, yotto*—something Japanese people say to themselves when they're making an effort. In this case, she was trying to maneuver onto the toilet. I summoned my strength to help her to the right spot, and I pulled down her pants and underwear. She urinated. Only two of her fingers were working so she couldn't wipe herself. She said, I'm sorry, I hate to ask. . . . So I helped her wipe. She'd done a greasy bowel movement in the toilet, but she hadn't seemed to notice, making it harder for me to wipe her clean. Luckily, it was one of those fancy Japanese toilets with a bidet option—push a button and a stream of warm water shoots out. I turned it on, stuck my hand into the stream of water, and sloshed it around to clean her dirty bottom. It didn't bother me that she had defecated without knowing it. It didn't even bother me that I had to help her wash, but it was hard to watch her grip her food with her two claw-like fingers and carry it to her mouth. And her shit was just that. Shit—it smelled terrible. But that's life. Yeah, we eat, we shit. And our shit stinks. Honestly, those are the most natural things in the world.

I WOKE AIKO AT SEVEN.

Every morning, she asked me in Japanese, do I have to go today? She whispered, I don't want to go to school. She looked at the school menu and read the hiragana syllables one at a time: Today's lunch is going to be *sa-ba no te-ri-ni* (mackerel with sweet ginger glaze), *nat-to ji-ru* (fermented bean soup), *na-su no so-ku-se-ki-zu-ke* (pickled eggplants). That just made her whine even more. Do I really have to go? As if she could no longer hold back, her complaints started gushing out in English: So-and-so's mean to me, there's another mean one too, they're mean for no reason.

I put Aiko in the car and dropped her off by the school gate. The bell rang. It was time for the children buzzing around the school-yard to go in. I watched as she put on a tough expression and disappeared into the crowd. Next, I stopped at Dad's. The dog was barking, barking happily, barking and shedding hair. A little after nine, I went to pick up Mom from the hospital. I pushed her to the car in the wheelchair. I took her in my arms, helped her stand, then grabbed the top of her pants to drag her into the passenger seat. Mom said *yotto* like she did getting on the toilet. I folded up the wheelchair and put it in the back seat of the little car. I'm good at dealing with such things. I'm a down-to-earth, practical person, so I get things right the first time around. I joked to her that I could probably get a job as a caregiver, then I drove to the big hospital and got the wheelchair out again. Then I grabbed Mom by the top of her pants and maneuvered her into the chair. *Yotto*. She sank in heavily. Then I wheeled her through the automatic doors. I walked and walked down a long corridor, then parked her in a corner of the waiting room. We spent half the day there.

Mom said, oh, goodness, I need to go to the toilet, there's a diuretic in the medicine I take for my high blood pressure. In the restroom, I grabbed the top of her pants and hauled her over to the toilet. She urinated. Mom said, oh, it feels like something's coming. A soft, slippery bowel movement slid out, and I wiped her clean. I said, Mom, come forward a little bit, and she swayed her body as she leaned forward. *Yotto*.

As a young mother, I'd done the same thing countless times. My baby's bottom was smooth and pale pink. What came out was yellow and green and so pretty I could almost imagine mistaking it for pudding and giving it a taste. It smelled slightly sour like spoiled milk, so it seemed a gross exaggeration to label it "shit." That's why I started using the cuter, more benign-sounding "poop."

Compared to those baby bowel movements, Mom's loose stools were shit. They had the same foul smell as the ones I make.

Each time she used the toilet, I had to stick my hand in and help her wash. It wasn't long before my hand started to smell. It didn't matter how much I washed up afterward, the smell never completely went away. As I stuck my hand into the jet of water shooting out of the toilet to clean her up, I said a prayer: May this stink be taken from me.

At such times I think of Lord Jizo
The Jizo on the bustling pilgrimage route where I once walked
The temple with the large cauldron out front
Inhale the burning incense, let it permeate her body
Through mother's fingers, mother's toes
Through the nerves running to the ends of her limbs
Pull out the deep, deep thorns penetrating her body
Take away the scent of shit clinging to my hands
As I pour clear water
Upon your small stone chest and stomach
Let me scrub away
Let me scrub away
All our suffering

NOTE FROM THE AUTHOR

Some of the voices in this chapter come from Kenji Miyazawa's novel *Matasaburo the Wind Imp*, the manga artist Naoki Yamamoto, the poet Sakutaro Hagiwara, the singer Momoe Yamaguchi, and the lyricist Yoko Aki.

Mother Leads Ito from Iwanosaka toward Sugamo

ONE OF THE MOST NOTICEABLE things about Tokyo dialect is that instead of pronouncing the sound *hi* like the English pronoun "he," people add an "s" sound and pronounce it *shi*, like the English word "she."

As a result, the statue of the loyal dog Hachiko, a popular rendez-vous spot, is located in "Shibuya"—that, Tokyoites can pronounce without much problem—but Hibiya, a part of town known for its movie theaters, is "Shibiya." The atomic bomb was dropped on the city of "Shiroshima" (which is Hiroshima, of course), and on festi-val days, crowds of people—"*shitode*" (*hitode* in standard Japanese)— gather at the local shrine while cats bask in the sun—*shinatabokko* (*hinatabokko* in standard Japanese). No wonder it's so difficult for Tokyoites to get the name of the newspaper *Asahi Shimbun* right. (No, it's not *Asashi Himbun!*)

That's why, when I was little, I thought for the longest time that my name was pronounced "Shiromi." That was what Mom and my aunts called me. Across the narrow street from the house where I grew up lived a boy. Day and night, I heard his mother yell at him, "Masashiro! Masashiro!" Later, when I learned they were pronouncing his name right, and the second half of his name was indeed *shiro*, not *hiro*, my impressionable young self felt cheated somehow. Why was mine the only name with the funny pronunciation?

IF YOU GET OFF THE train at Itabashi Honcho Station and follow some of the twisting lanes, you soon come to the hilly streets of Iwanosaka. Many years before I was born, a series of murders took place there—a bunch of foster parents killed their infant adoptees. In the mid-nineteenth century, Itabashi was a stop on the Nakasendo highway where travelers could rest and find lodgings for the night. Even at the beginning of the twentieth century, there were still many wooden apartment buildings and cheap rowhouses near the station. All sorts of people congregated there: beggars, the homeless, vendors selling incense for the Jizo temple in Sugamo, and men who hung around waiting to push carts full of luggage for spare change. Locals started adopting unwanted children, but many of those children met with mysterious deaths. When the authorities finally took notice, it became apparent that the crime wasn't the work of one or two rogues—the entire neighborhood was involved. In Japan, when parents send their children out for adoption, they usually send money and clothing along with them. In Iwanosaka, each time a new child arrived, the neighborhood confiscated those things, and the people drank, ate, and celebrated. Sometimes the community raised the child and put it to work. Sometimes they simply killed it. Dozens of infants were killed because they were too young to be of any use.

All of this took place way before I was born, back when Mom

was a little girl. At the time, she was living with her down-and-out family close by Ryusenji temple in Shitaya, an old working-class neighborhood near Asakusa. At first, the family had no real connection to Iwanosaka, but their lives were hard and they decided to try their luck and moved into one of the shacks there. Their situation didn't improve, and eventually Grandpa left to work in the gold mines on the island of Sado, far from Tokyo. About a year later, he had a stroke and returned home, partially paralyzed. Grandma had a really difficult time after that. And with five or six children to take care of too. Mom was the second oldest of the kids. The oldest was my aunt—in reality, Mom's half-sister from a different father. She was sickly and weak. Mom, next in line, was healthy and strong. They said she worked hard—harder than anyone else.

Harder than anyone.

SOMETIMES I THINK ABOUT RECOUNTING our family's story in the style of a Japanese folk tale. I might begin with a song and then launch into it, like some old-fashioned storyteller. Here, let me give it a try:

Come, come
To Iwanosaka
Where a bridge of tears
Crosses Oshito Stream

Once upon a time, there was a man named Tatsugoro who was tall and ruggedly handsome. He was educated and willing to do anything to make money, but he loved gambling, liquor, and ladies.

(Ladies of the night, that is.) Still, he was a good man at heart. He had a strong sense of justice and got along well with everyone. He was a defender of the weak and enemy of the powerful. Because of that, a widow named Toyoko fell in love with him and brought her young daughter to live with him. She was a good woman, skilled at needlework and singing.

As soon as they moved in together, they started having children—not just one, but lots. Life grew harder and harder, so Tatsugoro went to work in the gold mines of Sado to provide for his family. While there, however, he suffered a stroke, became half-paralyzed, and had to return. Toyoko's life grew even harder. She sent her oldest daughter out to work. Toyoko did anything and everything she could think of to make money. Anything and everything. Worked her fingers to the bone. She sewed, sang, and worked like mad to support her children and husband.

One day, a god possessed her. Day after day, she had been praying in the morning and at night, praying with single-minded devotion in front of the little Buddhist altar in their home. As she prayed, her voice suddenly rose, froth poured from her lips, and she collapsed. But then she sprang back up, glared at her husband, and started heaping abuse on him in a low voice. This had happened once before, and her second daughter, Mako, was the only one who could understand what she was saying. It was clear to Tatsugoro and the neighbors that Toyoko had been possessed, but no one knew which god it was or why it had chosen her. At that time, Mako was working as a nanny for a merchant family in Otsuka, so she was immediately sent for. Mako rushed home, and sure enough, she was able to understand her mother's every word.

What's she saying?

She's saying, I'm the god of such-and-such, and if you don't listen to what I'm telling you, you'll be in a ton of trouble.

What else?

She says, the wallet you lost is behind the dresser, right where it fell. She says so-and-so is too stingy. He's sure to be punished for not giving people more time to repay their loans.

Sure enough, the wallet was discovered behind the dresser, and that evening, on his way home from work, the stingy fellow she mentioned fell into the gutter. When the rumors got out that her predictions had come true, people began to show up at the house.

She says so-and-so's husband is in Sueshiro in Itabashi. (That was how she pronounced the name of the brothel Suehiro. Tokyo dialect, you see.)

She says so-and-so's son is either in Shinagawa or Gotanda somewhere in that direction.

Something something (There's some song that appears in narratives like this, but I've forgotten it. Too bad, or I'd use it here.).

Come and see
The backside of the arrowroot leaves
Curling to show their backs
Curling to show their grudge

Her predictions were so accurate that before long, her half-paralyzed husband Tatsugoro, defender of the weak and enemy of the powerful, got to thinking. Lifting his pipe to his mouth with his trembling hand, he said, lots of people are coming to listen to the god speak through her. Let's ask for offerings.

But the instant they started taking money from visitors, the god stopped speaking through her.

She lamented, I've lost everything, I've lost everything. Even the gods have abandoned me. My husband's half-paralyzed, my sons and daughters are all too young to help. We can't feed all these mouths. To make matters worse, my oldest daughter is sick. One of my sons is weak in the head. All my youngest daughter does is cough. As if that wasn't enough, my half-paralyzed husband is playing around. He'd be a tall, rugged, handsome man if it weren't for all his health problems. When he doesn't come home at night, all I do is sit and worry.

One day she heard a rumor about the miraculous bodhisattva Jizo in Sugamo, said to relieve a visitor's suffering as easily as if he was pulling a thorn from their body. In one of the nearby rowhouses lived an old woman who sold incense to offer Jizo. Just the other day, she'd visited Toyoko to borrow some rice.

Toyoko lamented, the incense vendor comes all the time, even though we're desperately poor. Even so, my husband tells me to help her and shares our rice. She tells me, Toyoko-san, try going to Jizo, try praying to him just once. He'll take away your suffering. So I did. There was such a huge crowd there that even when I looked for the incense vendor, I couldn't find her. I ended up buying my incense from someone else. The crowd jostled me as I lit it and tossed it into the large burner. I swept the smoke toward me with my hands and rubbed the throat of my youngest daughter, praying her cough would go away.

I rubbed her head and prayed she'd be beautiful.

I rubbed her head and prayed she'd be smart.

I rubbed her shoulders and stomach so she'd be strong.

I rubbed the spot above my uterus so I wouldn't have any more children.

I rubbed the spot above my legs so Tatsugoro would stop fooling around.

I rubbed my chest so all my suffering would end.

I rubbed my neck (so my coughing would end).

I rubbed my eyes (so my eye strain would end).

I rubbed my shoulders (so my stiffness would end).

So that Mako's suffering would end.

So that Chiyoko's suffering would end.

And I stood in the long line so I could wash the small stone statue.

So this suffering
And that suffering
Would all
Come to an end.

IN 1966, THE TOKYO METROPOLITAN Bureau of Transportation shut down the Shimura trolley. The idea was to install a subway. As they worked on the new subway line, they started running buses back and forth to Sugamo. In addition, the government was building an elevated highway nearby, so there were huge holes and piles of dirt all over the place. The new subway line would stop at Honcho, Nakajuku, the Itabashi Ward Government Office (it ran much closer to the Itabashi gas tanks than the old trolley had),

Koshinzuka, Yatchaba, and then Sugamo. The buses wove their way through the construction, which left almost no place for large vehicles to stop and park. Finally, in late 1968, Subway Line Number Six opened, connecting the ten kilometers between Sugamo and Shimura.

Sigh . . . There are way too many stairs in Sugamo Station. Twenty-four steps, then another twenty-four steps, then thirteen steps, then out the ticket gate, then another forty-five steps, forty-five steps, and another forty-six steps. That's one hundred ninety-seven altogether. It's really far, really, really far, and the stairs only make the distance feel that much greater. I was running out of breath. The new subway made it much harder to visit Jizo than before. Pilgrims have to expend so much more effort that I couldn't help but assume Jizo would be even more generous to anyone who makes the trip.

Up the stairs. One step. One step at a time. Then another. I ran out of breath climbing. I exited just outside Itabashi Honcho Station on Subway Line Number Six. I thought I'd be completely outdoors once I left the stairwell, but I found myself under a raised portion of Loop Number Seven, the highway that encircles much of central Tokyo. Something felt vaguely unsettling to me. It was there that the slope to Iwanosaka started. Downward it went.

At the top of the hill were a few shops, then a street lined with regular houses. Another street much the same. Then a funeral parlor so well camouflaged one could almost miss it. Then a bar, a pharmacy. A tea shop, a tobacco shop, a store selling electrical goods, another selling work uniforms, and in front of that, an old lady sitting outside on a chair.

A rice shop. A tiny police box for one or two policemen. Behind that, the entrance to a public bathhouse. Behind that, the entrance to some student lodgings. Then halfway down the slope on the left-hand side was the "relationship-ending hackberry tree."

Why is it called that? Well, get someone to swallow the bark of that tree, and your relationship with them will end. We've all tried it: Grind some up and slip it into miso soup. Not just me—everyone around there. Lots of times. I've been known to get embroiled in bad relationships from time to time, but the bark of the tree saved my hide every time. I ditched all those guys. And good riddance too.

So much bark had been peeled from the trunk of the hackberry tree that the bumpy wood underneath was in plain sight. Behind the tree was a small Shinto shrine. A three-legged chair sat there. Across the street was an antique store and a barber shop. To the left beyond the tree was an elementary school, but I couldn't hear any voices. The place was completely silent. Beside the school was a paper mill. It was surrounded by a wall, with a narrow alleyway beside it. Walking down the alley, I looked up and saw barbed wire running along the top of the wall. More than once when I was looking at the stained splotches on the wall, they started to talk to me.

Get stuck by this rusty wire, and it'll be the end of you.

Soil the wire, and it'll get you faster.

Nah, no need to bother, just steer clear.

I went down the alleyway alongside the talking wall and came to the house where Tatsugoro used to live. At some point in his eighties he developed what we'd now call Alzheimer's. From time to time he'd disappear, and the family would have to go to the police.

Eventually he grew weak and died at home. The official records list the cause of death as pneumonia, but who knows? Mako whispered to Chiyoko that the doctor who had come to check on him had given him some sort of injection, promising it would make him feel better. Was the doctor responsible? Who knows. Toyoko died several years later in hospital.

I walked further down the alley along the wall and came out along the Shakuji River, partway between Banbabashi bridge and Itabashi bridge.

I wasn't the only little girl in the neighborhood who was told she'd been discovered underneath Banbabashi bridge and brought home. My cousins, uncles, and aunts were all told the same thing as kids. In fact, I used to say it to my daughters too.

At first, I repeated this local legend to tease them, but I'd be lying if I said there weren't moments when, somewhere deep inside, I wished they really weren't my kids. I told them the story to provoke them, but now just thinking about it makes me feel bad.

The path descended along the river from Banbabashi bridge. From the path, I could see into the nearby houses. I could catch glimpses of people's lives that way. No one seemed to care that someone might be peeking in. Sometimes I even witnessed scenes of birth or death. No one seemed to care that someone might be watching as they died. They crawled around. They fell into the stream. They climbed back up. Or if they didn't, they were carried away by the water's flow.

My imagination is carrying me away. Let me get back to the story.

It was the twenty-fourth.

Old women were coming out of the woodwork from every direction.

Backs bent,

They wear kimonos covered in intricate gray designs.

They tie their sashes loosely to expose their chests.

Backs bent,

The women spill from the narrow alleyways

And converge on the old Nakasendo highway.

They pass through the store-lined streets,

Slowly, slowly climbing toward Iwanosaka,

And are swallowed by the subway entrance

On their way to the Thorn Puller in Sugamo.

THE NURSES TOLD ME MOM was disoriented. Every night she would chatter on and on about all sorts of things. It seemed to happen only after dark. It never happened during the day when the sun was shining.

One evening the nurse said, your mother was crying and repeating, "Mommy, Mommy," then "Daddy, Daddy." She said, "I want to go live with Daddy." She said, "It's the fourteenth of the month, I need to cook some rice," then she asked in a loud voice, "How did I end up this way?" She kept asking, "How did I get here? Where am I going tomorrow?" She repeated this over and over until darkness fell. Then she started crying, "Mommy, Mommy" all over again.

Without thinking, I asked the nurse what she was talking about. Did Mom think she was a little girl again?

During the day, Mom was in her right mind, but she hardly ate, so her caretakers had to keep telling her to eat—you've got to eat, you're on an IV, but you've still got to eat. She had lost a ton of weight, and her arms and legs were especially thin. Her face was still super wide, square, and grumpy-looking—exactly like mine. There are *dodomeiro*-colored spots spreading all over her face. (Hold on, I'll say more about the word *dodomeiro* in a second.) Whiskers sprouted from her upper lip, and little skin tags had appeared here and there. Sometimes I would use my fingernails to pinch them off. Ouch! Ouch! she said. That hurts, just leave them, I don't care, I'm an old lady, I don't care. My efforts only seemed to irritate her.

I used to believe that the word *dodomeiro* was a vulgar word that referred to the purplish, bruised color of someone's private parts after tons of sex, but I looked it up in my dictionary. It told me that *dodomeiro* is dialect from central Japan, and it refers to the color of ripe mulberries. My goodness, I thought. There's always something new to learn. I've never seen the ripe fruit of a mulberry tree, but I do know what well-used genitals look like.

My mulberry-colored mother asked me the same question over and over: How did I end up like this?

How did I end up like this? Did I do something bad?

No doubt you did. Lots of bad things. I'd be telling the truth if I said that, but I bit my tongue. You did lots of bad things, and lots of people did bad things back.

She'd convinced herself that her condition was the result of her own actions. That everything that had happened during her life had created this inescapable suffering. Her life experiences were like needles piercing her body as her days dwindled. She had been mistreated by her parents, she was alone, she was beaten, she was sold, she was bought, she was forced into sex, she hated people, she was reviled, she picked on people, she was picked on, and she shouted back. Every one of her experiences was a needle piercing her flesh. Like so many other women, she gave birth to children she couldn't care for. She got pregnant and had an abortion, then later, a miscarriage. She had seen so, so, so many demons. Still, I wanted to ease her suffering, even if it was just a little.

So I made up a story.

Mom, you must've killed too many spiders.

Spiders? Spiders? I wonder. Did I really squash that many?

Sure you did. You killed them on first sight. You hated spiders, positively hated them. So much that you couldn't stop yourself.

Spiders, eh? Well, if I ever get out of the hospital, I'll go make some offerings for atonement.

For a moment, it seemed she'd accepted my explanation and returned to a normal state of mind, but then she got herself all worked up again.

No. No way. Couldn't have been the spiders.

If she'd just believe me—if she could just believe in something, even my ridiculous assertion that spiders were the cause of all her suffering—then she'd feel so much better.

THE NURSE PHONED ME. IT was five o'clock in the morning.

Your mother is calling out, "Mommy, Mommy!" She called us and said, "I want to see Shiromi. Shiromi works at night so she'll still be awake. Call her for me." She asked us over and over to call you. (In her mental reversion to her youth, Mom's Tokyo accent had returned.)

It's true I work at night, but even night owls are usually asleep by five in the morning. Me, for instance. I threw something simple over my pajamas and headed out. She was in bed, and her eyes were full of tears. It was perhaps the first time I ever saw tears streaming down her face, but I couldn't help feeling that it was somehow an all too familiar sight.

She said to me, I had a dream. I saw Jizo's face with thousands of needles sticking out of it. Mom said, I thought, oh, my goodness, and as I stroked his face, the needles started coming out wherever I touched. I thought, oh, my goodness. I opened my clothes, and the wound in my chest had healed. (In reality, she had no wound on her chest.)

It was beginning to grow light outside. As I stroked her chest, caressing the wound that wasn't there, I asked, on which day of the month did you go see Jizo?

The fourteenth.

Not the twenty-fourth?

Nope.

Why the fourteenth?

There were more people out then. There were so many people it'd be packed all the way from Sugamo Station to Koshinzuka. If you tried to get off at Sugamo, it'd be so crowded you couldn't get off, and you'd have to go back. That's why I'd get off at Koshinzuka instead.

So what did you do when you got to Sugamo?

I went to the temple, of course. They've got that big iron cauldron full of burning incense out front, and I'd rub the smoke on the parts of my body that were giving me trouble. Then I'd wash it, of course.

Wash what?

The statue of Jizo, with his clothes off.

Are you sure it was Jizo you washed? People who go there usually wash the statue of Kannon, the bodhisattva of mercy, the one outside the temple.

Nope. (Mom's response was emphatic.) The statue didn't have Kannon's face. It had Jizo's. They've got scrub brushes there, and if you scrub the part of the statue that's giving you trouble, Jizo takes your thorns of suffering away.

Are you sure you're not talking about the statue of Kannon right in front of the temple? It's famous. Lots of people go there to wash it, hoping that Kannon will help them.

Nope. (Once again, Mom fired back without hesitation.) I'm telling you, it was a Jizo with the face of a young child. That's not how Kannon looks.

By that point it was light outside.

I tried to change the subject. What do you call the kind of clothing Grandma wore when she went to the temple?

Those? Tokiyo took them all away.

No, Mom. That's not what I'm asking.

I've still got one left, so if you want to wear it, I could lend it to you. You'd have to look through the chest of drawers, but I know it's in there.

No, Mom. I'm not asking because I want to wear it. I was wondering what you call that kind of clothing.

It's an *akashi*. In June, you used to wear an *akashi*. There was also something called a *jofu*. I've forgotten. Back in the old days, you'd wear certain things during certain months. In June you'd wear a such-and-such, in July a such-and-such, and so on. And then in July, you'd wear a silk gauze kimono.

The kind I'm thinking of is a single-layered kimono. It's light gray and has a small intricate pattern.

Oh, that one. I've got one of those at my place.

Mom, I don't want one. I'm just trying to find out what it's called.

The reason I wanted to know is that I wanted to write about Grandma's kimono. Whenever I think of her, that's what I remember her wearing. Mom's answers to my questions showed that she was thoroughly confused. Was her memory failing?

You think I'd remember something like that?

She looked so relaxed and comfortable wearing it.

She looked stylish and sexy—because of the kimonos she wore and the way she wore them. She'd wear them so loose in front that you could catch a glimpse of her breasts.

How'd she wear her hair?

Like you're wearing yours now. In a bun. She'd wrap her hair around and around and pin it in place. She'd shave around her eyebrows to keep them nice and neat. And if anything happened, she'd immediately go to Jizo. Anything difficult or frustrating, she'd set off right away.

You mean she'd go on the special days for pilgrims?

That's right. The fourteenth.

Isn't the twenty-fourth the usual day to worship Jizo?

Yep, that's right.

But just now, you said she'd go on the fourteenth.

Oh, I did? Well then, I guess I was right, maybe it was the

fourteenth. I wonder why the fourteenth. Maybe because it was empty? If my daughter was with me, I'd hold her hand. I suppose it was easier when the place was empty. She was weak and always, always sick. We had so many doctor's bills that we never knew how we'd pay. Your grandmother and I prayed. We even gave up drinking tea as a sacrifice to make Jizo more likely to listen. We went to pray and wash Jizo every month.

Hold on, Mom. I'm confused. Which daughter are you talking about?

Mako. No, wait. I'm Mako. It couldn't have been Aiko, so who was it? Oh, I'm thinking of Shiromi. Shiromi was the one with the weak constitution. You know, when we were naming her, her Grandpa was steadfastly opposed to the name Shiromi. He kept on saying, you can't give a kid a name that you can't even pronounce properly!

(Of course, Mom was talking about me.)

I asked, did the wishes you made at the temple come true?

Shiromi got stronger so I knitted a little red bib for Jizo to thank him. I also bought two or three scrub brushes. Do people still do that these days? Probably not.

When Grandma went to visit Jizo at the temple, did she dress up or wear regular clothing?

I think she wore a cotton kimono.

Those are nice—those light-gray kimonos with intricate designs.

You're talking about the ones Tokiyo took away.

No, I'm not talking about who took what kimono.

I've just got that one left.

No, Mom, that's not the point. I just want to find out what that kind of kimono is called.

Mom said, in June, we'd wear an *akashi*.

Then she changed the subject.

I'm going to sleep.

And she closed her eyes.

Yes, go to sleep.

I left her hospital room and went outside. It was midmorning by then. The sun was shining brilliantly overhead. It was so bright I couldn't help feel it was looking askance at how crazy I looked, with my coat thrown over some worn-out pajamas.

NOTE FROM THE AUTHOR

I borrowed from the article "Research in Crime 2: The Foster-Child Murders at Iwanosaka" in volume 3 of *Who Are You*, edited by Shunsuke Serizawa, Minoru Betchaku, and Tetsu Yamazaki.

Ito Crosses the Ocean and the Slope of the Underworld, Throwing Peaches

TRANSPACIFIC.

I've boarded more planes and trans-ed my way across the Pacific more times than I can count. And no, I'm not talking about the kind of trance Grandma Toyoko, the spirit medium, used to go into. I'm talking about flying east to west, west to east. For some reason, going from west to east is much longer, much darker, and much more difficult. In fact, it's so difficult it's less like traveling and more like dying and trying to make your way back from the underworld.

The oldest book ever written in Japan, the epic *Kojiki*, describes a wide-open, broad slope at the entrance to the underworld. It tells the story of Izanami, the first goddess on earth, dying and going to the underworld, like Eurydice. When her partner, Izanagi, the first god, tries to rescue her—like Orpheus—she tells him she's already eaten the food of the underworld and can't go back. He sets his wooden comb on fire to create some light and sees that her body has rotted beyond recognition. Terrified, he flees. Izanami shrieks and runs after him. He throws his hair comb and then some peaches at her—whatever he can lay his hands on.

When I arrived in California, I told myself I was just going to have to grin and bear it. There's a word in Buddhism, *saha*, which means "the world that must be endured." California was like that to me. I had to just grin and bear it.

The sun was blazing, the sea was bright blue. This country has all sorts of things: big houses, parks, nature, an overripe consumer culture. It's overflowing with food, people are chubby and well-to-do, and give generously to the poor. Make eye contact with a stranger on the street, and they'll smile in a friendly way. As I dragged my heavy luggage through the airport toward the exit, I didn't feel like eating a hamburger, sandwich, burrito, pizza slice, or anything else from the restaurants lining the hallway. Just the sight of a muffin or cinnamon roll got on my nerves. But I realized that the moment I set foot outside, my husband would be there to pick me up. No sooner would I utter the first word of English than I'd find myself wanting a sweet treat. I've been known to get sucked into a Cinnabon and buy a roll on the way home—and not just once or twice either.

My sky. My house. My life.

My life with my family.

So, let me say a few words about husbands. . . .

Here's what people say. Husbands make meals, manage expenses, make love, care for kids, and if you're lucky, even bring home some dough. They're dependable, take care of their families, and they feel good when they get nice and plump and hard.

I wanted—really wanted—a good husband, a kind husband, a user-friendly husband who I would look at with a heart brimming with everlasting affection. I wanted him to love me forever. Eternally.

Well, that was just a pipe dream. And that's why my marriage was such a farce.

I didn't have a sweet tooth at first, but Americans love sweet, rich, heavy food. Their cinnamon rolls are so sugary they make your head spin. In America, the cookies are brimming with chocolate chunks, and brownies are huge and heavy. The doughnuts are greasy, fried in oil, and the carrot cake is smothered in cream cheese icing. The country is overflowing with sweets. I used to think about how sad it was that people who live here end up eating such things. Sometimes you just can't help feeling sorry for folks. But at some point, I started to eat those things too. I ate and ate. And I ate and ate and ate and ate and ate and ate and ate and ate and ate. I ate until the fat and sugar swelled up inside me. And that's when I realized something—eating their sweets is like eating the food of the underworld. Eat them, and you'll never be able to go back.

AIKO AND I WERE RETURNING from our long stay in Japan. We'd fled the snowy skies of Kumamoto to Tokyo, where there was no snow but it was bitterly cold. With Aiko in tow, I tottered through the ticket gate of the monorail. I'd sent most of our luggage ahead to the airport so that we could pick it up before the international flight, but earlier, while packing, I realized I needed to bring all sorts of things as carry-on luggage, not just my laptop. I was loaded down like a packhorse. I had bags in my hands, bags slung over my shoulder, and bags dragging along behind me. On the way across Tokyo, we stopped and spent our last night in Japan at a friend's place. The next morning, as we transferred from one subway line to another, the muscles in my neck grew stiff, and I squeaked out a warning to my daughter. Aiko, don't do that, come this way please, Mommy can't turn her head that way.

We had made it this far, and as it just so happened, it was December 24, the last possible day we could get home before Christmas. If we made our transpacific flight, it'd still be the twenty-fourth when we arrived in California, and we could spend Christmas with family—we'd just barely make it, like a baseball player sliding into home. Safe! I'd promised my husband we'd be home for the holidays. He's Jewish and I'm Buddhist, so it was crazy we gave a damn about Christmas at all, but hey, that's how our household works. Welcome to my world.

So there we were, early on the twenty-fourth, going to the airport, me with a neck so stiff I could barely move it. We got on and off the subway and the Something-or-other Express, and by the time we emerged at ground level, we were already inside the brightly lit airport at Narita. The pain was killing me. I bought a compress for my neck, went into the bathroom to apply it, then wrapped my head in a scarf to cover it up. I was sitting absent-mindedly on one of the hard waiting room chairs when Aiko said, Mom, you look sick.

Do I really look that bad? I asked.

No, that's not what I mean, she said. So-and-so's mother (one of her friends in California) got cancer and had to do chemo, then all her hair fell out. Afterward, she kept her head totally covered with a scarf. You look like her.

Hugging Aiko, I said, let's come back to Japan again someday. She answered in Japanese, saying, ummmmm, I think I like it over there better.

Over there. In Japanese, that's what people sometimes say when they mean "abroad." By over there, she meant California.

She said the last part smoothly in Japanese, but at times there was something weird in her speech. I was glad she'd been listening and learning from other people, adding to her vocabulary. Even so, there was still something off in the way she used her Japanese. It was like an accent would suddenly appear here and there—sometimes she'd even stick in a word, sometimes a sentence, sometimes even an entire paragraph in English.

I wanna go home soon, I wanna see Daddy and my friend (she said that in Japanese), ah, I really miss her (in English), she's my best friend after all, when we get home, I'll call her right away, we'll play together, forever, I've already promised (in Japanese).

Ten hours in the plane. The compress was still on my neck. I repeatedly drifted in and out of sleep. My neck was constantly warm, and my head and neck so heavy I hardly knew if I was sleeping or awake. There were no decent movies. I didn't feel like reading. The movie sound was switched off, but I gazed at the screen anyway. At times Aiko's Tamagotchi whispered at her. Aiko slept like a log, like she'd completely melted away. I kept on applying new compresses over and over. I repeatedly opened the window shade a crack to peek out. Each time, a sliver of sunlight filtered in.

When we got off the plane, we walked for a long time through the artificially lit hallways. Outside, we were bathed directly in the light of the sun itself—so bright I couldn't open my eyes. Palm trees swayed in the wind, the sky shone blue, cars came and went, and the buildings and the street looked like they were caked with grime. People shouted angrily, cars squealed, lights blinked, doors opened and closed. Our heavy luggage clattered behind us as we walked between terminals toward the gate where we'd board our next plane. The next plane was so small it looked like you could fold it up and put it in your pocket, but it carried us south along the coast to our destination.

My husband was waiting.

It'd been four months since we'd seen each other.

So, let me say a few words about husbands. . . .

They look like men, but kneaded and plucked.

They swell up like balloons.

They look thick, big, and sturdy.

Like a good hard squeeze would make them hard.

Like they might let out a passionate cry.

Everyone says they're great, but I know better.

My brain wasn't switched on until I saw him. I was too busy climbing the broad slope that leads out of the underworld. But to be fair, he was too. He'd been with me at all stages of my life in America. He hugged me, but I let out a shriek and pushed him away. My neck! Without thinking, I started throwing things at him—I threw a comb, I threw peaches. My neck. He pulled back and gave Aiko a hug instead, rubbing his cheek against hers.

And with that, I watched Aiko quickly slip away from me, retreating into the distance.

No, actually, Aiko was still with us. She was there in the house, but it wasn't long after we got back that her language began to change. Her daily habits changed, her way of thinking changed, the foods she liked changed, and even the things that amused her changed. For four months, we'd lived together, just the two of us, but when we returned to America, hand in hand, we crossed over a slope. And in that instant, Aiko reverted to the person she was before.

My neck was still killing me.

In English, there's the expression "pain in the neck," like "He's such a pain in the neck, I'm totally sick of him."

And then there's the expression "pain in the ass," for when you're more fed up, when you've dispensed with moderation and want to let someone have it. "Damn it to hell, what a pain in the ass."

Damn it to hell, the pain I was experiencing was literally a pain in the neck. And yeah, what a pain in the ass.

After two or three days, my neck still hadn't improved. I followed my neighbor's advice and went for a massage. I went to a dimly lit massage clinic scented with incense. I lay down, and as the tan, blond masseuse worked on me, she smeared on some Tiger Balm. She said, this'll be sure to work, we sell it here, then she asked, do you want to buy some? I told her a lie—we Asians always have Tiger Balm—then I left. The momentary relief from the massage quickly faded. The next morning, my neck was stiffer than ever. I couldn't move it at all. I was as stiff as a shirt doused in starch. I called the masseuse from the previous day, and she told me to apply my Tiger Balm.

Damn it to hell, what a pain in the neck.

I had to bend my neck to look down. As I tested the limits of my mobility, I happened to see rodent droppings on the floor. Still fresh and soft. To make matters worse, they weren't from a mouse but a rat. I wished I hadn't found the droppings, but I had. We'd have to exterminate. I put small packets of poison in key locations—I know all the strategic spots. The rats probably don't know I know, but yeah, I do. I remembered even though I'd been away for four months. The poison was gone in less than half a day. The following day, a rat ran across the corner of the room. I reflexively pounced, chased it, and caught it in a sealed container. It was a rat all right but still a baby. With lovely round eyes. And a twitching nose. Shaken by the death of its parents, it'd fled the darkness and come out of hiding.

My husband praised me as he looked at my prey. How many live rats have you caught? Damn, that's amazing. Your neck might hurt, but it hasn't affected your rat-trapping technique at all. Maybe you're a cat in the guise of a woman.

I gave him a confident little look.

"Come see me, you will find me. . . . Where the leaves of arrow-root rustle their complaints." The words of this old story rose to my tongue, but I suppressed them. Might as well, no way he'd understand. Over the decade we'd spent together, I'd given up on my husband more times than I could count, thinking there was no way he could understand me. In fact, I used to like it that he couldn't. That's one of the reasons we started living together. Originally, it was okay—at the beginning, I felt a special thrill when there was something about me he didn't get. And let's be honest, he didn't have a clue. He didn't understand my language, the things I was writing, the things I was thinking, or even the things I was trying to do. He didn't understand the sights I see, the scents I smell. He didn't understand the things I wanted to eat or even the things I didn't want to eat.

But people are people. We always want more. There'd been

times I'd really wanted him to understand me. I fell under the illusion that if I explained things carefully, he'd finally understand. I tried countless times to explain my thoughts and feelings. I tried telling him about my background, my language, and my culture, but it didn't work. Now and then I thought we were on the same wavelength, but I'd soon realize I remained a mystery to him. I'd realize my feelings of closeness were an illusion, and I'd get disappointed and angry. In my rage, I'd do all sorts of things—maybe pick a fight, maybe have sex with him, if I couldn't think of anything else to do.

So I gave up. I gave up talking to him about me and my rat-catching. I gave up on the prospect of telling him the old Japanese legend of the female fox named Arrowroot Leaf who takes on human form, moves in with a man, then is driven out when he discovers her true identity. As she leaves, she utters a poem to express her despair.

If you should miss me
Come see me, you will find me
In the forest of Shinoda in Izumi
Where the leaves of arrowroot
Rustle their complaints

No, I didn't talk about these things. Instead, I just talked about how good I was at hunting—it's not hard to catch a rat if you don't mind hurting it. It's much harder to catch one without doing damage.

He listened and watched me with the same expression one might have while gazing at an animal, but I could tell he didn't intend to investigate any further. My pride and motivations didn't seem important to him.

Nighttime. I went to the beach to let the baby rat go, though I suspected releasing animals like that was probably illegal. I turned off the headlights so no one would see, and I stopped the car on the road by the shore. I quickly removed the lid from the container, and the baby rat bounded off into the darkness.

The house began to stink from the rats I'd poisoned. The baby rat's relatives were all dead. The baby rat had probably snuck into one of the fancy homes on the beach. By that point, it had probably grown into a healthy adolescent and was going into heat. Meanwhile, my neck was still stiff as a board. It wouldn't move, still wouldn't move, still wouldn't move.

My husband began to get fed up. He said, you ought to take better care of yourself, you're just being negligent. Don't put your trust in those damn masseurs, you need a real doctor, but you won't listen to my advice—same as always.

I resigned myself to fate and went to the doctor. He prescribed a muscle relaxer, which I started taking right away. I began to feel like it might be getting a bit better.

Aiko went back to school.

I prefer it—this school, my friends here too.

Why? I asked.

'Cause I'm American.

She said this as if she was proclaiming her faith in some religion. Every morning I saw her pull on a slovenly T-shirt and baggy pants, grab a sandwich, and leave home with unkempt hair. In those moments, she looked like a little zealot to me. I couldn't help but sigh.

Then I began to itch all over.

I'm constantly getting bug bites in California. I was sure there were flesh-eating insects in the house. Maybe in the beds or the rugs. I don't get bug bites in Japan, but when I return to California, they start up again. Every time. It was so bad last year that I took up all the rugs and put down new ones on the hardwood floors. My husband told me that wouldn't help.

After the next trip to Japan, I got bitten all over again, so I replaced all the mattresses and pillows. (Despite having bought a new bed only two or three years before.) He berated me, are you satisfied now? To tell the truth, I think the whole thing is weird, I'm not sure if it's bugs or some kind of sickness, but I sleep next to you and nothing ever happens to me. I find it hard to believe we've really got bugs. I find it hard to believe you don't want to scratch yourself when you keep doing it. I find it hard to believe you.

The itchiness got worse again. I took so many antihistamines you'd have thought I was an addict, but I still itched. It didn't matter what lotion I put where, it didn't go away. I couldn't take it. I didn't just scratch myself, I tore at my flesh. I clawed at myself with my fingernails. That still wasn't enough, so I took a hairbrush and raked it over my body until my skin tore. I imagined the insect's saliva mixed into my blood. Maybe I'd stop itching if I could rub the blood out.

That's where trying to think scientifically leads you.

He found me clawing at my body with the hairbrush. His whole body trembled as he shouted in exasperation. What the hell? Are you out of your mind?

There was a mark next to my nipple where I'd been bitten. My fingertips sunk into the soft flesh making it hard to scratch. To make matters worse, I couldn't scratch there unless I bared my breasts completely.

I went into my room alone so I could bare my breasts and scratch the bite. The puppy we had just adopted came plodding in. He was just a little thing and reminded me more of a sparrow or a cat than a dog. He spied my nipple, then slowly came up to me and bit it. No, not a mean bite. A love bite, I'm sure, but a puppy's teeth are sharp. My other dog also bit me on the nipple when she was little. And the dog before that too. Every puppy I've ever had did the same thing—they couldn't help it. My exposed nipples made them come right up to me and bite. Maybe because my nipples stick out? Do the well-used nipples of all mammals look alike?

Who knows? Maybe they like me because they're attracted to my stink.

My nipple itched terribly where he bit me. If he bit harder, maybe hard enough to make me bleed, maybe that would relieve me of the itchiness. But it was just a little love bite. That's all.

I lay in bed that night scratching all over. My husband, who was supposed to be asleep, woke up angrily. You just keep scratching. All night. It never stops. He spoke in a clear voice as if he'd been awake and listening to me the whole time.

I tried to defend myself. I'm scratching because I itch, if I weren't itchy, I wouldn't scratch, there's nothing more natural than that.

He rolled his eyes and looked at the ceiling for a moment before shifting all the blame to me. I told you to see a doctor, but you never listen.

I resigned myself to fate and went to the doctor again. He

prescribed a steroid and a strong antihistamine. I already had a cold when I started the drugs. I'd caught it from Aiko. She had come down with it and had been coughing for a while, but she was already on the mend when she gave it to me. As my throat grew sore, I imagined it feeling warm from her body heat. I imagined my fever smelling of her. The sore throat and fever weren't too terrible, but wow, the cough!

One day my husband said, your cough is getting worse, isn't it? The next day, he repeated the same thing. He sounded critical. I tried to defend myself: I just caught a cold. When I catch a cold, I cough, nothing more natural than that. My body is pushing the foreign substance out. I'm cleansing it—my body, I mean.

But you've done nothing about it, you're just being lazy and leaving your body to heal itself. Your cough is getting worse, the days keep going by, and you're doing nothing to fight it.

The cough continued. In fact, it got worse. I was coughing so hard I thought my bronchial tubes might fly out of my mouth. Not just my bronchial tubes, but my lungs, my stomach, and everything I'd eaten too.

I resigned myself to fate and went to the doctor again. He pre-scribed an antibiotic and a strong cough suppressant. I greedily swallowed them down, but there was no change. My body shook as I bent over in paroxysms of coughing. I panted as I brought up chunks of phlegm. I started worrying the phlegm would stick to the back of my throat, so I did my best to clear it. I was so desperate that I cleared my throat while cooking and eating dinner, cleared my throat while reading, cleared my throat even in bed. I had trou-ble sleeping because of the coughing. My husband, who was trying to read beside me, gave up. His book slipped from his hands and he slumped over, but realizing he was falling asleep, he removed his glasses, set them on the bedside table, turned off the light, and turned to face the other direction. For a long time, I lay in the darkness coughing, panting, trying to clear my throat.

I thought he was asleep when he rolled over to face me and said, I get it. I totally get that you've got a cough, but can't you do something about the noise? I can't get away from the sound of you clearing your throat, it's everywhere, in my ears, in my mind, in my bronchial tubes, in my heart—what the hell are you trying to get out of your system? Me maybe? You told me the doctor said it must be allergies, but what are you allergic to? This place? Our house? The weather? Me?

So, let me say a few words about husbands. . . .

We've been together a long, long time.

We spend our nights on the slope.

The broad slope into the underworld.

Or perhaps this is Iwanosaka,

The slope in Tokyo where so many murders took place.

NOTE FROM THE AUTHOR

I borrowed voices from the ancient chronicle *Kojiki* (An Account of Ancient Matters), Kenji Miyazawa's children's story "Gauche the Cellist," and the medieval Buddhist narrative *Shinodazuma* (The Wife of Shinoda).

The Peach Ito Threw Rots, and
She Becomes a Beast Once Again

ON FEBRUARY 24 I RETURNED to Japan. This time I was alone. Just before I left, I bit my husband. Yes, you read that right. I *bit* him. A big bite too. It sort of scared me that I'd lost the ability to behave like a normal human being. He freaked out when I left for Japan, and now I wasn't sure I'd ever see him again.

I left Aiko behind. If worse came to worst, I could go to the bank and shift money between our accounts, send my most important books to my oldest daughter who lived elsewhere, and I could leave the rest behind—yes, I could leave everything behind, bringing only a flash drive for my computer. I could kidnap Aiko as she came out of school, put her on a plane, and take her with me. These thoughts passed through my mind over and over as I planned how I might get her back.

When my husband and I weren't face-to-face but talking on the phone, we'd sometimes settle down, but before long we'd start arguing about god knows what. I hated, absolutely hated the way he'd fire off arguments, one after another like he was trying to win a debate. I couldn't take it. When I asked him why he was speaking to me so aggressively, he repeated the word *aggressive*. I couldn't see him on the other end of the line, but I could tell he was rolling his eyes, and he let out a contemptuous sigh. *You're* the aggressive one. If you think what you did to me the other day wasn't aggressive, then I don't know what is. I'm still having trouble walking.

He said, my thigh's black and blue, so swollen it's like a peach got stuck in it, and the peach has started to rot.

That's too bad, I said—a simple, straightforward answer with no ulterior motive. To be honest, that was the only way I knew to express in English what I was thinking, but I must have sounded nonchalant, perhaps even unrepentant. When I suggested he go to the doctor, he responded in a very, very low voice—so low it was hard to hear.

Just what am I going to tell him? That my wife did this? Just try telling that to the authorities in this country. You ought to thank your lucky stars I'm keeping my mouth shut.

Why were we fighting? I don't really know. I'd already forgotten. That's how it is when couples fight. This is always how things begin, and when a couple splits up, there's never any resolution. When I split up with my first husband, my second husband, and my third and fourth too, it was always like that. Fights start over dumb things but can still end relationships. When a Japanese couple reaches some sort of compromise, even if it's only lukewarm, like a kettle left too long after it boils, the couple clams up and sticks it out. But my current husband was entirely different. He was British, Jewish, and raised in an intellectual environment. For him, debates were the stuff of everyday life. He'd made his way through the world, navigating the unsheathed blades of language for longer than I'd even been alive. My English, by contrast, is faltering at best.

During our fights, he'd pick me apart word by word. Like he was picking up my poor English with chopsticks and dropping it into a sizzling hot vat of tempura oil.

He'd deep-fry and sizzle me.

I'd curl up like a shrimp.

In reality, our footings weren't all that uneven. I'd made up my mind to master his style of aggressiveness, and though I could still barely read and write English, my English fighting abilities had progressed so much over the last ten years that even I was impressed. Still, I come from a culture where one either slashes at an opponent while saying nothing or commits hara-kiri. *Slash at the opponent, or commit hara-kiri, how jolly.* That's probably what my husband would say in response. *Jolly.* The word usually means "pleasant," but in my husband's vocabulary, it meant something else. He used it sarcastically to mean "shameful" or "incorrigible." When he said it, I felt like he was putting himself on a higher plane than everyone else. No, I couldn't hold my own through words alone.

Deep-fried and sizzling. Scooped up by my feet. Knocked down hard. Driven into a corner. Caught in a hail of bullets, I take my last breath.

I say this all metaphorically, of course. The peach is a metaphor, the thorns are metaphors, my husband and mother and father are metaphors, the summer heat and winter cold are metaphors, everything is a metaphor. The only thing that isn't a metaphor is me living as myself, and that's all I had to hold onto.

So I fired back.

He's a big man. Stand him next to me, and he'd look about twice as tall and three times heavier, but fortunately for me, he was getting old and his movements slow. I was also lucky he wasn't the kind of guy who'd inflict physical harm. It was me who lashed out at him. My ability to catch rats barehanded served me well. He was about to grab my hand to stop me but didn't intend to hurt me. I seized the opportunity to start throwing hard unripe peaches his way, without taking time to aim, but I had trouble hitting him even though he was standing right in front of me. (All of this is a metaphor, of course.) The peaches rolled around on the floor, running into each other, as if electrified, knocking into each other. Most missed, but one hit squarely and lodged in his thigh.

I was being unfair. I shouldn't have resorted to projectiles to get back at him.

But did I regret it? Not really. I wanted to hurt him. You shouldn't hit people—that's just common sense. So I bit him. At that moment, I couldn't resist the urge to hurt him, it didn't matter how. Seeing the bite marks swelling up on his arm, I figured that now he'd know how angry I was. At the same time, I recognized I'd done myself in.

American culture abhors physical violence above all else. You can't even lay a finger on a person—actually, that's a huge lie. Americans think it's okay to own a gun and shoot it, but you mustn't inflict violence with your own hand—never, ever, ever. It's all or nothing. You should not kill, but if you do, do it completely.

NEITHER OF US DARED REMOVE the peach lodged in his flesh, so there it remained, a visible reminder of his injury.

I supported you, I supported your children, I supported your work, I supported you while you took care of your parents, but what am I to you? Just a monster you want to slay, or someone who supported you, cared for you, and deserves your love?

My husband sent that to me in an email. (Trying to talk on the phone was so unproductive that we'd given up on it altogether.)

I supported you, I supported your children, I supported your work, I supported you while you took care of your parents, but you still don't believe in me, do you? That's what he wrote. Thinking it over calmly, I realized he was right. I didn't believe in him. These ten years, I hadn't believed in anything.

You're right, I replied. Like you said, I don't believe in you. In a sense, I haven't believed in you this whole time.

I was being honest, but I could hear him groaning all the way through the internet when he opened the email, and the rotting peach sank even further into his flesh.

Our family's happiness was shattered to smithereens.

My wife is ferocious, faithless, shameless, unfeeling, she doesn't believe in me—her own husband. She doesn't love me, she's a beast. He was beating on the keyboard. He beat on it and beat on it. And as he did, he spelled out his abuse.

When he's mad, he uses lofty words like Jane Austen and speaks with that special form of circuitous sarcasm unique to the British. Sometimes those things slip out even when he's speaking normally. People often get ticked off at him, and he turns away, sighing that Americans just don't get British humor. Honestly, I can't say we Japanese get it either. Everything he writes just comes at me like a great big aggressive jumble of words—after all, I live in an English-speaking country but am practically illiterate. It took me hours just to digest his email.

He wrote, I supported you, I supported your children, I supported your work, I supported you while you took care of your parents, let me repeat, I supported you, I supported your children, I supported your work, I supported you while you took care of your parents—my freedom came second, and it's caused me all sorts of emotional stress and loneliness. The peach is still buried in my thigh, and it still hurts.

I wrote back, I understand. But you're so aggressive, so negative, you make everything impossible, you're always 100 percent right and I'm 100 percent wrong. There's a Japanese proverb, "the cornered mouse bites the cat." That's what happened. And let me tell you, it's not fair to bring up money during a domestic dispute.

He responded.

Read this, and read this carefully, I'm *not* talking about money.

I could tell. The injury to my husband's leg smarted as much now as the moment I inflicted it.

I supported you, I supported your children, I supported your work, I supported you while you took care of your parents, let me say it again! I supported you, I . . . He kept beating angrily on the keyboard.

You talk about compromises, but a compromise involves both parties giving something up. What are you giving up? Do you intend to give anything up?

You say I'm being negative. Negative? In my work, I've accomplished things no one has done before, do you think that's negative? How can you say that?

You feel guilty about leaving the house.

You feel guilty about your work.

You feel guilty when you leave me for so long.

EVERYTHING MAKES YOU FEEL GUILTY, I'M SICK AND TIRED OF YOU FEELING SO GODDAMN GUILTY ABOUT EVERYTHING.

The last part was all in capital letters. He was screaming at me through the internet.

HE'D BLOWN HIS LID, BUT I did think about what he said.

His view of me was way off base. Is that how he really saw me? Do I feel guilty about leaving home? Do I feel guilty about doing my work? Heavens no. Not me.

That's when I remembered why we'd started fighting. The reason behind it all.

We were having *o-nabe* for dinner. For those of you unfamiliar with Japanese cooking, *o-nabe* is a hot pot full of vegetables and meat cooked in broth. Usually it's made over a portable burner on the table so everyone can sit around, cook, and eat together. I'd recently bought a brand-new electric burner, and we'd been having *o-nabe* every night. That meant that we were eating *hakusai* every night, since it's one of the most common ingredients. In America, *hakusai* is called napa cabbage or simply napa—and in California there are piles of it in every grocery store. Napa makes you think of Napa wine, so it didn't sound right to me. One evening as I was adding some to the *o-nabe*, I used the word *hakusai* instead of the English word. My husband didn't understand, so I had to explain. That evening, I'd already had to say "enoki mushroom" instead of just enoki, "shiitake mushroom" instead of just shiitake, and "bean noodle" instead of *harusame*. I'd had to use the absurdly general word "sauce" to mean something specific like citrus-flavored *ponzu*. I always have to rephrase myself for him. So by the time we got to the *hakusai*, I was already in despair. We'd been living together for ten years, and during all that time he couldn't even learn a simple Japanese word like *hakusai*? He was always saying, "I love Japanese food" and "I love *o-nabe*," but could he prove it? To make matters worse, he was trying out the Atkins diet. That meant he was eating lots of high-fat, high-protein, low-carb food. He wouldn't touch rice with a ten-foot pole. How could he possibly claim to understand his wife's culture if he didn't eat rice?

I shouted at him, and he shouted back.

I wondered what would happen if, somewhere down the line, Aiko asked us why we got divorced. *Because of napa cabbage.* How could I possibly say that with a straight face?

Several days later, I saw our parakeets kiss.

Originally, we just had a cockatiel. One day I tossed some of its old food into the yard, and that attracted a green parakeet. I caught it and brought it in to live with us. When the cockatiel perched on my hand and the parakeet was near, it got excited. When the cockatiel was free in the house, it spent the whole day flying back and forth over the parakeet's cage, showing off. It talked non-stop. *You're a bird. Look! I'm a bird too! You're a bird. Look! I'm a bird too! You're a bird. Look! I'm a bird too! You're a bird. Look! I'm a bird too!* The cockatiel stopped perching on our shoulders and coming to the dinner table. Now it was a plain old bird who didn't interact with us. My older daughter decided to take it to her apartment, and that made the parakeet lonely. Far away in Japan, Dad was home alone, with Mom now in long-term care. I hated the thought of bringing more tedium and loneliness into the world, so I went to buy another bird.

Aiko came with me. She pointed at a white bird and said, that one. It was a pure white parakeet with none of the usual yellow, blue, or green on its back. We tried putting it in the same cage as the other parakeet, but the cage was too small, so we bought a new one—a cage for newlyweds. We also bought a birdhouse so they could raise babies. As the birds flapped around wildly in the old cage, trying to get away from each other, feathers puffed out, and dancing around, I managed to catch the wriggling green parakeet and held it in my hand. It bit me hard. The white one was no problem. I let the birds go in their new home. The white parakeet sat still on a branch while the green one approached it as if to say, how handsome you are!

From then on, they couldn't stop kissing. Lucky them, they had chemistry. Their kisses got deeper, and while I knew they were birds, I imagined them like people, tonguing one another, and I watched them with excited interest, wondering what would come next. They went on kissing shamelessly, oblivious to my husband and me. He snarled, those birds are the only ones in this goddamn house who get along. We don't have that kind of intimacy anymore. His tone and expression made it clear he was in an especially foul mood.

And it was true. We weren't close anymore. If, occasionally, we did show each other some intimacy, there was a one-in-three chance it'd lead to sex. We should have reconciled ourselves to not having sex anymore, but when a man gets older, that can become a sore point, and it's easy for him to feel slighted. I wanted to avoid that.

But I didn't just think it. I broached the subject of age out loud.

Oh, damn it. You've gone and done it now.

I shouldn't have brought projectiles to a fight, but I did, and now I'd gone and used them. As we argued, I threw peaches at my husband. One buried itself in his skin, grew inflamed, and started to swell. It looked exactly like a bite mark.

I'm getting old.

I don't have time.

My body won't move.

His insecurities had mounted, but now he had the perfect excuse—his own wife had bitten him. His rage boiled over. I was wrong, no matter how I looked at it. I'd hurt him. My own spouse. Violently. I'd crossed the line. He was justified, and he exploded.

I'm getting old. I don't have time.

My work isn't getting the attention it deserves. I don't have time. I don't have the time to wait. My health is going downhill. My body doesn't move like I want it to. Surgery isn't helping. I don't have time to wait. I'm old. I'm a sexual failure. I've failed over and over. Over and over. I don't have time for this. I'm old, I've never been in this situation before, and I don't know how to handle it. I don't have time to wait. I don't have time to come up with new ideas. I'm not satisfied. Things aren't getting better. I don't have time.

His anger was unrelenting. He had no time for me. He vented his anger at me. At himself. At me. But more at himself. At his limp cock. At his eyes. At his ears. At his heart. At his knees. At his shoulders. At his lower back. At his elderly, failing body. At his old, decrepit self. Yes, at himself.

THE DAYS WENT BY, THE weather cooled and then warmed up again.

I was walking to the clinic to see Mom when I noticed a grassy spot in the sun. There were clumps of a particular plant in it. I was thinking how lush it looked when I realized it must be henbit. Little reddish-purple flowers stuck out like tongues, and right before my eyes they seemed to puff out, and individual stalks began to grow. I noticed another flower, something like a white shepherd's purse, scattered among them. It seemed too close to the ground for shepherd's purse. I was thinking that it must be some relative when it too began to grow. As it did, it made a quiet rustling sound. There was mugwort too—impudent clumps had died and were giving birth to a new generation—and vetch, which had grown vines and looked like a baby sticking out a hand. I saw something twinkle in the grass. The more I looked, the more I saw. Speedwell flowers warmed by the spring sun. Their twinkling hurt my eyes. Near them, soft stitchwort plants bloomed quietly, revealing neatly arranged white petals. Scattered around were clumps of dried-up weeds. They lay dead and dry, motionless.

MOM WAS LYING IN BED.

She couldn't move, but she was conscious.

Was she responsive? No. Was she out of her mind? Not at the moment. As the waves of her dementia crashed and retreated, the numbness in her body had spread. Her right hand was gnarled. It couldn't move—it had died. A hand that was no longer a hand. A hand that had neither the shape nor color of a hand. Like dim sum chicken feet. Like it had been boiled. She had also lost movement in her legs, which had grown thin and frail. They wouldn't have supported her even if she could have stood. She couldn't urinate so the clinic had inserted a catheter. Previously she'd raised a fuss when they put in a catheter, but this time she didn't make a peep. She was still taking a diuretic for high blood pressure, but she didn't seem to be having problems with that. Still, she was so weak that it was all she could do to press the call button for the nurse with the pinky of her left hand. She couldn't even turn the pages of a book or use a TV remote. She had been languishing away like this for ages and ages, unable to do anything, unable to move. Meanwhile, at home, Dad was experiencing unending tedium and loneliness.

I sat by her bedside, and she asked me, will you scratch me a little? I'm so itchy I can't stand it.

I rolled up my sleeves, pushed her hospital gown aside, and scratched her all over—her back, her arms, her thighs, her belly.

Higher, harder, use your nails.

Her arms were slack and wrinkled. The skin on her belly was dry and worn. There was nothing left of her on the backs of her thighs. She was as thin as a bat. As a dried fish.

She moaned, oh, right there, right there, more, more. Don't be namby-pamby, do it harder, use your nails. Harder.

I felt a tiny bump as I was scratching her. Just a teeny-tiny one. A rough, dry spot. Rather than hurt her by trying to scratch it off, I used the tip of my fingernail to press into it. Mom moaned, right there, right there, there, there.

I know how terrible it is to itch. Her suffering was contagious—as I scratched her, I grew itchy all over. Moving the ring finger and pinky of her shriveled left hand, which no longer obeyed, she had tried in vain to scratch herself, but ended up just stroking her own skin. She repeated, I'm so itchy but I can't scratch myself, I'm so itchy! She didn't seem to be suffering from extreme anxiety or depression, but she was living one day at a time, never fully present for any of it.

Long ago I saw a nature program on TV that showed a lion on a savanna eating a gazelle. The lion grasped it at the base of its neck, and the gazelle shook and twitched, but then it went limp, eyes open wide. I thought it was dead at first, but no, it was still alive. The lion sat down and began to eat. Was it dead yet? No, still alive. The animal was being eaten, and its eyes were open wide in a catatonic state. The voice-over explained that some chemical substance was being secreted inside the gazelle's brain. The gazelle felt neither suffering nor fear, even as it was being consumed. I wondered if Mom's brain was secreting the same chemical. Was that why she lay there all day distracted, suffering so little? Was that why she wasn't worried about her growing paralysis or afraid of death?

Across the room was an Alzheimer's patient about Mom's age. She did all sorts of things—shouted, walked out of the room, came back in, then repeated these things all over again. In the bed next to Mom was another woman close to her age, but she lay quietly without moving. She didn't even eat. Once when I was moving a metal chair, I accidentally knocked it hard against her bed, making a loud clang and shaking her bed. She opened her eyes wide but didn't move a muscle.

Mom said, it's probably easier when you get like that. (Mom wasn't looking at the TV, wasn't reading. She just stared at some fixed point.) The lady on my left sometimes talks to me, but I don't have a clue what she's saying. It'd be a lot less trouble for me if she just lay there on her own like the other one.

As night fell, Mom and the other old folks changed personalities and began to remember things. The wanderers wandered, the emotional patients laid their emotions bare, others ranted and wept. A visitor arriving at the dark clinic in the evening would pass the receptionist and go up to the patients' rooms on the fourth floor to find a world without night. The lights shone bright as day. Nurses were busy jotting down notes as if all this was normal. Artificial anemones and lilies stood on the nurses' desks.

A world without night.

A world of nothing but night.

I heard a wild howl. A deep male voice. Ohhhh, ohhhh, ohhhh. The man's voice reverberated, filling the entire floor.

The lights shone for all they were worth.

As sleek as a clump of growing grass, the nurse jotted down some notes. As if nothing was the matter.

Ohhhh, ohhhh, ohhhh, ohhhh, ohhhh.

Ohhhh, ohhhh, ohhhh, ohhhh, ohhhh.

Someone was angry.

At old age. At their aging self. At the world. At the night. At their aging wife.

I WAS WALKING HOME AT night after visiting Mom when I smelled it—a violently fragrant aroma that clutched at my head and spun me around. That scent—a memory of desire—penetrated my brain, but for a second I couldn't remember the plant's name. I hadn't smelled it for the longest time, but I thought, I know you, I definitely know you, I've missed you, I've missed you, I've been wanting, wanting, wanting to see something nice like you again—and that's when I remembered. Sigh.

A daphne.

It was hiding in the shade of a wall about two meters away.

A gecko darted right in front of me, and with lightning speed, I reached out and grabbed it. Catching a gecko in the early spring is nothing compared to catching a rat. I put the gecko in my pocket for a while. The way it squirmed in my palm struck me as incredibly cute, and I wished I could keep it. I wanted it to live with me, I wanted it to be part of my family, but that was absurd. A gecko is a gecko. I let it scamper away into the darkness.

Even at times like this, you're daydreaming about making a family? I let out a sad chuckle, hollow and alone.

NOTE FROM THE AUTHOR
I borrowed voices from Franz Kafka's *Metamorphosis*, Kenji Miyazawa's "The Acorn and the Mountain Cat," and the *Kojiki*.

Evil Flourishes, but Ito Encounters Jizo in Broad Daylight

THE DEADLINES THAT COME ONCE a month are much like menstruation.

My friends who are about the same age tell me that they've gone through menopause or are at least on the verge of it. But I haven't stopped menstruating yet. I've spent these last forty-some years bleeding. Once a month. Once a month. Once a month. I'm completely used to it. I've grown close to it—in fact, I know how to live with it far better than I know how to live with my own husband. I ought to treat these installments of the novel that I submit monthly to the literary magazine *Gunzo* the way I treat my menstrual cycle. I ought to just keep writing, linking one installment to the next like the periods that just keep on coming.

Mom's suffering, Dad's suffering, my husband's suffering.

Loneliness, anxiety, frustration.

Various forms of suffering rain down on me, but my suffering is no longer really suffering. When I use the suffering that rains down on me as material for writing, I put it under a microscope and observe, and then I find myself forgetting that suffering causes pain.

So what's really happening? Is Jizo not answering my prayers and pulling out my thorns?

THE OPPRESSIVE ATMOSPHERE CREATED BY my sick husband's anger had grown even worse, and I struggled with the very thought of it. My return to California grew closer by the minute. I had no choice but to go back and face him. I had to face the question of where we'd go from here. Would our family split up? Would we go our separate ways?

While I was in Japan, I had plenty of friends to talk to. Every one of them had some sort of problem in their lives. Some had trouble with men, some had conflicts with their families, some faced financial troubles. I had all sorts of female friends who would sit down and listen to me. All I had to do was open up. The problem was that none of them really understood what my husband was like. True, some had met him. A few had even exchanged pleasantries with him and said, let's get together sometime. To them, he might look a little disheveled, but when he opened his mouth, he seemed to be a pleasant, intellectual, well-mannered, quiet *gaijin*. *Gaijin*? Why the non-P.C. word to refer to a foreigner, you might wonder. Well, what's the matter with a *gaijin*'s wife calling her husband a *gaijin*? He is a *gaijin*—an "outsider"—after all. I couldn't think of him in the abstract as just a "foreigner." He was a stranger. It had been my mistake to let him in and start living together under the same roof.

I didn't know what to do, so I gave in to my other daughter. I'm talking about my oldest daughter—Aiko's half-sister. She had flown the nest and was now living elsewhere, but in a certain way she was still with me. She listened to my feelings and even shared her frustrations about men. When I divorced her father, she was about the same age as Aiko is now. She went through all sorts of suffering, not all of which was entirely necessary. The bittersweet life she'd experienced since had matured her, so I turned to her for advice. She listened obligingly at first, but before long, she wrote me the following email.

> I feel sorry for Aiko, but to tell the truth, I think it's okay to be a little selfish and call it quits. Then you'd be living in a way that's true to yourself. It makes me excited just to think about it.

She was barely twenty years old, but the tone of her message made it sound like she thought she knew everything. My rage boiled over. I felt like an on-demand water heater that had been in storage for the last twenty years. I might not have boiled anytime recently, but my daughter had pushed my buttons. I clicked "reply" and began angrily jabbing at the keyboard.

> Keep quiet when it comes to things you know nothing about.
> When have you ever seen me living in a way that wasn't true to myself?
> Come to think of it, have I ever shown you how I act when I am really being true to myself?

This might not have been fair of me, but I was in turmoil, and I didn't know where to direct my indignation and resentment. If anything, that was the way I'd been living.

I'D BEEN THINKING.

Maybe I'd go back to California. As I mentioned before, one thought that had crossed my mind was taking the money out of our savings account and sending my most important books to my daughter—the cheeky one, I mean. I'd leave everything else behind. Abandon everything. Just grab my passport and flash drive, meet Aiko in front of her school, and whisk her away on an airplane.

Or maybe I'd find a cheap apartment somewhere nearby and move in. Aiko could go back and forth between us; maybe she could move in with me and visit her father on weekends. If so, she'd be just like all the other kids with divorced parents. Many of Aiko's friends went back and forth between two houses.

The other day Aiko said, Mom, I should get a cellphone. So-and-so has one, she brought it to school, it has a long strap on it. So-and-so—you know, that other girl—she's also got one.

I told her, kids don't need such things, cellphones are nothing but trouble, a cellphone wouldn't do you any good, but Aiko kept insisting.

Our teacher let so-and-so and so-and-so have a cellphone, our teacher said it'll help them stay in touch with their parents because their parents are divorced. *Okaasan* (she drew out the word "Mother" in Japanese), the first morning I take my cellphone to school, I want to hang my Tamagotchi from it (the rest was in English).

I'd been thinking.

One of those little cabins for surfers would probably be enough for me. I'm Japanese, I've lived in single-room apartments before, I could sleep in a tiny space and pile everything next to my bed. In that case, maybe it would make things easier for Aiko if she had her own phone. But when I looked up the prices of those surfer cabins online, I discovered that they're ridiculously expensive, especially considering they have so few conveniences. Plus, if I were to leave Aiko, her Japanese wouldn't get any better—it would grow worse, and soon we wouldn't be able to communicate as mother and daughter anymore. Once that thought crossed my mind, a cloud passed over me, and I felt despondent. This is, to borrow the words of a famous classical poet, the darkness of loving a child.

I STARTED TO NOTICE SOMETHING odd. People were talking about Jizo all the time. Here, there, everywhere. No one knew that I'd been thinking so much about the Thorn-Pulling Jizo, yet everyone seemed to be talking about Sugamo and the power of the miraculous Jizo there.

One of the nurses by Mom's bedside said as if to encourage her, Sugamo, Ito-san, Sugamo.

Sugamo. Hearing that took me by surprise, especially since we were so far away in Kumamoto.

Seeing my reaction, the nurse said, your mother talks about Sugamo so often. Actually, I'm fond of the place too. I have a daughter in Tokyo, so every time I go there, I visit Sugamo too. I promised your mother that if she gets better, we'll go there together. "Sugamo" has become like a secret word we share, just the two of us.

As the nurse said this, Mom, who by this point could only communicate with facial expressions, smiled and nodded.

I told the nurse that I hadn't been to Sugamo in a long time. How many years had it been? Recently, I'd been thinking I should go again.

The nurse said, you know the honey shop there? On the street that leads up to the temple? The one that sells honey and other stuff? Well, they started selling "sudden dumplings" too. It was like the Tokyoites were imitating us or something—as they ate them, they kept saying how great they tasted in their funny Tokyo dialect, how nice the texture was. They kept buying them and gobbling them up as if the dumplings were some Sugamo specialty.

Let me interject here. A "sudden dumpling," or ikinari dango, is a Kumamoto specialty. You take a slice of raw sweet potato and some red bean paste, wrap it in dough, then give it a brief but intense steaming—that's why it's called a "sudden dumpling." I could imagine how surprised she was to find them for sale in Sugamo, far away in Tokyo.

As if answering my thought, she said, I couldn't have been more surprised than if I was in Hell and had run into Lord Jizo myself! So I did what anyone would do, I bought some and ate them—those same treats I've been eating ever since I was a little kid. And ever since then, whenever I see one of those dumplings, I always think of Sugamo.

I WAS IN TOKYO TALKING to the widow of a famous poet when suddenly she said, say, why don't we get together in Sugamo? That'd be perfect. From there, we can go visit my husband's grave.

I was surprised. What are the chances she'd suggest meeting there?

I'd only met her husband once when he was alive. Even at that meeting, I was completely in awe of him. He was a super-famous poet, after all, and I listened carefully to take in everything he said. Every sound he made was familiar; in fact, his manner of speaking reminded me of Grandpa Tatsugoro, Uncle Tatsuo, Uncle Kazumi, and all my other long-gone male relatives. But then I realized, no, the similarity wasn't in his voice. It was in his pronunciation. Changing the first sound in my name—*hi*—to the Tokyo pronunciation—*shi*—he whispered, my wife's reading your work, Shiromi-chan. His Tokyo accent made me feel as if I'd ascended to heaven.

He died not long after that. I was busy in California when it happened. When I published my next book, I sent a copy to his widow, even though we hadn't yet met. In response, she sent me a postcard expressing her thanks in generous but not at all flowery terms. Again, the next time I published a book, I sent it to her, and once again, I received another postcard. Once again, I sent a book, and once again I received a card. That continued for ten years. It was like a long thin thread of connection had formed between us despite the fact we'd never met. But I hadn't received a postcard lately. Judging from the poet's age at the time of his death, I guessed she probably wasn't any spring chicken either. She might be having age-related health problems too. I began to worry. Soon after, the postcard I'd been expecting finally arrived.

I wrote her back, saying, I was worried when no postcard arrived. I'm pleased to hear there's no change on your end. I write books to make a living, but when your postcard didn't arrive, I began to feel that maybe the real reason I'm writing all these books is because I'm actually just hoping to hear from you.

A box of chocolates arrived from her. I called to thank her, and in doing so, I heard her voice for the first time. Like her postcards, her speech was quick, generous, and concise. Her accent wasn't as strong as her late husband's, but I could still detect traces of Tokyo.

While we were talking, I thought, Sugamo! There's the Sugamo connection again! Her husband's grave was located there. Once on a previous trip, I'd tried to find his grave on my own. If you walk from Sugamo Station, the temple where he's buried is before the shop-lined street leading to the Jizo temple. I'd managed to find the graveyard, but the graves were packed tightly together, and I couldn't find his.

I explained I'd gone to the cemetery, but I'd been unable to find his stone. I told her, I must have some sort of karmic connection to Sugamo. I've been thinking about the Jizo temple constantly, and I'd really like to make a trip to see it again.

Oh really? Well then, why don't we meet in Sugamo? That'd be perfect. I'll invite so-and-so—she mentioned the name of a poet who was a mutual friend of ours. It was through that particular friend that, more than a decade before, I'd met the dead poet in the first place. The poet's wife sounded so happy that I could imagine her jumping for joy. Why don't we visit his grave together?

I don't remember exactly when, but some years before, my husband had come to Japan to visit. We were out with Aiko, who was still little, when we passed a small statue of Jizo standing next to a city street. I stopped, bought a stick of incense from the little window beside him (a stick and a candle cost a mere twenty yen), and gave them as an offering. Aiko and I would sometimes do things like that when we were on our own.

When my husband saw us, however, he began berating me, saying, so my wife is giving my daughter a religious education without consulting me, eh?

It took quite a while to clear up the misunderstanding. In fact, we only really managed to clear it up the next time he came to Japan. A friend of mine took him to a bunch of places. They were at a Shinto shrine together when she threw a coin in the offering box and pressed her hands together in a gesture of prayer. He asked, who are you praying to? Not looking the least concerned, she answered, to anyone who listens. Later, back in California, my husband repeated that story over and over, saying, there's nothing stranger than what passes as faith among the Japanese. You might call it religion, but it's not religion as we know it.

I have no strong feelings about religion one way or the other. But it's a whole different story when it comes to Jizo. I'm not sure if I should call it habit or belief or what exactly. It's like how I want to use Japanese when I really need to express myself, like how I want to eat when I get hungry—Jizo is like that for me. I keep coming back to him because it's the natural thing to do. There's a part of me that wishes I could be like my Grandma, the spirit medium, and pray and pray and pray so ardently that I fall into a trance. But since I can't, well, the next best thing is to buy an amulet at the Jizo temple and keep it close.

I TOLD MOM, I'M GOING to Tokyo soon. I'll visit Sugamo while I'm there. I'll pray to Jizo and ask him to remove your thorns of suffering.

Mom said, if you're going there, buy a good luck amulet for me. She said, they sell them just inside the temple gate. The so-called substitute amulets are the best—they take away troubles on your behalf, allowing Jizo to act as your substitute. They've also got "portrait amulets" that have images of Jizo on them. You swallow them to heal yourself from the inside out, but the substitute amulets work the best.

She told me a substitute amulet won't work if you just carry it around. It's best to burn the little piece of wood it's printed on and then eat it. It's like the bark of the relationship-ending hackberry tree—grinding it up and putting it in soup or something is what makes it work.

She said if you want to break up with a man, you should walk along the road in front of the Sugamo Jizo temple. Keep going toward Koshinzuka until you reach the tracks. The grave of Oiwa is right where it stops. That also works. (Oiwa is a famous ghost from kabuki. Her husband betrayed and then poisoned her, so she returned as a ghost and took revenge on him and his lover.)

I say to Mom, but isn't Oiwa's grave in Zoshigaya?

No, she insisted, no, the demon-mother goddess Kishimo is in Zoshigaya. Oiwa's grave is in Koshinzuka.

Get off at Koshinzuka and walk in the opposite direction from the Jizo temple. It's right by the tram tracks. Back when you had that problem with that guy, I worried myself sick. I went there and prayed for help, and sure enough, it did the trick—the two of you broke up right away.

She was right. When I was twenty-two, I had a love affair that totally broke my heart. The experience was so awful that I cried in front of Mom more times than I care to remember. Still, I'd never have dreamed of asking Oiwa's ghost to help break us up. After that, I had a whole string of painful love affairs. Come to think of it, I've never had a relationship that was completely pain-free. I wondered how many times Mom had gone there to pray to end my relationship. There was no way of knowing which prayers had worked.

I've done tons of bad things in my time. I couldn't help it. If a woman wants to be her own person, she doesn't have a lot of choice.

She has to steel herself and do some down-and-dirty things—that's why I've experienced so much pain. I felt as if I were being shunned by all the buddhas. I had trouble with my previous partners and with my children, and now I was having trouble with my husband. No sooner did I work myself free of one set of problems than new ones came along with my aging parents.

When I was a little girl, once a month someone would take me by the hand to the temple. Even if I was shunned by many buddhas, when we arrived, I put my tiny hands together in prayer, and Mom or Grandma would rub, rub, rub, rub the smoke from the burning incense all over my hands, legs, and head. I told myself, everything will be fine as long as I trust Jizo. And now I thought, he's still there waiting for me.

THE POET'S WIFE AND I decided not to meet on the twenty-fourth, the most popular day for pilgrimages, since the place would be mobbed with people. We met on the nineteenth, a blustery spring day.

Sugamo looked different from how I remembered. My most recent trip was ten years earlier when I took an American poet and his wife there. That visit fell on one of the pilgrimage days. The place was packed, and I grew exhausted trying to lead them through the crowds. They tried to tell me not to worry, commenting, this is still better than Disneyland—this place fulfills the need to believe in something, it keeps local culture alive.

I bought some flowers at a shop near the station. I was worried I'd be late for my rendezvous with the poet's wife, so I didn't take the time to choose them properly. I just grabbed three bouquets of smaller chrysanthemums—white, yellow, and reddish purple—from the bucket by the entrance. I went inside and asked the florist to bundle them together. He responded, if you want those colors, why don't you take these instead? He went over to a bucket with fresh chrysanthemums of various colors.

Now then, you wanted white, yellow, and red, right?

Well, how about if you just give me all white?

Okay, white then. Wrap them up together, right?

He spoke with a rich Tokyo accent. It had such a familiar ring.

The wind was blowing through the temple grounds where the poet's wife was waiting. Moments later, our poet friend showed up, followed by yet another poet. Together, the four of us went to the grave. The cherry trees were in bloom. The other visitors in the graveyard were carrying buckets of water to wash the gravestones. Near the entrance someone was selling bundles of branches and flowers of various colors. When I stopped to reflect, I realized it was the equinox, the time we go to pay our respects to the departed. I'd totally forgotten the date. The poet's widow called to her husband under the gravestone, Minoru darling, Shiromi has come to see you. The way she pronounced my name was halfway between *shi* and *hi*, giving off just the faintest whiff of Tokyo.

THANK YOU. THAT WAS A really nice meal.

I bowed and said, well, I think I'll be off.

Where are you going next?

I thought I'd go to the Jizo temple and get one of those substitute amulets for Mom.

Mr. So-and-So chimed in, mind if I go too? It feels as if it was meant to be.

I bowed and said, well then, we'll be off.

As we parted, everyone agreed we ought to get together again.

The poet and I walked side by side. It had been ages since we'd seen one another.

It probably sounds disrespectful to call him "Mr. So-and-So" just to preserve his anonymity. After all, he's much older than I am, and we're really, really close, but it had been ages since we'd seen one another. We used to see each other more often and talk on the phone. He loved to talk trash—mocking people's foibles and sharing gossip. Then he'd break off to recite a new little poem—always sincere—peppered with classical allusions. His voice would become strong and clear as a boy's, and I'd listen, my heart swelling with appreciation and affection. In those days, I never had new poems. All I had were piles of old ones, so I never had anything to share in response.

On that day he had a bunch of poetry manuscripts in his backpack, and he carried the kind of walking stick you'd use for climbing a mountain. He leaned forward as he walked, and the cluster of tiny bells at the end of his walking stick jingled with each step, as if casting a spell.

He asked, is this your first time visiting Sugamo?

No, it's not, I said, I came here once with an American poet. You know who I mean—that guy you met and his wife. It was the twenty-fourth, and the place was so packed you could hardly move. We bumped against strangers with every step, and lord help us if we got separated! He wanted a statue of Inari, the fox god, and so even though it was super-crowded, we stopped to buy one at a shop that sells religious goods in front of the temple.

The poet nodded and said, he must have found it very exotic.

There were fewer people on the approach to the temple than

you'd encounter on the special pilgrimage days. There weren't too many stalls either, no crowds of ladies jostling against each other to get where they were going. Just grocery stores, plant stores, florists.

I commented, it's early spring, but all they're selling is chrysanthemums.

To that, the poet responded, it's the vernal equinox. Chrysanthemums make the best offerings.

But why? It's not the right season. It's spring.

It's because it's customary to offer a thornless flower with a long stem. They say that in ancient times, when the disciple Mahakasyapa was rushing to the Buddha's side, he encountered a Brahmin on the road who told him to go offer a flower to the Buddha. That's how Mahakasyapa learned the Buddha had died. In such situations, they say, offering a flower with thorns is like sticking the soul of the deceased with a thorn. Plus, you need to offer a flower that can dispel evil. If not, then the person doing the offering might be next to die. That's why chrysanthemums are best—they have no thorns, and they dispel evil.

A pharmacy, a shop selling salty Daifuku mochi, a clothing shop, a pickle shop, a shop selling senbei rice crackers, a shop selling undergarments, a shop selling knitted goods, a shop selling vegetables simmered in soy sauce, a shop selling sweet potato confections, a fabric shop, and the honey shop where Mom's nurse had gone. A shop selling kumquats, a shop selling Chinese medicine, a shop selling ginger, a shop selling goji berries, another clothing shop, a shop selling beaded handicrafts, a shop selling eels, a soba restaurant, a dessert cafe, another senbei shop. A shop selling wooden clogs, a shop selling shoes, a shop selling work clothes, a shop selling shawls, a shop selling furoshiki wrapping cloths, a shop that cleans kimonos, a shop selling clothing, a shop selling fabric, a shop that provides acupuncture and moxibustion services, a spice shop, and everywhere, people selling bundles of incense.

The poet was transformed as we walked.

An incense vendor stood there with his face covered.

The poet's whiskers disappeared.

His spine slowly straightened.

His walking stick grew into a staff as tall as he was.

Surprised, the incense vendors all bowed in respect.

The creases in his face smoothed, and the streaks of white in his hair disappeared. His face grew younger and younger—as he walked forward, eyes shimmering with curiosity, he looked like a boy of fourteen or fifteen. He was no longer gaunt. His chest swelled, grew thicker, and I thought I saw his breasts jiggle. He had become both man and woman, yet at the same time, neither. In previous lives, he had certainly been both a man and a woman. He was a bodhisattva who felt sorry for humankind. He'd transformed himself into Jizo so that he could inhabit the six realms of existence and alleviate our suffering. Jizo was walking beside me.

I bought a bundle of incense. We walked through the temple gate, and I threw my lit bundle into the gigantic cauldron of burning incense that stands in front of the main hall.

How strange.

I hadn't been there in years, and yet I still remembered how to do it.

First you wash your hands to purify them.

Then you throw some incense into the cauldron to burn.

Visitors to the temple always get trapped in the crowds, but you can't let that bother you. Unless you push your way through, you won't be able to approach the big incense burner. Once you're there, use your hands to fan the smoke toward you, then rub it on any part of your body that might be afflicted—your head, face, shoulders, breasts, fingers, or throat. Next, proceed to the temple's main building, toss a coin or two into the offering box, and pray.

Ordinarily, the next thing would be to get into the long line to wash the statue of Kannon in front of the temple, but we skipped washing the statue that day. The poet-turned-Jizo stood there with his backpack and staff and watched me silently as I prayed.

WE LEFT ALONG THE SAME street on which we had come. I talked about the problems that I'd been having with my husband. The people walking past us produced a steady hum, but I ignored them.

And so, I don't know if I can go back, I don't even know if I want to go back.

Jizo asked, why on earth did you do such a thing?

I have to level with you about a couple of things.

Jizo nodded. Sure, you can tell me anything.

And so I started telling him all sorts of things—about my husband's erections (or his lack thereof), about my husband's willingness to go down on me (or his lack thereof).

It's clear that there's some sort of problem between us, but we're not able to talk it out. I'm not able to tell him my true feelings.

Jizo nodded. Sure, makes sense.

But if we can't talk those things over, then he questions what kind of couple we are. I only want to spend time together without getting in each other's hair, but he doesn't seem to feel the same way, it's like there's some Judeo-Christian delusion—some ideal that he believes in. He seems to think the romance between husband and wife ought to be eternal and unchanging. It doesn't leave any room for growing older or dying, but in reality, that's what's happening—we're getting older and dying little by little. He gets dragged down by that delusion and keeps on complaining, I can't get it up anymore, I can't get it up, I just can't get it up. It's not like it's anyone's fault he can't get hard. When our eyes meet in the mornings and at night, we don't even smile at one another. We're on pins and needles.

We crossed to the opposite side of the street. The crowds of people going to worship the Thorn-Pulling Jizo were already behind us. We walked along the shopping street in front of the station, filled with ordinary people coming and going. There were none of the big piles of chrysanthemums we had seen in the stalls near the temple. Instead, there were rows of potted plants—flowering quince, small flowering peach trees, Calanthe orchids.

Jizo commented, it only makes sense, we're all the same, he's no spring chicken, the fact he was able to keep it up so long is impressive—a dream come true really. There's no need for him to feel bad, but of course, telling him that won't make him feel any better.

Then Jizo turned to me and said, I have some advice.

Here's what you need to do. Praise his work, praise it to the skies. Tell him his work is the best thing about him. He'll stop worrying about his impotence then. You've got no idea how much a man likes having his work praised. Praising someone's work is even better than praising his cock.

Jizo said, say this to him: I've been too embarrassed to say it until now, but you've got no idea how much your work has influenced my poetry. That's probably not a lie, in any case.

As soon as we descended the stairs to the platform at Sugamo Station, Jizo resumed the form of the poet, carrying his backpack filled with handwritten poetry and his walking stick. Bent over like before, he disappeared into the crowd boarding the train for Komagome. I stood there for a long time, hands pressed together as if in prayer as I watched the green Yamanote train retreat into the distance.

NOTE FROM THE AUTHOR

I borrowed from a poem in the late-twelfth-century anthology *Songs to Make the Dust Dance*: "Passing through this fleeing world / as I labor on the sea and mountains, / I am shunned by many buddhas— / what will become of me in the next life?" In addition, I borrowed the voices of the food writer Moeko Akatsuka, Yoko Yoshioka (the wife of the poet Minoru Yoshioka), and the poet Mutsuo Takahashi.

Ito Goes on a Journey, Making a Pilgrimage to Yuda Hot Springs

I'VE BEEN THINKING CONSTANTLY ABOUT Oguri-san. Then yesterday I got an email from him. (Hold on, I won't tell you what it said just yet. Be patient!) I stood up and cried out in a voice that wasn't really a voice at all. I'm not exaggerating when I say he'd been on my mind every single day. I first met him through work. That's the reason I affix the polite suffix -san to his name and always use formal language with him, even though he's more than twenty years younger. I'd been brooding, really worried about him, so when his email arrived, it felt like I'd cast a spell that worked. I suppose I should call it "prayer," but I'd been thinking of him with such single-minded devotion that it felt more like a spell than a prayer. That's when I remembered. Perhaps it was a spell, but the other day I'd given him the amulet I'd bought a while back when I was visiting the Thorn-Pulling Jizo in Sugamo.

I DON'T MAKE RIGHT TURNS. That's what I told him when we first met three summers ago. I said I really wanted to go to the literary museum where he works, but the location was a problem. To get there, I had to follow the streetcar tracks away from Kumamoto

Castle, go through the intersections at Suidocho and Taikobashi, then turn at Shin'yashiki, Miso Tenjin, or Suizenji, none of which had a special right-turn lane, and all the while I had to brave oncoming traffic and crossing streetcars.

I said, it's in my father's last will and testament—his dying words were that I should never make a right turn under any circumstances.

But Ito-san, you just told me that your father was alive and had a caregiver.

That's true, I said. I was just exaggerating, trying to show him how much I hate right turns. I also hate squeezing through narrow streets when there's oncoming traffic, but I still do it. Right turns across traffic, however, are where I draw the line. When I'm on one of those little streets where there's no right-turn lane and I'm waiting for a break in the oncoming traffic, which just keeps on coming and coming, ignoring me completely, I sense the cars behind me getting pissed, and I end up completely losing the courage to turn. If I do pluck up the courage to do it, I feel as if I'm taking my life into my hands, and by the time I get close to the museum, my fear has left me completely breathless. The parking lot is behind the gymnasium, and the museum is even farther, behind the library. To get there, I have to make my way through bushes and thickets. My nails get broken, my feet get scratched and irritated, I get caught in spiderwebs and eaten by mosquitoes. As if that wasn't bad enough, the neighborhood is called Izumi, which means "the spring." Every time it rains, the place quickly floods, as though water is bubbling up out of nowhere. I couldn't get to the museum even if I wanted to.

So Oguri-san taught me a way to get there by turning left in front of those intersections, veering right in front of Suizenji Park, then passing directly through all the stoplights. He also promised to clear a spot in the embarrassingly thick tangle of jasmine wrapped around the large camphor tree right in front of the museum, since that would give me a place to stop the car and enter.

After learning his special route, I started driving to the museum to see him whenever I returned to Kumamoto, even if I didn't really have any business there—I turned left, followed the road as it veered to the right, then proceeded straight ahead.

He loved literature. He spoke passionately about all sorts of things, telling me how the museum built its collection and how the new displays were going to look. Until then, I'd never bothered to tell people I'm a poet, because as a poet I'd only just scraped by. The only way people might have known I'm a poet was because I'd use my profession as an excuse, saying things like, hey, don't hate me, the reason I put the trash out on the wrong day is because, well, I'm a poet, you know. But with Oguri-san, things were different. His work involved putting together displays featuring the museum's literary collection, so I didn't hide my poems or books from him. We got lost in conversation, chatting on and on about famous poets like Kenji Miyazawa and Chuya Nakahara.

In the museum there were life-sized papier-mâché statues of the novelist Soseki Natsume and the haiku poet Teijo Nakamura sitting there quietly, and in the back stood a silent statue of the haiku poet Santoka Taneda. Once I started going to the museum regularly, I got to know all the staff, and they would call out to me, ah! Ito-san!

Twenty years ago, I moved to Kumamoto with a newborn in tow. My parents also left Tokyo for Kumamoto more than a decade ago, but in the meantime, I had relocated to California and returned to

Kumamoto only a few times a year. My memories of Tokyo faded. When I passed through Tokyo on my way to Kumamoto, I encountered new subway lines and lots of new places to visit, but they were all unfamiliar. When I talked about Tokyo, I talked about "going there," rather than "going home." On the other hand, if you asked me if I felt like I really belonged in Kumamoto, I probably would have said no. I lived like an orphan, depending on no one. I felt akin to the fleabane and goldenrod growing wild on the riverbank near where I live in Kumamoto. But then Oguri-san and his colleagues started calling out to me, ah, Ito-san! And with that, everything changed.

Oguri-san and I'd been talking about going to a festival dedicated to Chuya Nakahara. It was held every year in Yuda Hot Springs in the city of Yamaguchi. I sent him an email suggesting we drive my car.

My car is bigger, he wrote back.

I responded, my car is a rental anyway, so we might as well use it.

The problem was my discomfort with making right turns or squeezing through narrow streets with oncoming traffic. It was impossible to drive the small backstreets of Kumamoto without yielding to cars coming from the other direction. Renting a tiny compact car was how I kept from killing myself.

I added, don't worry, even the smallest compacts are pretty big these days.

Oguri-san accepted my offer. This whole exchange took place over email while I was in California.

Before long, another email arrived, telling me something personal had come up on the afternoon we wanted to leave. I suggested we head out after he was done. Plus, I needed to make sure Dad had dinner. Would six o'clock work? He responded, I took off a half-day in the afternoon, I'll finish what I have to do, then go back to work and wait for you. We can go whenever you're ready.

Aha, I thought. Occasionally, the chance arose to ask him about his personal life. I tried to entice him into spilling the beans by asking, you got some dumb thing you've got to do that day?

He wrote back, I'll tell you on the road when we've got time to talk.

A few days later I arrived in Kumamoto. It was toward the end of April.

The camphor trees had spread. Where the camphor grew between the rocks in the castle walls, it had bushed out, covering the stone. Not just there, though. All over town the camphor grew thick and looked out, dominating the city with its firm stare. No sooner did you notice the green clumps growing restless than the branches began to laugh with new leaves the color of bright yellow and bronze, and before you knew it, the foliage was growing over everything. The camphor trees had no ill intent—they were just so hungry they couldn't stand it and gobbled up whatever they could. The ginkgos were thick with new leaves. The cherry trees weren't just green, they had a bluish hue to them, perhaps even the color of blue-green seawater. The trunks and branches sucked in the color, and where the sunlight fell on them, the trees sucked it in, turning a dark indigo. The rhododendrons had started to bloom, producing patches of color. It was as if red and white paint had been spilled on them—the colors mixed in some places and not in others, but either way the color seeped through the teal and viridian leaves. Sorrel,

green with touches of red and yellow, grew tall on the riverbank
and shone in the light. The grass sweated and wound its way into
whorls, while the wild raspberries worked to produce sweet fruit.
The trees and plants had pulled out all the stops, giving birth and
living life to the fullest.

APRIL 28. I TURNED LEFT, followed the road as it verged right, and
reached the museum. Oguri-san was already waiting.

Hold on a sec, I'm going to move my car to the parking lot, then
I'll be back, he told me, I've rented a parking spot for my car out
back. The camellias are blooming back there, you want to come see?

I went with him. The space, behind the museum at the edge of
someone's garden, was so tiny there was no way I could've gotten
a bicycle in there, much less a car. The place was lined with huge
camellias, which were blooming and dropping their open flowers.
Long ago, the goddess Izanami vowed to strangle a thousand people to death every day, and the god Izanagi shouted back, well then,
I'm going to make sure a thousand five hundred people are born
every day. The blooming and falling flowers reminded me of that
exchange. The camellias were at the end of their season, with newborn blooms far fewer than those that had already been strangled.
Even while he was moving the car, blooms died and fell before my
eyes. *Sheets of metal eat senbei, and the spring twilight is calm. Low-thrown
ash grows pale, and the spring twilight stills.*

Oguri-san was a big fellow, so he had to fold his limbs and stoop
a little to fit in the passenger seat. The tiny gray car got onto the
highway and sped up. The forests of trees with their shiny leaves
throbbed with life and new growth, while the wild wisterias wound

around themselves reluctantly, eager to finish whatever they hadn't yet completed. Yellowish bamboo thickets stood here and there, stupefied. Bright yellow rapeseed blossoms and white herons stood out against the background, but eventually, all these things faded away in the encroaching darkness.

OGURI-SAN STARTED THE CONVERSATION, SAYING, let me level with you, I've developed a lump on my side, below my chest. I didn't know what it was, and it's just got bigger and bigger. I went to the doctor, he did all sorts of tests, and he told me it was either cancer of the lymph nodes or some complicated illness named after the guy who discovered it. The illness is rare and not well researched. It looks just like cancer but it's treatable if the lump is removed. The tests have taken forever, I was supposed to get the results today, but when I went to the clinic, they told me they couldn't figure it out, so they decided to send me to the university hospital. That just leaves me hanging for another two weeks. Calmly, quietly, he told me, I ought to know by the time the Golden Week holiday break is over. That'll be early next month. *In the slippery state of moonlight, is spring twilight that which submits?*

He told me, I've lost a bunch of weight. My appetite's just fine, I thought maybe the weight loss was because I was too preoccupied with work, so I didn't think much about it until the doctor brought it up.

The last service area in Kyushu was in Koga. I drove that far, and we switched places there. As he drove, I stared into the distance. We saw a truck lying on its side at the edge of the road. The lights on the police cars were shining, shining, shining brilliantly.

It's hard, Oguri-san muttered, when things are so up in the air—all I do is think about it.

We chatted about all sorts of things—about champon noodles from Nagasaki, about the poet Chuya Nakahara, about my parents, about the displays he was preparing for the museum, but neither of us could avoid thinking about death, nothingness, and suffering. Nothingness, suffering, and death weighed heavily on our minds.

WE ARRIVED AT YUDA HOT Springs. It was probably after ten in the evening. All the poets and other folks associated with the Chuya Festival were out eating, so we walked to the restaurant to join them. It was late at night, but *here and there, we could hear the sound of people scooping up water in the public baths.* On the street corners were steamy mini hot springs known as "foot baths" by the locals. Everyone was at the restaurant. I greeted them excitedly. My goodness, it's been so long! Looks like you've put on a bit of weight. So-and-so isn't here yet? He's supposed to arrive tomorrow.

Some people I knew, some I didn't. I watched everyone bob up and down, bowing and exchanging name cards, until a poet I know well said, there's an outdoor bath on the roof of the hotel, they usually turn the lights out at midnight, but apparently, it's open all night.

It was almost one o'clock by the time I got to the hotel room. It was an ordinary hotel with Western-style rooms, and Oguri-san was in the room next to mine. I put on the cotton yukata the hotel provided and quietly tiptoed up to the hot bath on the roof. The light was shining on the women's side. Not a soul was there—no one had left slippers at the entrance. I could tell there were a whole bunch of people on the men's side though—lots of slippers there. I guessed that's where all the poets were, probably Oguri-san too. It was a new moon and partly cloudy. I slipped into the rectangular jet-black bath and spread out my arms and legs. The water sloshing around my skin was just the right temperature—comfortably warm. I thought of Oguri-san's side, about suffering, death, and nothingness. I sank into the pool and watched the night slide by for what seemed like eons and eons.

CHUYA WAS BORN ON APRIL 29, 1907, and every year on his birthday, the Chuya Nakahara Memorial Museum, built on the site of his birthplace and childhood home, holds a big festival in his honor. I won't say much about the festivities, but lots of people recite Chuya's poetry. We heard all his most famous lines. *Look, look, these are my bones*, and *On this bit of soiled sorrow*, and *Sheets of metal eat senbei*, and so on. I read too. *Will you flow, flow away? And One morning I saw a black flag flutter, up there in the sky*. That was why I was there—to read. I chatted with old acquaintances and the people I'd just met. *Here, tonight, a party like no other. Here, tonight, a party like no other.* Of course, Oguri-san was with me too. *It rains, it stops, the wind blows. The clouds flow, the moon hides. Ladies and gentlemen, a spring night. The wind blows, wet and warm.* I say he was "with me," but our circle of acquaintances didn't entirely overlap—*this time, and that time, are so far apart, and this place, and that place, are not the same*—so even though we were together in the same place, we spoke with different people. Nonetheless, I was thinking about him the whole time.

Yuaaaaan yuyooooon—swinging back and forth. I imagined all sorts of things. Oguri-san's suffering. *Yuya yuyon—back and forth.* His death. *Yuyon*. And nothingness. *Yuya yuyon*. I imagined that even if I turned left, veered to the right, and proceeded straight to the literary museum, one day there might be no one there to greet me, ah, Ito-san! *And so life puffs away like smoke, your life and mine puffed away like smoke. Yuya yuyon—back and forth, back and forth.*

In the middle of the night, I crept back to the rooftop bath. The lights were off, but I took a dip in the lukewarm water anyway.

And I rocked back and forth—*yuya yuyon*.

I thought of the cluster of banana trees behind the literary museum swaying back and forth—*yuya yuyon*.

Water flowed along, flowed along, feeding the banana trees, which drank up the water and spread. Over countless summers, they had spread in the heat and humidity. Over countless winters, they had died back and grown quiet. The place was incredible. Any time someone came to visit, I showed it to them as one of the sights of Kumamoto. I'd also take them to the eight-hundred-year-old camphor tree known as "Jakushin-san's camphor" because of the samurai-turned-priest buried beneath its branches.

THE NEXT MORNING WHILE OGURI-SAN and I were eating breakfast, he suddenly stopped smiling and asked, do you want to touch my lump?

I extended my hand. *Yuya yuyon*—I hesitated, hand shaking back and forth. He lifted his arm, and just as he said, there it was—hard like a bean—but it wasn't just a single lump as I'd imagined. There were a few of them.

Oguri-san said, you see? Then he smiled again, but he looked like he might cry.

The previous night, when I returned to my room from the rooftop bath, I checked. Yes, I still had it—the substitute amulet that I'd bought on my most recent pilgrimage to the Thorn-Pulling Jizo.

Mom had told me you're meant to keep it against the afflicted part of your body until it becomes soft, then you swallow it—it's also okay to burn it, put the ashes in miso soup, and swallow it that way. I'd bought the amulet for Mom but giving it to her had completely slipped my mind.

I called out his name. *Oguri-san.* At that moment, every sound that issued from my mouth was a spell.

I have something good for you.

Something incredibly good.

I took the amulet

Out of my wallet and put it

Trembling back and forth—*yuya yuyon*

In his hands.

As I spoke, I hid within my words a spell: *This is not just an ordinary amulet, no, it holds great spiritual merit, it is one of the Thorn-Pulling Jizo's amulets, and this one has the greatest power, Jizo will take away your suffering, so I bequeath it to you—place your faith in it.*

A FRIEND OF MINE JOINED us on the return trip. She offered to drive, but I told her that in America, it's not uncommon to drive five or six hours. I took the steering wheel, and we left Yuda Hot Springs behind.

It had rained the previous day, but that day the sky was completely blue. She suggested we stop along the way at Akama Shrine in Shimonoseki to enjoy the view of the sea, so I set my GPS and took off along the Chugoku Expressway.

She kept talking about her boyfriend. *Although he is kind to me, I am firm in my ways,* and so nothing has happened between us yet, she said. I responded, he probably doesn't really want you, and honestly, it doesn't seem you want him either. She said, no, I do. *I am fond of him, I've spent these nights and days submerged in the clear waters of affection and amicability.* Because I've been around the block a few times, I told her that wasn't enough—if she really wanted him, she had to go for it. We drove on the expressway for a while, then got off just before crossing over to Kyushu. As we followed the GPS's instructions, turning corners and driving straight, my friend continued talking about her boyfriend. She said to me, *I don't want him to think about anything when we're together, I don't like it even when he thinks out of consideration for me,* so I started teasing her. I teased her, and we had lots of fun laughing as we drove into the city. Oguri-san listened quietly in the back seat. The GPS told us we'd arrived.

My friend shouted, ah, there it is! There it is! Turn right! But since I had to turn right, I missed it. I kept going, made a careful U-turn, traveled back along the way we'd come, and made a left turn. No one said a word.

My friend told us, some things here are amazing, but the rest are nothing special. There's the statue of Hoichi the Earless and the mounds erected to the dead Taira samurai—they're totally creepy, like they're cursed, full of resentment somehow.

A famous naval battle had taken place just offshore in the late twelfth century. The result was the defeat of the Taira clan. The Genpei Wars, which dominated much of the late twelfth century, came to a close. The shrine had been erected to appease the souls of the defeated warriors, and so on the grounds of the shrine were several memorials dedicated to the Taira samurai whose bodies were never recovered.

Then a few centuries later, something incredible supposedly took place there. According to a famous folk tale, Hoichi was a blind musician who lived in the shrine precincts and recited stories of the Genpei Wars and the defeat of the Taira. The ghosts of the dead Taira warriors who were enshrined there began to visit Hoichi and asked him to perform the part of the story that described their own demise. Hoichi didn't realize at first that his patrons were ghosts, but when he did, the priest at the shrine took a brush and painted Hoichi's entire body with holy texts to protect him. The next time the ghosts came, they could see nothing but his two ears, which the priest had forgotten to cover with protective writing. One of the ghosts ripped off his ears and took them back to his grave. After that, the legend of Hoichi the Earless became famous throughout the country.

As luck would have it, the Festival of the Previous Emperors was about to take place in a few days, and a stage had been set up inside the grounds of the shrine. We were there in late April on a national holiday—Greenery Day—plus it was an auspicious day according to astrologists, so it was a good day for weddings. Several wedding ceremonies were taking place under the sunny skies, and there were also lots of visitors to the famous shrine. The crowds were making noise and having a fun time, but we went directly to the statue of Hoichi the Earless and to the memorials to the samurai who had haunted him.

The shiny leaves on the trees were thick and dusky, filled with spiderwebs. The camellias looked shabby, with the blooms falling to the ground. Seven memorial mounds stood in a row. One was dedicated to Taira no Tomonori, a historical figure I rather like. The mounds were off to the side, where there were no other visitors. The ground was slightly higher than the surrounding area, giving a good view of the Dannoura straits where the naval battle had taken place. Standing there in the shade, the mounds did seem cursed or full of ghostly resentment, just as my friend had said.

Right then, she let out a small shout and jumped back. Surprised, I turned and heard her say, oh my god! That statue of Hoichi gives me the creeps!

Hoichi? What's the problem?

Look, he's staring at us even when we turn our backs.

Inside the little shrine building behind us, Hoichi gazed at us intently with his dark, blind eyes.

As we left, we realized we could see the shore of Kyushu beyond the strait.

That's probably where the naval battle took place all those centuries ago, said Oguri-san. I imagined the water red with blood.

I looked at the water thinking, so this is where it happened. As the Battle of Dannoura was coming to a close and the Taira boats were sinking in defeat, Taira no Tomonori said, "I've seen all the things I should have seen," and jumped into the sea. He had done everything he could do, and he chose to kill himself with dignity rather than be killed or captured.

My friend said, Kyushu looks so close, when I think about those samurai, I feel really, really sorry for them—they must have wanted to get over there so badly. The water is so rough and the current so strong that even if they'd tried to make it to shore, they would've been carried away or crushed in their armor.

Oguri-san took over the driving. We got on the Kyushu Expressway after Shimonoseki. I suppose young men are good drivers after all. He drove fast, pedal to the metal. The tiny compact shook as the wind struck the side of the car.

New Moji. East Kokura. South Kokura. Yawata. The towns sped by.

Once we got on the expressway, we saw camphor trees everywhere, their leaves tinged with red and yellow. Wild wisterias were blooming, with flowers that crawled down the hanging stems. And here and there were paulownia trees, their flowers the same color as the wisterias but rising into the air.

I asked, you know the expression "mountains laughing" that they use in haiku? When they use it, what season are they describing?

This season right now, Oguri-san answered, keeping his hands on the wheel. It's used to describe the moment in spring when the hillsides develop their color and look nice and bright.

They sure seem to be laughing all right, my friend said as she started to laugh too. Do you suppose the camphor trees are the only ones who laugh? Don't the others do it too?

Wakamiya, Miyawaka. These similar-sounding names made it seem the sign-makers had forgotten the town's name and were trying to remember. We had a bowl of champon noodles in the roadside stop at Koga. Fukuoka. Sué. The names were becoming more and more historic. Lots of early history took place here.

Now we were getting into the region that was once the main point of contact between the ancient Japanese nation and the Asian mainland. Dazaifu. Tofuroato. That's where the ruins of the ancient sea walls erected in the seventh century are. The site of the medieval Karukaya checkpoint was there too.

Oguri-san said, occasionally you can find bits of ancient rice by the ruins of the sea walls. I found a single grain, and I treasure it to this day.

Chikushino. Tosu. The highway parts there, one way going to Nagasaki and the other toward Oita.

We reached Kurume. Then Hirokawa, literally "broad river," named after the river that flows through it. At Yame, famous for its tea, we stopped for a drink.

Nearby at Nankan lived a biwa player named Yoshiyuki Yamashika who, like Hoichi the Earless, recited the stories of the decline and fall of the Taira clan. The last time I heard him play, he was over ninety years old. That was over a decade ago.

My friend, cellphone to her ear, was speaking clearly so she could be easily understood, yes, darling, Mommy will be back in Kumamoto before long. It was a calm day. Outside the car, the spring landscape flowed by. The mountain trees looked so plump they seemed ready to burst. Spring was full on, and as twilight fell, the landscape felt full of erotic passion. *Somehow, the air is ever so slightly blue, as delicately pale as the root of a young spring onion.*

The delicate waters of the Kikusui River. The delicate town of Ueki. Then finally Kumamoto. *One roof tile has gone missing. Starting now, the spring twilight will silently march onward, into its own silent fetal duct.*

SOME TIME WENT BY. I returned to California, and although May is usually dry and sunny, it was so wet that year that the water seemed to be permanently suspended in the air. There were no blue skies, only *overcast skies* in which *flags fluttered back and forth, back and forth*. It was on one of those days when I received an email from Oguri-san.

> Last night, someone invited me to go on a drive with them
> in the middle of the night to the valley south of Mt. Aso.
> The pale moonlight was like out of some fantasy.
> The rice paddies filling the valley were brimming with water,
> frogs were pleasantly peeping, and for a little while, I felt
> refreshed.
> However, my friend only lets me ride in the back seat
> so I sat back there sipping some coffee, and thinking that this
> must be like the pilgrimage that Oguri made.

OGURI-SAN WAS REFERRING TO AN old Japanese story about a fellow with the same surname. According to the story, a man called Oguri Hangan was unjustly murdered, but through a series of miraculous events, the Lord of Hell returned him to life in the form of a *gakiami*—a deaf, blind, sick man who had a distended stomach and couldn't walk. Fate brought him to the lodgings of Terute, the woman he loved, who didn't recognize him but out of kindness dragged him along on a wagon for several days. After her, other generous people also pitched in and eventually took him all the way to the hot springs in Kumano. There, the miraculous springs healed him and restored his original form.

I wrote back, so you've just figured me out, eh, Oguri-san? What we did was exactly that—a *michiyuki*, a long journey in search of healing. I wrote about taking journeys—an important element in the classical literature we both like so much. I wrote about how plant, animal, and place names are so important to the old stories. I wrote about tenderness. About finding consolation. About other unimportant things. Soon I received the following response.

I realized something.
When you don't know what to do and
can't see any way out of a predicament,
when you can't simply sit still and
just want to bolt out and run away,
sometimes simply getting out and moving
can save you.

SOME MORE TIME WENT BY. Oguri-san wrote me again, but this time his email was like a cry of surprise. The doctors were right. It wasn't cancer. It was the other illness he'd mentioned—the one named after the guy who discovered it. That meant it was treatable.

The substitute amulet had worked. The spell had worked.

I'd been Terute for him, taking Oguri on the journey that brought him back to health.

I'd just turned fifty years old.

I'm no longer young. I've gotten flabby, and my spots, wrinkles, and gray hair are second to none. I may look old now, but when I was young, I was like the young maiden Terute in the story, pulling along countless sick, wounded, and decrepit men. I've pulled along lots of them, lots of sick and damaged men to the hot springs on the slopes of Kumano, where I dunked them into the rejuvenating baths. And it always worked. The power of pilgrimage hasn't lost its strength. This time, however, instead of going to the hot springs on the Kumano slopes, we made our pilgrimage to Yuda Hot Springs, where Chuya was born, and instead of a wagon, we took a compact car. Oguri didn't just get pulled along passively. Sometimes he also took the wheel, despite his sickness and wounds, but I suppose that's to be expected. We're modern people after all. There's one line in the story of Oguri Hangan that goes, *how kind of them, they are asking after the maiden*. I thought of the twittering of the skylarks, the calling of the black kites, and the high-pitched voices reading the poems of Chuya Nakahara that spoke to me so much. . . . And to top it all off, the gray compact that had carried us along was a Daihatsu Move.

NOTE FROM THE AUTHOR

I borrowed the voice of the poet Chuya Nakahara many times in this chapter. Most of the passages in italics are from Chuya Nakahara's poetry. The onomatopoetic expression *yuya yuyon* comes from "Circus," where he describes the movement of a trapeze artist swinging back and forth through the air. There are places where Chuya's words appear slightly differently than the way they originally did in his poetry, but this is a result of me uttering them in my own voice. If this bothers you, please forgive me. In addition, I have borrowed the voices of the *sekkyo-bushi* narrative *Oguri Hangan*, the epic *Kojiki*, and the four-teenth-century *Tale of the Heike*, as well as the voices of my friends Junji Baba, Yukiko Ono, and the poet Mikiro Sasaki.

With Tongue Intact, Sparrow Chases the Old Woman Away

I OWE A GREAT DEBT of gratitude to my dogs.

They saved the life of one of my daughters. I'm talking about my oldest daughter. I'm glad I brought her to a new life in America, but it wasn't easy. She didn't adapt well to the culture or the language, her new household or her school, or even to her new self. That's when we decided to get a German shepherd puppy. She came from a pedigreed line of police dogs and required special obedience training. I let my daughter take care of all that. My daughter has since flown the coop and lives far away. Last year when I went to Japan with Aiko for four months, she took care of the dog, but the life of a college student is irregular, and she found it difficult to live with such a big pet in a small apartment in the city, so as soon as we got back to the States, I brought the dog back home. She has been at my feet ever since.

One evening, I was watching a movie by myself. I was feeling miserable and wanted to let out a few tears. Since I'm fifty, I don't cry over little things—tripping and falling over or getting criticized isn't enough to do it anymore—but irresolvable conflict and anxiety leave me weepy, and when I've got some thorn in my side, crying helps to work it out. At such times, the tears feel really hot, so hot they practically burn my eyes and cheeks.

That day, I was watching *I Am Sam*. I'm familiar with *Green Eggs and Ham*, the Dr. Seuss picture book with the character Sam-I-Am, so I immediately understood the title reference. It's not hard for me to get swept up in movies that make unscrupulous plays for our emotions, evoking childhood memories, familiar books, songs, and parent-child relationships. At the beginning of the film, a small girl lisps, "Daddy, you're not like other Daddies. Why?" From that point on, the film is a real emotional rollercoaster. Daddy, Father, Dad, Papa, Pops—this story about fatherhood evoked all sorts of emotions, and the tears came flooding out. They ran down my cheeks and nose, to the back of my reclining head, down my neck, and to my shoulders. Then, just as the thorn was working its way loose from my side, the dog stood up, started sniffing around, and pushed her nose into my face. My daughter had told me, she'll come if you cry—that was what she was doing. But I wasn't crying out loud. I was crying silently, and she still knew.

She was telling me with her wet nose, you're not alone, I'm here with you. Strange. What was she responding to? The scent of my tears? Changes in my body temperature? To the emotions welling up within me, then working their way out to disappear into thin air? When my daughter was thirteen and struggling, feeling all alone in the world, she didn't have a creature with a mysterious ability like this at her side. I realized how thankful I was to have the dog and wanted to press my hands together in a gesture of gratitude.

THERE'S A KIND OF DOG I refer to as a "sparrow-dog."

That's not the real name. I'm not sure what language the real name comes from—French? Dutch maybe?—but in any case, the word is so hard to say that I'm afraid I'll bite my tongue, so I just call them sparrow-dogs. They're tiny lap dogs, nimble, friendly, and clever. I hear that in Europe, people used them to chase away sparrows, but who knows? Maybe they even inspired the old folk tale about the sparrow with the cut tongue.

Here's how the Japanese version of the folk tale goes. An old woodcutter finds an injured sparrow, takes it home, and nurses it back to health. His wife resents the fact that her husband is sharing their food with such an insignificant creature. In anger, she cuts out the sparrow's tongue and releases the bird. When the tenderhearted old man learns what happened, he is shocked and goes to look for the sparrow in the mountains. Eventually, other sparrows lead him to the bamboo grove where his sparrow lives, and they have a joyful reunion. When he's ready to leave, the sparrows offer him the choice of two baskets. The old man takes the smaller one, thinking the large basket might be too heavy for him. Back at home, the elderly couple finds treasure inside it. When the old woman learns her husband didn't take the larger basket, she decides to go to the bamboo grove herself. There the sparrows warn her not to look inside the basket before she reaches home, but she's so greedy she can't help herself. The basket is full of terrifying creatures and filth. She steps back in horror and falls down the side of the mountain to her death.

I was surprised to learn there are versions of the same story outside Japan. I guess I shouldn't have been surprised since, after all, sparrows live everywhere. Even if the other versions don't take place in a bamboo grove, the fundamentals are the same. A husband (the old man in the Japanese version) had a sparrow that he loved, but it was killed (or had its tongue cut out, as in the Japanese version) by his wife. The husband goes through a series of hardships (repeatedly drinking horse and cow urine to survive in the Polish version), and then he goes to the underworld (the bamboo grove). As he leaves, the kind husband is given a small package of gold and silver, whereas the wife grabs the large basket (full of poisonous snakes and excrement) and dies as a result. There are many overlapping elements—it's a tale of marriage between different types, a tale of traveling to the underworld, and a tale of reaping what one sows. Just as there are elements of fantasy in the story, there are lessons to be learned as well.

I hear that in one central European variant of this story, a sparrow-dog plays the role of the sparrow. Sparrow-dogs are almost small enough to fit in a pocket, weighing less than ten pounds. Their heads are round, their jowls are black, and they have lovely round eyes with dark shading. These features give the impression you're looking at a sparrow instead of a dog—so much so that it's rumored you'll find little bits of sparrow DNA mixed in with theirs.

I'll never forget it. Five years ago, my parents were losing so much strength that I was worried about them making it through each day. I came up with the idea of buying them a dog. They were so eager to see me and their grandchildren return to Kumamoto each year that I thought they needed something to lavish their affections on. I repeatedly suggested they get a dog. Dad agreed, but Mom refused.

She hated animals—in fact, I don't know anyone who claims to dislike animals as much as she does.

Even so, when I was little, I kept bringing animals home. We had lots of dogs, cats, and birds over the years. Dad did nothing for them, and I was busy being a child, so Mom was always left to care for them. She'd grow attached to them and even affectionate. She might claim to dislike animals, but I saw her countless times teasing and playing with the cats, and the dogs following her around as she did chores. Now that my parents were old, I thought a dog might bring a gentle rhythm to the household—Dad could take it out for walks, and Mom could feed it. So I moved forward with my plan.

After looking into various breeds, I decided on a sparrow-dog.

Sparrow-dogs are small enough that an elderly person can pick them up, light enough that they won't pull their owners off balance, energetic enough that they don't need a walk if their owners have leg or back pain, hesitant enough that they won't attack other dogs, humble enough that they don't put on airs, even in front of children. They don't bite, howl, ignore, or forget. They're easy to groom, and don't shed a lot or stink too much. They have cheerful personalities and noses that aren't too long or too short. They don't need much praise, aren't high-strung, and their chic, unusual looks are enough to fill the emptiness in a senior citizen's heart.

THE TWO-MONTH-OLD SPARROW-DOG PUPPY ARRIVED on a plane, and I went to pick it up. It was quaking in a small cage in a dimly lit corner of the airport. I took it to my parents' apartment, but as luck would have it, they were out shopping. I was playing with the dog on the rug when it suddenly started yapping. The door opened, revealing my parents standing there with the light behind them, staring down at me.

My god, what've you done?

Mom was then still able to move her hands and feet. She let out a sigh and put her bags on the floor.

Dad shut the door.

No way, out of the question. You shouldn't have done that.

I don't know how many dozens of times I've heard him say that. Dad's still saying it to me, even now that I'm old? It's hard to forget the sad, pathetic feelings that well up inside you when you have to take an animal back to where you got it. But this puppy had nowhere to go. Once that sunk in, Dad took it in his arms. I told him it was a sparrow-dog, and on the spot he named it Chunsuke after the chirping sound a sparrow makes when it sings—*choon, choon*. Chunsuke has been with them ever since.

Chunsuke turned out to be smart, cheerful, and loyal—all the things people say about the breed. That made me really happy.

There were some errors in my calculations though. I didn't realize that when people get old, they can't bend over and pick up a little dog down by their feet. Old folks begin to lose their footing, and strength leaves their bodies. It's hard enough just to support themselves, so if they fall when bending over—well, they're down for the count. I also didn't realize that even the tiniest dog is enough to pull an old person off their feet. It makes sense that something like that might happen to someone with little feeling in their lower extremities, but I never considered how unsteady Parkinson's patients are on their feet. I didn't realize that people with Parkinson's generally don't go out for walks. I also hadn't anticipated that sparrow-dogs would run circles around owners who don't know how to handle them. And I had no idea sparrow-dogs are difficult to housetrain, despite their intelligence. Back when my folks were in Tokyo, the dogs were higher on the pecking order than I was—constantly biting, growling, and stealing food without repercussions. Dad swore unconditional allegiance to the pets. He couldn't help falling in love with small things, but he was no longer any good at training dogs. In his old age, he'd lost all desire for dominance and authority. Or perhaps he simply didn't want to put in the effort—I'm not sure.

Each of my parents loved the dog in their own particular way. They reminded me of the elderly couple who finds a boy inside a peach and takes him home to raise as their own. During our phone calls, all my parents talked about was the dog: We've had all kinds of dogs over the years, but never a dog as smart as this one, this dog's so smart, it's a shame it's a dog, if it was human, it'd probably go to Harvard.

At the time, I was phoning my parents every other day from the States. I say "parents," but in reality Mom did most of the talking. Dad kept making excuses for not getting on the phone—he'd say, I can't hear you, or, it's a pain to talk on the phone. It seemed he had no desire to converse, and I didn't know how to change that. At times I couldn't help feeling like Dad had died and left me behind.

MOM SAID, THE DOG'S REALLY smart, it learns really quickly, and when your dad isn't feeling well, it looks at him all worried. And when Dad gets out of the bathtub, it licks him all over his body to dry him—gross.

She told me, I don't like it when dogs do that, so I got angry.

Chunsuke stopped coming to me after that—that shows you how much it understands. I get mad when it picks up my slippers, so it only brings your dad's. I don't know how many pairs of slippers it's ruined. Your dad just thinks the whole thing is funny.

Mom kept complaining that they were having trouble house-training Chunsuke. That dog wakes us up in the middle of the night to go out to pee, but we're old, so we bump against things and fall down. Chunsuke peed on the floor so many times that we had to change the flooring.

Even when dogs aren't peeing on the floor, the homes of old folks get messy, especially as they lose their eyesight. Mom used to be such a clean freak. Anytime there was a mess, she'd lead an all-out assault. I'm not talking metaphorically here. She'd assault everyone in our family, alive or dead, in her efforts to destroy every speck of dust in the house. She cleaned the place so thoroughly from top to bottom that her daughter—me, in other words—was left bruised and battered. Everything had to sparkle. Now she put little energy into housekeeping and no longer cared much about messes. She didn't even care if there were dried-up pieces of poop lying in the corners or sticky floors in her kitchen. I'd been told sparrow-dogs didn't shed, but that wasn't true. Clumps of fine white fur blew through the room, dancing from one corner to another.

So was Chunsuke a boy or a girl? Mom kept doting over the little dog as though Momotaro the peach boy had come to live with them. And Dad had named it Chunsuke—a boy's name—right off the bat, so naturally you'd assume Chunsuke was male. In reality, however, Chunsuke was a girl, and it wasn't long before they had to get her spayed.

Mom complained, if I'm going to be honest with you, I really hate dogs. They stink, they shed, they're not cute to me at all. Your father only liked to play with the cats back in the day—never the dogs—so I'm the one who gets stuck playing with Chunsuke. Mom took a ball and played fetch with her. Chunsuke took off running like a bullet, leaving puffs of hair floating in the air behind her.

She said, I hate dogs, especially female dogs—female cats too, by the way. Do you remember that cat we had who gave birth to a bunch of kittens and then wandered off, leaving them all behind? When I came home and found them, I was so angry that I could have sworn.

She'd repeated this story over and over since I was little. She hated females. She hated female cats. She hated female dogs too.

Mom yelled at the cats because they were female. But do you think our cats just meowed and curled up in a ball? Nope. They didn't care, they just went outside looking for a male to screw.

Back in the day, I went through a series of bad love affairs—a whole string of marriages, divorces, and abortions. I was lost in a fog of confusion. When Mom scolded the animals, I couldn't help wondering if she was venting at the cats or at me, or perhaps at her younger, pre-menopausal self? Or was she yelling at me, her daughter who was too old to have children but was still menstruating, her body still wanting to produce?

Mom said, I hate females, I don't like them at all. Females don't do anything but give birth and make messes, that's why I don't like them.

I was the one who decided to get a female dog. That's what I wanted. They go into heat. They have lots of sex and give birth to children. I thought, damn it, that's what females do, and that's why I want one.

Five years went by.

Mom had a blockage in her brain that left some damage. She recovered, but she kept getting new blockages that sent her back into the hospital. She was constantly checking in and out. Then Dad had surgery for stomach cancer, and the trauma of the surgery was so great, I thought he'd never recover. He was diagnosed with Parkinson's, and it got harder and harder for him to walk. He hadn't been doing much before that, but now he did even less. His desire to live dried up, along with all his energy. Mom supported him, but purple blotches appeared on her legs, and her joints stopped working properly. She became forgetful and lost her ability to cook. Eventually, the health system determined that Dad was eligible for assistance, and a homecare helper started coming to the apartment. It had just been the two of them until then. The sparrow-dog made three. Then, while Aiko was with me in Japan for a summer visit, Mom's condition worsened, and she had to check into the rehab clinic full-time. And that was it. Dad and the dog were left behind at home.

FOR FOUR MONTHS, WE COULDN'T find a place for Mom to land. She kept getting transferred from one clinic to another.

Dad and the dog were alone for the first time.

Aiko and I went back to California.

While we were away, Dad and Chunsuke were left alone with only the helper to rely on.

I came back to Japan alone.

I went back to California, then came back again.

Everyone got used to my back-and-forth life.

Dad got used to life without Mom by his side.

He got used to his life alone with the dog, relying on the helper for meals.

I called Dad faithfully when I was in California. I called him morning, afternoon, and night. Although he used to be reluctant to chat on the phone, he started talking a lot. Our conversations were disjointed since he couldn't hear well, and our topics of conversation were increasingly limited to the few things left that interested him, namely the dog, Mom, samurai stories, and baseball. But even so, we talked. To me, it was like Dad had come back to life again—the same Dad who stank of body odor and cigarettes, the same Dad I didn't necessarily want to get close to but had no choice but to care for now.

Dad said in a sad tone of voice, I had a dream, but I don't have anyone to talk about those things with. Your mom also has lots of dreams, but Chunsuke's the only one here I can share mine with.

I said, Dad, that breaks my heart. I could tell he was nodding on the other end of the line.

He said, I'm tired.

I told him, that makes sense, Dad. You've been doing everything on your own.

Sheepishly, he told me, I had diarrhea, and some leaked into my underwear.

Oh no, did you clean it up yourself?

Dad nodded on the other end of the line.

After Mom was hospitalized, Dad started moving around more briskly. In fact, the change was so noticeable that Mom got angry and shouted, your father was acting like he was half-senile until just recently. Do you think he was faking it?

She was so upset that I could practically hear her shouting across the Pacific—I can't believe it! He made me take care of everything, but just look! He's able to do things by himself—he can get the newspaper, clean up Chunsuke's messes, prepare breakfast, make coffee, wash off the balcony where Chunsuke poops, do the shopping and cleaning and laundry by himself. Just look, he can even change Shiromi's diapers!

RECENTLY, DAD ASKED ME TO take the dog to the vet. The receptionist shouted, oh my! Look at you, little Chunsuke! You've put on so much weight! I was a bit taken aback at this, thinking she was being critical, but I had to admit, yes, Dad had been lavishing all kinds of affection on her. That's par for the course with dogs. They get nice and plump, then eventually their bottoms sag and wiggle when they walk. When Chunsuke waddled along, she looked more like a goose-dog than a sparrow-dog.

When I told Dad the vet had said we needed to help Chunsuke drop some weight, he flatly refused, saying, eating with Chunsuke is the only joy I have left in life, right, Chunsuke?

At the dinner table, Dad would let Chunsuke sit in Mom's seat, and she'd put her paw on the table and lean over, staring at Dad's mouth. He'd put bits of food in front of her, and she'd gobble them down. When they were done eating, the dog licked Dad's mouth clean. I dared him to try that sometime when Mom was there. She would've given him a piece of her mind and pushed the dog away from the table.

One time, Dad gave Chunsuke the meal the helper had made for him, without ever taking a bite himself. The proof was the plate, licked clean, still on the floor. Pieces of burdock and shiitake mushroom were scattered all over the place. Not the least bit fazed, Dad just said, you sure love chicken simmered with vegetables, don't you, Chunsuke?

When Dad and I chatted, Chunsuke would get between us and start howling like she was singing. Dad would say, awwww, you're jealous, aren't you, Chunsuke? If we continued the conversation without paying her any attention, she would pad over on her little feet and pull one of Dad's slippers off his foot. Dad would groan, oh no, not again! Then he'd say with love in his voice, look here, Chunsuke, give it back to your old man. But she would pretend she hadn't heard him. Dad would stand up and sigh, what's a person to do? But that would send Chunsuke pitter-pattering off behind the bamboo. If Dad stood in one place (after all, elderly people with Parkinson's can't make quick movements), she'd come back to within arm's reach and lie on her back with her belly facing up. Her brown and black fur closed in around her snow-white underside and pink nipples. Her bright, round eyes smiled at us, highlighted by the dark corners of her eyes and black cheeks. Dad rubbed her with his rough fingers, saying, Chunsuke, you're a good little doggie, aren't you!

DAD AND I WERE TALKING on the phone. Today I took Chunsuke to see Mom in the clinic again. Chunsuke was waiting for me to come downstairs—such a good girl.

He had said the same thing yesterday.

He had said it the day before that too.

Every day when he came home from the clinic, he'd give me a report. I could picture everything vividly. Every day, every single day, just before lunch. Dad would say, wanna go, Chunsuke? She would jump with joy and run around in circles yapping. They'd call a taxi, Dad would put her on a leash and get in first on his unsteady feet, followed by the dog.

Little sparrow, where is your home?

Little sparrow, where is your home?

Dad would sing this folk song the whole way to the clinic full of paralyzed and unconscious senior citizens. That's where Mom was. Before he went to her room, he'd tether the sparrow-dog near the front entrance, where she would stay. People going in and out would comment, what a good dog you are, Chunsuke, waiting so nicely for Grandpa!

A QUICK OBSERVATION—WHEREVER YOU FIND the Japanese folk tale of the tongue-cut sparrow, you'll find the folk tale of the old man who had a lump removed. That's generally the way things are in books. Where you find the folk tale of the old man who had a lump removed, you'll find the folk tale about the rabbit who took revenge on the mean trickster *tanuki*. The punishments the *tanuki* endures go on and on. (It takes some time to reach the end where the rabbit pushes the *tanuki* into a lake and complains, "Man, I'm really working up a sweat!")

In any case, I'm getting ahead of myself.

Dad developed a lump.

NOTE FROM THE AUTHOR

I borrowed the voices of Kenji Miyazawa in his poem "Strong in the Rain," Osamu Dazai from his story collection *Fairy Tales*, *Madison's World Dog Encyclopedia*, Doctor Seuss's *Green Eggs and Ham*, Dakota Fanning's performance in *I Am Sam*, the late-tenth-century noblewoman Sei Shonagon's *Pillow Book*, and the performers Hitoshi Ueki and Yukio Aoshima.

The Rainy Season Continues, and
Mother Suffers on Her Deathbed

I'M REALLY WORKING UP A sweat, said Aiko. She held out her arms as if to catch some nonexistent wind. Colorless fuzz had started to sprout under her arms. Blackheads had appeared on the end of her nose, and her shorts revealed legs that had grown long, hairy, and tan in the sun.

We were in Narita Airport waiting for a bus to take us across Tokyo to Haneda where we'd catch our southbound flight to Kumamoto. The air was filled with sharp-stinging bugs, feasting on our flesh—bugs of humidity. I was completely exhausted.

The bags weighed so heavily on my shoulders that they felt like they might break my bones, damn it. It had been a terrible trip. Aiko hadn't fallen asleep until just before the plane landed, damn it. I found it impossible to sleep in the plane's tiny cabin, damn it. I was at the end of my rope. Flying west across the Pacific, you leave in the afternoon and arrive late afternoon the following day, but where you started, it's still the middle of night. There I was, lugging our suitcases from one airport to another in what felt like the wee hours of the morning. Ugh. My brain had completely stopped working, and the only thing carrying me forward was my homing instinct.

Exiting the airport, we were assaulted by the humidity. June 24—it was hell.

SINCE SUMMER VACATIONS AT SCHOOLS in the U.S. start a month earlier than in Japan, I'd once again tricked poor Aiko into coming with me to attend school in Kumamoto, even though she really wanted nothing more than to relax and hang out with her friends in California. I'd been doing this off and on since she was in first grade. Japanese society is rather closed, and I wanted her to be able to function in Japan as an insider. A year earlier she'd spent two full semesters in a Japanese elementary school, and her language abilities improved to the point where she was able to read for pleasure. She was now absorbed in a manga called *InuYasha*, using the phonetic guides next to the kanji to make sense of whatever words she couldn't read. She could sing loud parodies of songs in both languages, inserting references to puke and poop wherever she wanted—the sign of a true bilingual. But now she was an adolescent, and she was having a hard time relating to the world. When I brought her with me to Japan again this year, I did so fearfully, feeling like I was treading on thin ice.

We were a pair of mother and daughter ducks. Guided by our homing instincts, we crossed humid wetlands and marshes, growing wet, wet, wet in the swamps as we swam home. We swam through the humidity all the way to Kumamoto.

The first stop was my parents' place.

When I'm away, I leave our place in Kumamoto empty. Dad lives five minutes away with the sparrow-dog.

When I reached his apartment, the stench and humidity

practically knocked my socks off. My sniffer detected all sorts of things: dog, cigarettes, unchanged sheets, mildew, dried pee, even Dad's faint B.O. (Since I was a girl, I always used to think, Dad, you stink, you stink!) The *kotatsu* table with the heater underneath—designed to be used in the winter—was still smack in the middle of the room. Dad wasn't using the air conditioner at all.

I asked him, what? No A.C.? Dad responded as if it was no big deal—it's not that hot yet. I told him he had to be kidding, the humidity was nightmarish, but he simply responded, that's 'cause it rained yesterday. I asked if he wanted the *kotatsu* put away, but he told me he wanted it out until at least the end of the rainy season. Chunsuke bounced around like a rubber ball. I stuck my fingers in her mouth (something she really enjoyed), and she wriggled happily.

If this is how you want to live, you'd be better off living outdoors.

If only I didn't have a home to take care of.

The same thought crossed my mind every summer. Modern Japanese buildings are built to withstand storms and earthquakes. Unlike traditional Japanese houses, breezes can't pass through, and the heat gets trapped in, bad smells too. Every time I return to my place in Japan, I feel as if I'm stuck under a cover with a stinky fart, and I find myself wishing I could abandon home altogether. I've felt that way for a long time. I felt trapped in the house way back when I was living with Mom and Dad. I felt that way when I was living peacefully with my Japanese husband in Japan. I still feel that way.

Smash the home.

Smash the family.

Destroy the home.

Destroy the family.

The same thought went through my head every summer. Eventually, the same thought preoccupied me fall, winter, and spring too. Smash the home, smash the family. Then, I finally did it. I destroyed our family. I moved to California.

The rain had been falling constantly for a week. When it finally stopped, the humidity rose sharply. But still the rainy season wasn't over yet.

IN HER ROOM AT THE clinic, Mom was looking beautiful again.

You're probably surprised to read that, but it was true. Of course, she was still bedridden, tossing about, unable to go to the toilet by herself. She relied on a catheter to pee, and the faint smell of urine wafted through the room, never disappearing entirely. Her facial expression, however, was so much more vivid that she seemed like a whole different person. She looked refreshed and lively—the dark spots had vanished, along with the spots and wrinkles on her pale skin. She had transformed into a lovely woman.

I couldn't help asking, are you wearing makeup?

She replied confidently, I was brooding over ending up this way, and it didn't seem like anything mattered any more. But now things are much better. I realized things couldn't stay the way they were. That's what I always do. I start out worrying and feeling depressed about something, but eventually, I take stock of where I am and start thinking about the future. I've done that ever since I was little.

Her tone of voice was that of a ten-year-old. She was emotional as she spoke, and tears welled up in her eyes.

She told me, something happened the other day. One of the

nurses in training came into my room quietly during the night and told me she was desperately in love with one of the young doctors. She asked, Ito-san, will you do me a favor and find out if he's in love with anyone? So I said to the young doctor, I hope you don't mind me asking a question, you'll probably think it's strange for an old lady to ask something so personal, but do you have anyone special in your life? He told me, I do, so I said, what a shame. There's someone who's really in love with you, and she wanted me to ask you. He asked me who, but I told him, if you've got someone, you can't do anything, but fate works in mysterious ways, you never know. I gave him her name. Later, the student nurse asked me what I found out. I told her not to stray from the path of decency. (Mom can't abide people having affairs.)

Since then, Mom told me, the nurses had been coming to her with all sorts of personal problems late at night. Mom told the young woman who wasn't getting along with her mother-in-law that she had to start living completely for herself, that would change her perspective on things. Mom sang the melody of the most difficult part of an *enka* ballad for a young woman who wanted to learn it. Mom became a storyteller for the young woman who liked old stories, recounting the one about the outlaw Bamba no Chutaro in the classic movie *In Search of Mother*. The young woman, I understand, left the room with tears in her eyes, commenting how wonderful those old stories can be.

Mom told me that when night came, a tall, long-haired young male nurse would come in and scratch her wherever she wanted.

She was bedridden. She experienced moments of dementia during which she felt she was in a different world, but those moments came and went. I came to realize that late at night in her room, when all human noise had retreated, the nurses' visits allowed her to become someone different from her usual self. That seemed to be a major factor in keeping her alive. Her arms and legs weren't working right, but she could still offer a listening ear and give advice, she could still have meaningful relationships, she could still root around looking for her wallet. That was one way to stay alive, I suppose. Grandma Toyoko would probably say, you can't compete with blood—your mom has had energy rushing through her veins ever since she was little.

Dad said, I don't like the way she looks, like some calm and collected bodhisattva.

I remembered that Grandma had that kind of bodhisattva look on her face before she died. I asked him if he remembered.

As if in agreement, Dad added, yeah, she also thought she wasn't going to die.

THE RAINY SEASON STILL HADN'T ended. Nonetheless, the sun came out nice and bright when it dared show its face. I took walks along the riverbank. I was about to cross the river when I noticed a little old lady. She couldn't have been more than a meter tall, standing at the side of the path like a small stone statue of the bodhisattva Jizo. She looked as confused as a little girl whose mother had sent her out on an errand but had lost her money on the way. She seemed at a complete loss.

I called out, are you okay?

We were in a place along the river where few people go. The summer plants were at their full height, growing thick and lush on both sides of the path, and just beyond it was a marshy area covered in tangled kudzu. What would happen if the little old lady collapsed from sunstroke? No one would ever find her to help, and her dried-up, little-old-lady corpse would decompose, consumed by plants.

Is Dr. So-and-So's ophthalmology clinic this way?

I started to explain she needed to walk across the riverbank, cross the bridge, go out by the big national highway, and so on, but it was clear she wasn't following a word I said. I told her I was headed in the same direction—that was a lie—and I'd walk with her. She nodded, and we started off together. Despite her age, she seemed accustomed to walking and was steady on her feet. Judging from her backpack and sun visor, she probably took daily walks for exercise.

Indeed, it's quite the hot day today. She spoke in formal, old-fashioned Japanese.

Indeed, it is. Her formality pulled me in, but when I commented that usually the rainy season should have ended by now, she quickly spat out, not at all, it's not going to end anytime soon. She looked up at the sky and spoke. It'll end when it ends. Damn, this cursed Kumamoto summer!

She kept chatting as we walked on.

I had a husband, but he died a little while back, a few years really, he went to the hospital for a little checkup and never came out again, I felt sorry for him, what with the way he died and all—a single checkup led to the discovery of something bad, and one thing led to another. Checkups and surgeries, checkups and surgeries, the doctors stabbed him and cut him up, and then after a couple of years in the hospital, he died suddenly, poof, just like that! It was at the university hospital, you know the place—it's like a prison there. Even if they give good medical treatment, they don't have the time or energy to think about how exhausted the patients and their families must be, mind you, their parking lot is way down at the bottom of a cliff so to get there you have to climb a set of stone stairs a few hundred steps all the way up from the bottom, but that only takes you to the back entrance, if you go in there, you're at the morgue, every time I went, I'd slink by with a sense of foreboding, thinking it wouldn't be long before my husband ends up there, I felt miserable when I slid the shaky sliding door open, the place was such a mess that even the sign that said "please keep door closed" had been ripped off, I suppose it didn't matter since even if I tried to close it, I couldn't get it shut, but that was the way in, once inside, you've got to walk through a labyrinth of hallways. A long time ago, a kind woman like you called out to me, she said, the gods and buddhas are so much greater than us that we must follow the paths they have created, no matter how difficult that may be, but now that things are over and done with, I can speak my mind—that's nothing but crap.

I pointed out to the old lady that we'd reached the crossroads. Over there is the national highway, do you see the red sign? Hiding in the shadow of that building is the ophthalmology clinic you're looking for, you'll be there in five minutes.

She said, thank you for coming all this way with me, I won't forget your kindness, I can get there by myself now, if I just think back on the pleasant conversation we just had, I'll be there before I know it. The old lady bowed deeply to me, raised herself up, then bowed again. I thought she was going to fold in half like origami when I heard her say something quietly. It sounded more like a groan than proper speech. Missus, can I give you some advice from an old lady? If you go to the hospital, be sure to do everything the doctor tells you, 'cause if you don't, the doctor won't pay any attention to you at all. But if you implore him politely, he'll help—tell him, please deliver my mother from her suffering as quickly as you can.

DAD'S PREMONITION WAS RIGHT. THE next day, he got a call from the clinic. We rushed there and found that Mom's face had turned a bruised shade of purple. She had an oxygen mask strapped to her, and she was groaning, I feel terrible, just terrible. She'd already been connected to lots of lines and tubes, and now there were even more.

In her agony, she told Dad, thank you so much for everything you've done for me. These sixty years with you have been fun.

She fell silent, as if she had nothing else to say, so I told her, hang in there a little while longer. I was aware of what I was saying, but it just slipped out during a lull in the conversation.

All I've done is hang in there my whole life.

She said this straightforwardly, not for dramatic effect. I knew it was true. They say that when you speak to people suffering from depression, "hang in there" is one thing you shouldn't say. Depression and dying have a lot in common. I was immediately filled with regret.

Then she said, this is saha—the world of suffering that must be endured.

My poor mother, who had just been lamenting how terrible, just terrible, she felt, then added, it's no good, I'm done for. Turning to the doctor, she said, it's time, give me my cup of poison.

I DON'T REMEMBER WHICH PLAY it's in, but there's a passage in one of Chikamatsu Monzaemon's plays that has remained with me: "The four types of suffering, the eight types of bitterness—all of these suffered during the throes of death." It must have been in *The Love Suicides at Sonezaki* or *The Love Suicides at Amijima*. Both plays are about a woman who is killed by her lover, and both depict her as an object of pity and erotic attraction. The reason this passage stayed with me is that it describes what people experience as they die—it's about what happens right at that moment. People don't experience just one kind of suffering. It's not like one person has only one kind of suffering, and someone else experiences another. According to Buddhist doctrine, there are four fundamental types of suffering: birth, aging, sickness, and death. Then four more types are added— love, resentment, desire, and not attaining what one longs for—to make the eight types of bitterness. But really what this expression means is all suffering. Tens of thousands of instances of suffering. Millions of instances of suffering. The suffering of all humanity. The four types of suffering, the eight types of bitterness—then the four types of suffering, the eight types of bitterness repeat all over again.

When life ends, there's music in the heavens. When life ends, purple clouds enfold the body. I don't remember where I read this. If it were true, it should've happened right then. I listened, but the only sounds I could hear were the beeping and whooshing of the machines. Mom was clearly experiencing the four types of suffering, the eight types of bitterness, but there were no purple clouds or music. Just Mom lamenting, I feel terrible, just terrible. And now—no, probably over the course of her entire life—she was alone, without anyone who could help her. She was alone and helpless, weak and vulnerable. She was naked and exposed, left to suffer.

I was just like her in that regard. I'm her daughter after all. Alone and helpless, weak and vulnerable.

The nurse prepared to move her to another room, connecting her to even more lines and tubes. Then, with lines and tubes trailing from her body, she was loaded into an ambulance and rushed to the university hospital.

There were no purple clouds, no music. Mom didn't die yet. Standing in front of my suffering mother, the doctors told us her heart was failing. Fluid was accumulating in her lungs, and she was having trouble breathing.

I asked them, can't you alleviate her suffering?

The doctors didn't seem to think so. In fact, they didn't even seem to consider the possibility. They told me that things hadn't gone quite that far yet.

But she's suffering, I exclaimed. (As long as she is going to die) I want her to get some relief from this suffering (by being allowed to die on her own terms). I didn't dare say the parts in parentheses out loud, but that was what I was thinking.

One of the older doctors asked who I was. Everyone, every single person, he said, experiences thoughts of pain and suffering, that's what being sick is all about.

I started to protest but stopped myself. I knew there were times when it was hopeless to say what was really important. I had good-will in my heart. I wanted her to live. I wanted the power of science to work its magic. But this was far from reality. I'd been doing lots of reading—stories of rebirth into the Buddhist paradise, stories for the puppet theater about double suicides. I'd been reading classics like the *Tale of the Heike*, I'd even been reading manga like *Vagabond* and *Death Note*. In those books, people died easily. They die one after another. All sorts of deaths. But in a real-life hospital room, my own mother wasn't dying an easy death. She couldn't even if she wanted.

We've been consulting, said the doctors. We think we should do dialysis—that will likely bring the fluid out. Her condition will likely improve quickly, and her breathing will get a lot easier. The doctors spoke as casually as if they were on the news, predicting the weather.

IT BEGAN TO RAIN. THE news reports didn't just give a thunderstorm warning, they spoke of a record-breaking torrent. They were predicting eight hundred millimeters of rain for the Kumamoto region.

How much? asked Aiko. Eight meters, I told her—I was never any good at math.

How much? asked Aiko again. I didn't know how to tell her in the American system of feet and inches.

As much as that house? she asked. She pointed to an old wooden building. It appeared to have been vacant for some time, with vines covering one entire side. It was old and misshapen, and the foundations had sunk. Probably, I told her, maybe even higher than that. I imagined the rain reaching up to the sky from which it had fallen. Houses, cars, people, even Aiko were all underwater, floating.

The roads flooded. Cars were forced into long, circuitous detours. No matter which road, somewhere along the way they'd run into trouble. Still, I had to keep going to the hospital for Mom.

To get there, I had to go up a slope and take a winding road that snaked around the stone walls of Kumamoto Castle. Wet from rain, the stones, plants, shrubbery, and people all looked unusually colorful, as if yellow and green paint had been spilled all over them.

THE DIALYSIS WORKED. FIVE LITERS of fluid were extracted. The swelling and blemishes went away, but she lost her angelic, bodhisattva-like countenance. The power she'd temporarily inherited from Toyoko had also gone, leaving Mom far, far away.

She said, they tell me that I've been in a rehab clinic?

That's right, Mom. A whole year.

Oh, my goodness, that must have caused your dad all sorts of trouble. What's going on? How could I forget such a long stay? She seemed genuinely puzzled.

You've been under their care since last year. You remember when I came last year? I went home, came back, went home again, came back again, went home, came back again, and you were in the clinic the whole time.

I don't remember, she said, then fell silent. She seemed to be pondering something. Then she asked, was I really in the clinic all that time before coming here?

Yeah, Mom. A whole year.

Why's that?

You lost the use of your hands.

Oh, you're right, they won't move.

We've been to all kinds of clinics, all kinds of hospitals, the two of us. I put you in a wheelchair and took you to a big hospital with a dermatology unit, and you got surgery on your legs, then we went to a big hospital with a cosmetic surgery unit, and you had your nerves examined, then we went to a big hospital with a neurology unit and did some more tests, then when you checked into the big university hospital with the hematology unit, they did some more big tests, you've been tested over and over, but they didn't seem to know what was going on anymore, so we checked you into the rehab clinic where your primary doctor works, and he's been looking after you all this time. Now you're in a hospital room on the fourth floor with all sorts of doctors and nurses.

Do I have to stay? I'm putting everyone out, including you. And when is the surgery going to be?

I could see we weren't really communicating, and it tried my patience to pretend we were. It also terrified me. As we chatted, I could tell she was no longer really present, and a chill ran down my spine. She was still alive, but she no longer existed. In front of me was a shadow of the woman who used to be my mom. It'd be an exaggeration to say that what I was feeling was loneliness. Mom had never really understood me, and I'd never really expected much from her. But the version of me that was living there in the mossy, wet, wet wilderness holding onto Aiko—well, that was the real me. When that thought occurred to me, my sadness was boundless.

THE PARKING LOT FOR THE big hospital was at the base of a cliff. As we walked down the path, Aiko hung from my arm holding the umbrella. I tried to brush her off, but she grabbed onto my arm again. She kept holding onto me as she talked.

Mom, earlier when I asked Grandma where you went, she

scolded me, telling me not to interrupt you when you were talking to the doctor, then a minute later, she asked me, where did your mom go? I told her you were talking with the doctor, and she said, oh goodness, I didn't realize. Then, a minute later, she asked me, when is your older sister Yokiko coming back to Kumamoto? I told her August, Grandma. Then she asked me what month it was right now, and I told her July, Grandma. She said, oh goodness, I didn't realize, so what month is it now? I thought uh-oh, but said, July, Grandma. Oh, really? Say, I've been meaning to ask you, Aiko darling, what month is it now? Uh-oh, I thought, but I told her, it's July, Grandma, then five minutes later, when's Yokiko coming back again? August, Grandma. Oh, really? Then, what month is it? Uh-oh, I thought, here we go again. I said July, Grandma, but then she asked where you were. I said, she's outside talking to the doctor, Grandma. Oh, really? I wonder what they're talking about. Uh-oh, uh-oh, uh-oh, here we go again.

I told her to stop sticking the English word "uh-oh" into her Japanese. It sounded like the interjection of a cuckoo.

She said it again, uh-oh! Then she went on chattering. Her Japanese was really funny. It was fluent enough for her to express herself, but the words in her sentences were often in the wrong order, as if her speech was influenced by English.

But Grandpa's even worse. When I called him, he said, oh, is this Chunsuke calling? I don't think he was joking. Chunsuke was barking in the background.

Aiko burst out laughing. Uh-oh, uh-oh, uh-oh, she repeated, laughing. Then she imitated my mother, oh, really? Then rolled her eyes.

I couldn't help it. I burst out laughing too, and as we laughed, we sang, uh-oh, uh-oh, uh-oh!

There are times, uh-oh.

When conversations, uh-oh. Don't work out, uh-oh.

And here we go again, uh-oh.

IT RAINED, AND PEOPLE ALL over the region died. Then the rain stopped, and the sun shone bright in the sky. The moisture rose from the earth, becoming thick in the air. Even if you didn't have cardiac failure, your lungs felt full of water.

I was driving along a river when I saw an old lady at the roadside. I wondered, does she have another decade, or not? In another ten years, even an old lady like her who moves freely now will age dramatically like my mother and likely find herself bedridden in a hospital. I was preoccupied with such thoughts during Mom's illness. In that moment, the old lady took a step into the road and waved her hands. I stopped the car. She was covered in sweat and looked like she was about to burst into tears. She told me, the bus isn't coming, I mixed up the time and now it won't be here for another hour, I don't know what to do, there aren't any taxis around here, I promised to meet my friend at a hotel, but there's no way I'm going to make it on time.

I told her to get in, I'd take her.

She dropped heavily into the passenger's seat, saying, thank you so much, you're a huge help, it was terribly rude of me to stop a total stranger, but I didn't know what else to do.

I told her not to worry, I was happy to help. I drove up the hill to the castle grounds. Since the rainy season had let up, the moss had started creeping across the stone walls, and leaves and vines were peeking out from the gaps between the stones. The old lady told me her son lived far away, he came for a visit last month but had already returned home. Then she took a deep breath and said, thank you so much, you're a huge help, it was terribly rude of me to stop a total stranger like you, but I didn't know what else to do.

I told her not to worry, I was happy to help. As we drove through the woods, up and down sloping streets, I started telling her about my dying mother.

When we stopped at the hotel, she turned to me and repeated what she'd already repeated—thank you so much, you're a huge help, it was terribly rude of me to stop a total stranger like you, but I didn't know what else to do. She choked up, and tears welled in her eyes. I never imagined anyone would be so kind to me at my age. For a moment, she pressed her hands in front of her in profound gratitude.

The stone walls were colorful, as if yellow and green paint had spilled over them. As the sun blazed overhead, the trees and vines grew silent, turning a dusky hue, and when I closed my eyes, I felt I could still sense them crouching there. Everything was coming back to life and growing thicker and thicker. It was shocking how disorderly and uncontrolled all the new growth was. Filled with their store of light and shadow, clusters of different plants spilled out from the gaps in the stone walls and covered the steep hillsides. The plants grew brighter and brighter until they seemed about to burst. As branches struck the side of the car, they trembled and groaned, we're going to burst, we're going to burst, we're going to get rid of everything, we're going to get rid of everyone! And the vines continued to crawl out of the stone walls.

NOTE FROM THE AUTHOR

I borrowed voices from Osamu Dazai's *Fairy Tales*, the Buddhist priest Genshin's *Essays on Rebirth into the Pure Land*, the poem "The Buddha is always everywhere / but it's sad he remains hidden; / at dawn when human noise is still / in dreams, I see his shadows" from the classic *Songs to Make the Dust Dance*, and the Homeric "Hymn to Demeter," which I read in Yoshihiko Kutsukake's Japanese translation. I also borrowed the voices of the playwright Chikamatsu Monzaemon from the late seventeenth century, the tenth-century author Yoshishige no Yasutane, and the contemporary writer Michiko Ishimure. And of course, 800 millimeters does not add up to eight meters—I'm terrible at math! Still, 80 centimeters is a lot of rain!

Ito Travels West, Blooms, and Then Wilts Away

THE OTHER DAY A YOUNG woman asked my advice about a personal problem. She was working part-time for a professional musician and now found herself in her thirties, wondering what she should do with her life. I lent a sympathetic ear, but that got me thinking about things—steady incomes, guarantees for the future, and the like. That's when it hit me. I have none of those, do I? My only income is the paltry amount I earn here and there from writing. I publish books, but they don't become bestsellers. But is it enough to get by? Yeah, I suppose so. I don't live a life of luxury. If anything, I scrape by, but somehow I'd managed to raise three kids, pay for groceries and tuition, and secure places to live without too much struggle. I'd even had enough to fly back and forth across the ocean and take care of the many potted plants I'd collected over the years. To this day, I'm still not entirely sure how I managed.

AT FIRST, I HAD ALL sorts of plans for the summer holidays. When Aiko's school in Japan let out in late July, I'd take her on a trip, then when August came and my second daughter, Yokiko, came to Japan, I'd take them on another trip, then on the thirteenth, after avoiding the craziness of the Obon holidays, the three of us would cross the Pacific and return home. But before the rainy season let up, Mom fell into a precarious state. After much deliberation, I canceled the first trip. Cheap tickets come with a big cancellation penalty. I paid solemnly and silently. Then I bought a cellphone and programmed it with the numbers of Mom's clinic, the relatives I needed to keep informed, and the funeral home. I called my oldest daughter and asked her to come from California. Not Yokiko, who was set to come in August—her older sister, my eldest. She was twenty, and she'd had some success as a musician in the Bay Area, enough to get by. She hadn't been back to Japan in years. She was the first grandchild, and Mom had doted on her when she was little, so I wanted Mom to see her again. Time and money were tight, but I figured I ought to reunite them, even for just a few days, so I shelled out over a hundred thousand yen. Just for a couple of measly days in Kumamoto. I wanted to weep.

It was the end of July when the rainy season finally let up. It got so hot that I quickly became desperate. The news reported temperatures of thirty-six and thirty-seven degrees Celsius for days on end. Temperatures that hot are more like body temperatures than atmospheric temperatures. I didn't want to wear a thing. Anything with sleeves was unbearable. Collars and buttons too. I wore only thin, sleeveless clothing, but then my fifty-year-old arms and my love handles are on display. My hair hanging down my neck and shoulders was also unbearable, so I twisted it up in a bun, but that revealed the loose skin under my chin. For days, I kept looking at my sagging, droopy body spilling out all over the place. When I stepped outside, my makeup would immediately begin to run, no matter how thick I caked it on. Age spots, wrinkles, flab . . . all hopeless. I wanted to toss my entire body in the trash and start over. I spent those awful days solemnly and silently, hardly able to suppress the hatred I felt for myself.

That was when my husband told me he was going to London.

Not long before, a friend who thought highly of his artwork had come to visit. That got my husband's cock hard. A few weeks later, someone else came to visit too. That made his cock even harder.

I'd followed Jizo's advice and praised my husband to the skies. As a result, my husband's cock, as well as his sense of self-reliance, had grown long and proud. Its color and luster improved as well. And that's why he decided to go to London to try to sell more of his work. Forty-plus years earlier, he had left London after a tremendous fight with his gallery. When he contacted them again after four decades, they brushed aside the argument as ancient history and said they'd like to restart the relationship. My husband asked me if I'd like to go with him to London at the beginning of September. If he was away, then I wouldn't be able to take Aiko back to California.

I had no idea when I might have to rush back to Japan to help Mom and Dad, so I decided to stay in Kumamoto until mid-September, but that meant canceling my plans and making new reservations for international flights, domestic flights, and a rental car. I had to make arrangements with Aiko's school, juggle my work responsibilities, make new plans, and arrange dog care. The mere thought of all that work made me dizzy, but if I could help my husband's cock—his sense of self-reliance, I mean—then I'd do it. I quietly assented, changed my plans, and solemnly and silently paid the cancellation penalties. I wanted to weep. I got to thinking. By the time I returned, the weather would probably be cool. But I wasn't optimistic. The last two years, the heat lingered into September, October, and even November. I was practically guaranteed that the ferocious heat would continue to the moment I left the country.

August rolled around.

My oldest daughter came to Japan in July and then went to Europe. She emailed me from Berlin. Not long after, she emailed me from a rural village in the Czech Republic. She didn't really have much to say. She couldn't type in Japanese, only in a combination of romanized Japanese and English, and so it didn't feel like a real conversation. Still, she told me that she was playing music wherever she went, but the audiences found fault with whatever she did. How painful it sounded. And then the emails stopped coming. She must have continued her travels.

Yokiko got on a transpacific flight and made her way to Kumamoto. Earlier in the summer, she had stayed at college to take summer classes. She was an awkward type who spent her life completely absorbed in whatever she was doing. She called me from California every day, and I called her back to talk and help her through her worries. I solemnly and silently paid the phone bill. Now that summer classes had finally ended, she came to Japan, despite the horrible heat. She had grown lanky and thin and looked completely exhausted. No sooner did she arrive in Kumamoto than she began to joke around with Aiko. They would go on and on together in English—sometimes they'd fight, but then they'd spread out their futons side by side and fall asleep on top of one another. I looked at Yokiko while she was sleeping and saw that she had cuts and scars all over. Although she'd grown up and left home, she was still far from being an adult. Her life was full of pain.

THE HEAT WAS AT ITS peak when I went on a 46,000-day pilgrimage.

On July 10, I went to Asakusa in Tokyo hoping to gain 46,000 days' worth of virtue. Tradition says that a visit to Sensoji temple on that day is the equivalent of making pilgrimages for 46,000 days in a row. I'd planned to meet a gardening expert in Tokyo for work, and July 10 was the only day before the Obon holidays I had any free time.

It's no exaggeration to say that at that time, plants and gardening were what gave me a reason to live. The gardener I was to meet was just slightly older than me. We'd grown up in the same area of Tokyo, and we had similar tastes and inclinations when it came to gardening, so I'd wanted to meet him for some time. The opportunity finally arrived.

Let me tell you what I was wearing when I set out on my journey.

Since we were meeting for the first time, I wanted to dress nicely, but because of the heat, I ended up wearing my usual paper-thin camisole and skirt, with a top that was as see-through as silk gauze. I'd abandoned wearing bras ages ago. When I was young, it bothered me if my nipples showed, even if I wasn't entirely sure what to do about it. My nipples aren't where they used to be. They're a lot lower, more asymmetrical, and swing back and forth like crazy. Sometimes I even catch sight of them next to my armpits, pointing down.

Long ago, I remember Mom throwing her breasts over her shoulder like she was hoisting up a sandbag. Another time, she grabbed them the way an eagle takes something in its talons, then stuffed them into her bra as though putting on armor. Her breasts were covered in wrinkles, and her nipples were almost jet black. Beside her nipples were hard bits of scar tissue. For years, she reminded me that those were from me biting her. I knew. She cursed me when I was younger but later sealed the curse away inside of her. I worried that if that seal broke, her anger might come blasting out and destroy everything. Over time, her breasts swelled up and grew so dark that they seemed to suck in everything in the house—they sucked in the chopsticks and bowls and futons and mosquito netting, our Shinto shrine (we didn't have a Buddhist altar), our tables, our mirror stands, even Dad and me and the dog. When she went out into the back alley, her breasts threatened to suck in the fish crates left there in the narrow streets, the carefully planted flowers, and even the old folks and stray cats walking by. There were countless times I thought her breasts were going to suck me in too, but somehow, I survived. I imagined myself as an infant looking at her big breasts. It was probably like Ultraman or Superman staring down some great evil—I imagine that's how much hatred and fear I felt as I bit her and ran away. But when I saw her breasts yesterday, they were completely withered. What about my breasts? They've nursed three daughters, but they aren't nearly as big or evil-looking as Mom's. That's why I don't mind walking around with them sticking out.

I put on my earrings and necklace. About a year before, I'd ordered them from a friend about my age who was a designer. When she saw the stones I'd chosen, she commented, now that you're older, it would suit you to wear something with a bit more color and bling. I told her that for a while now I'd been wanting something like the dewdrop-shaped twinkling red stones I'd chosen, so she did what I asked and mounted them on a delicate gold background. The jewels look like I'd stuck my finger with a needle and squeezed out a drop of blood. I've worn them ever since.

I grabbed a parasol and towel to wipe away the sweat. Such things were indispensable in this heat.

Finally, I was ready to go out into the world and face people.

I left home, got in the car, boarded a plane, transferred to the train, and arrived at the Thunder Gate of Sensoji, where we'd arranged to meet. The place thronged with people, seemingly all foreigners. The shops lining the route to the temple gate were filled with cheap, tacky souvenirs. On the far side of the sloping hill, I saw the embankment of the Sumida River shimmering in the heat. The heat was so intense that the world hardly seemed fit for human habitation.

IF A HIGH-RISE APARTMENT BUILDING is more than ten stories, it allows a surprisingly strong breeze to flow through. That was one reason I felt so comfortable around the gardener during our first meeting. Also, something about his appearance seemed oddly familiar, as if we might have met before. Plus, I couldn't stand on ceremony—my makeup was running terribly. He was dressed casually, in shorts and a T-shirt, and he didn't seem to be the kind to care about things like makeup, so our meeting felt relaxed right from the moment he came to meet me.

We went up to his apartment, and he led me to a south-facing veranda while telling me about all the plants he had—an olive tree, datura, bitter gourds, rosemary, Arabian jasmine, bougainvillea, spider plants, air plants, succulents, peonies, hollyhocks. A real feast for the eyes, I said.

But what I saw was a heap of corpses—everything was in miserable condition. Nothing was lush, nothing reproducing, nothing even flowering. It seemed like the veranda wanted everything to die, and his collection of plants was solemnly, silently doing just that. It was as though he and the plants had decided to commit suicide together. The only watering can I could see was sitting among the pots. It was so small, the kind of thing elementary school kids might put their pet beetle in. And it was so covered with moss that you could hardly see inside. When I bent over and peered in, I spied two tiny fish—medakas, apparently—swimming around.

There used to be more, he told me, but they died.

I told him he ought to put in an air pump to give them some oxygen. I felt like I was lecturing a child. He told me not to worry, since medakas just die one after another. Perhaps he was trying to console me. I used to have medakas too. I scooped up their dead bodies just about every day, and soon wondered if I was taking care of them or their corpses.

Memento mori, he whispered.

It's practically necrophilia, I added.

He groaned.

DO YOU EVER CUT YOUR plants back so far you kill them? I asked.

He told me he trusted them to die on their own.

Really? Me too. Sometimes when I keep cutting one back, I eventually realize I can't resuscitate it no matter what I do, it just can't be saved. When that happens, I take my gardening shears and chop it off at the roots.

I don't go that far, the gardener told me, then made a strange contemplative face. He looked like he was thinking about death. Let them wilt, he said, let them wither, let them fade until they die and become a pile of corpses.

I asked him if there were any plants that he had trouble growing but he still tried.

He immediately responded, peonies.

They'll die anyway, there's no way they'll survive, maybe that's why I put them where they're sure to die on their own, maybe I want to kill them, I can't tell you how many I've killed, look at this one, I ought to pull it out. The gardener indicated a dead peony.

I said, the plants don't seem to care.

He nodded. They don't, do they?

I told him that for plants, dying doesn't mean death—not dying is what it means for them to live.

He smiled and said, you're right. It's okay to kill them. We humans can't think about the death of plants in the same way as we think about the death of human beings—it doesn't make sense to think of it as sad or scary.

Then, as if he suddenly remembered something, he spit out the word "thanatos." He paused for a moment, then repeated it to himself quietly. I suppose that's thanatos for you. Then he fell silent.

Was he right, or was what he was saying completely stupid? I could sense him wavering.

ON THE WEST-FACING PART OF his veranda were several pots that stood empty or contained only dirt, no plants. He told me that when the western summer sun beat down on them, it killed everything in those pots. The western summer sun's terrible, just terrible, he said.

But among the piles of plant corpses, I discovered some blooming flowers. I'd seen those flowers before—often, in fact. They had reddish leaves like crepe paper, and the center of the flower was yellow. I asked him what it was called.

Portulaca, the gardener told me.

Potalaka? You mean like the mythical dwelling of the bodhisattva Kannon?

No, that's Potalaka, this is portulaca. Moss rose. The words are similar but have different etymologies, he told me. These flowers bloom but the petals don't scatter. With affection in his voice, he told me that they bloom for a day, then wilt, bloom then wilt, bloom then wilt.

The reddish flowers blooming in the west-facing hanging pots were fully open, revealing their yellow centers as they stared down their own impermanence.

I'd finished what I'd come for. The gardener took me back to the station, guiding me through one small alleyway after another. In the narrow alleys, I saw a bunch of styrofoam boxes that had once been packed with fish. Some were stacked so that they looked like terraced rice fields, but they were all planted with periwinkles, portulacas, and other flowers that were now blooming beautifully. They were growing, growing, growing inside boxes that had once held death.

I suspected that in Katsushika, where he'd grown up in northeastern Tokyo, he had seen similar fish boxes all the time in the back alleys. I asked him, and he responded, yes, of course, that's what I used to think gardens should look like.

We had the same thing in Itabashi, where I grew up, I told him.

There weren't proper planters or terracotta pots or anything, just styrofoam boxes like this. Oh, how wonderful the green of that amaranth is! I spoke as if talking to myself, but he gazed in the same direction and nodded.

I'd never walked with anyone like this, looking at the same things and feeling the same emotions—not even my closest friends or lovers. I felt as if I was a plant he was carefully replanting, I felt his hands take hold of my sweat-soaked body as he carefully carried me to the station. It was early in the afternoon, and the heat was at its peak. The longer we walked, the darker the gardener's shadow became in the brilliant western sun. At the same time, he grew thinner and thinner, until he was as thin as a piece of crepe paper, and I could see the fish boxes right through him. At the station, when he took his leave and turned to go, his translucent body disappeared entirely.

I remembered a story. Something I'd read many years before. It was an unforgettable story about a man who turned to the west, the direction of the Buddhist Pure Land, and concentrated with all his might. He wanted more than anything to be reborn in paradise, so that was all he ever thought about. Eventually he realized that he couldn't rely solely on his own will to take him there. If he fell sick, started to suffer, and lost consciousness while dying, his suffering and attachment to this world would prevent rebirth in paradise. No, if he died of disease, all his dedication would come to naught, so he decided on self-immolation instead. That, however, might be really painful, so he decided to try it first to see if he could withstand it. He heated up two hoes until they were red hot and held them to either side of his body. His skin peeled, his flesh charred, and his fat melted away. It was a gruesome sight, but he was satisfied, thinking that he might be able to die that way. He treated his burns and started preparing a woodstove to burn himself alive, but then he reconsidered. If he set himself on fire, what would happen? What would his new life be like in the Pure Land? To complicate matters, he was just an ordinary person. It was possible that in his final moments, he might experience doubts, and the suffering that resulted from them might prevent him from being reborn in paradise as he'd hoped. That's when it hit him. He needed to go to Mt. Potalaka. He could probably manage to get there somehow. He made up his mind immediately. He stopped treating his burns, went to the seashore, had a boat made, and spent his days learning to navigate. He asked a professional sailor to let him know the next time a strong wind blew from the east. When he eventually got word of the eastern wind, he set sail solo for Potalaka.

The thin, crepe-paper-like flowers of the portulaca bloomed pink and red, then withered away.

Potalaka, portulaca. I imagined the gardener also looking west as he watered the flowers in the hanging pot that bloomed and withered, bloomed and withered. He was probably thinking about the day when he too would set sail for the next world.

AUGUST 10. THE HEAT WAS still unbearable.

Terrorists had attempted an attack on London, and my husband was getting cold feet.

He read in the paper that the baggage inspection lines at London's airports were so long that people couldn't get into the terminals and had to stand outside, waiting in the rain. Planes were taking off with more than half their seats empty because inspections had prevented passengers from reaching their gates on time.

The news he was reading was from just a few days after the terrorist attack. I told him, things won't be the same in two weeks, much less two months from now. No doubt the weather would change too.

I told him about something that happened to me long ago. Poland, 1981. All the newspapers had been running big sensational stories about how volatile the situation was with the Solidarity movement, but when we arrived, Warsaw was quiet.

I told him about something else that happened long ago. India, 2001. I was just about to go there when there was a terrorist attack in New Delhi. I reminded my husband that he got really upset and tried to stop me from going, but I took off anyway. It was quiet in the city and dusty, not because of the terrorist attacks but because of the lack of rain.

He snapped back angrily, you're being stupid, you don't think there's a terrorist threat? Do you think reporters would write about it in the papers if it wasn't true?

I said, usually you talk much braver than that, usually you say we shouldn't limit ourselves out of fear of terrorism, we can't give in to terrorists, but I've seen you cancel your plans every time there's been a terrorist attack. Once again, you're wasting an opportunity, you're wasting that hard-on you've finally got.

I'm not canceling, I'm postponing, he argued. How would late October be? You're planning to be here in California then, so you can take care of Aiko while I'm away.

I was struck speechless.

In late October, Aiko had two weeks of fall vacation from school. I'd originally planned to take her to Japan, but after making that decision, my husband begged me to let her stay. Then he told me I should be there too. It's such a long break, he said, don't you think it'd be nice to make plans as a family? So solemnly and silently, I changed my plans again. I called a whole bunch of places to apologize and rearranged all my late-October plans for earlier in the month.

I told him he'd forgotten he'd made me do that. I took a long pause, let out a dramatically big sigh, and rolled my eyes, hoping he could somehow sense that over the phone.

Then slowly, clearly, I spat out the words, *Have—you—gone—senile?*

On the other end of the line, he exploded.

Hey, HEE-roh-MEE, what did you say?

HEE-roh-MEE, what are you saying?

HEE-roh-MEE, what are you trying to tell me?

He kept sticking the word HEE-roh-MEE between his sentences like some sort of interjection. The heavy stress on the syllables HEE and MEE hurt my ears.

My name. More than ten years ago, I patiently explained to him that my name isn't *hee-ROH-mee*, with the second syllable stressed as most Westerners pronounce it, my name is *hee-roh-mee*, with each syllable pronounced evenly. But I suppose that's not the only thing that was hard to nail down. The sound of my H is also hard to get, my R too, and my M and my I and my O and even my second I—if you don't pronounce all those difficult sounds flatly and evenly, then you're not really talking about me. But as an English speaker, he couldn't stand not having a stress in there somewhere, so he started calling me *hee-roh-MEE*. To his credit, when he tried to get the H right, he stuck his tongue toward the back of his palate, thus getting closer to the sound Ç.

Long ago, a linguist told me that if you try to write the sound of H as it's pronounced in the Tokyo dialect, Ç is probably the closest approximation.

I remember people calling me çee-*roh*-MEE when I was young. When Mom was angry, she'd call out çee-*roh*-MEEEEEEE, çee-*roh*-MEEEEEEE. If I didn't come quickly when she called, she'd scold me, what the heck are you doing? You're so damn slow, why can't you ever do anything right? Maybe "scold" isn't the right word, sometimes she'd just yell, çee-*roh*-MEE! And for ten years, I've endured the same treatment from my husband. Every time he calls out to me, he sounds like Mom screaming my name.

Now that my husband was so enraged, he put his stress on both the first and last syllables. The Ç sound had disappeared, and his H was so explosive that I thought it might blow my ears off. HEE-*roh*-MEE, *yeah, come on,* HEE-roh-MEE, *come on, let's do this.* The more times he said my name, the more his anger seemed to grow.

I'D USED THE WORD ON purpose to make him mad. *Senile.*

Losing his mind is what he feared more than anything in the world. He denied it all the time, trying to reassure himself he wasn't going batty. Using the word senile was the only way to vent my anger. By choosing that word, I was telling him that though we had talked until we were blue in the face, compromising repeatedly, our compromises apparently didn't mean squat. I felt like I was walking in the dark—I'd canceled my plans, then canceled them again and again, remaking my schedule anew each time. He obviously had forgotten all that.

I thought, fine. I don't care if you stay there for the rest of your life. I hope the stupid airport shuts down forever. Who cares if one old fart goes and disappears? If he got blown to bits, no one would ever dream that a curse by his wife was to blame.

I knew, however, that I could curse him all I liked, but he'd never hear me. The next day, solemnly and silently, I changed all my plans and paid the cancellation fees. The one exception was that I wanted Aiko's older sister, who had come to Kumamoto in August, to spend the rest of her vacation with Mom like I'd promised, so I decided to ignore his repeated pleas for me to come home, come home, come home right away. I would stay until the end of the month. It was ridiculous how much I'd already shelled out for cancellation fees this summer. Not just hundreds of dollars—a thousand, at least. Ridiculous. It made me want to weep. How many poems would I have to write to make that much? I could write forever and probably still never fill the hole in my wallet. The money flowed away as quickly as a swollen river during the rainy season. There was a thorn in my side, and no matter how much I tried to pull it out, it just stayed there, stuck.

THE OBON HOLIDAYS BEGAN.

Lots of people sent me fruit.

Watermelons from Ueki. Pears from Arao. Grapes from Tamana. All places known for their produce.

I ate the watermelon from Ueki, but before finishing the pears from Arao or the grapes from Tamana, a box of peaches arrived from Okayama, and more grapes from Omuta. Then another box of grapes from Hiroshima.

The grocer got in some green and red ground cherries and some fresh sweet potatoes that were as thin as my fingers. My daughters used to love them when they were little—ten, twenty years ago. I couldn't resist buying them and throwing them in the steamer. We ate the pears and peaches and grapes and fresh sweet potatoes. We gobbled them up. We ate as if we were buddhas feasting on all the wonderful offerings we'd received.

Obon, the season when dead relatives return to this world to visit. At the beginning of Obon, there are fireworks and folk dances in town to welcome them back. Everyone has a raucous time before silence returns. At the end of Obon, people bid farewell to the spirits by launching floating lanterns on the Tsuboigawa, the river that surrounds Kumamoto Castle and flows by our building. That year, we'd been lucky. No one in our family had died, so we didn't need to light any fires to welcome them or send them off.

Aiko's breasts had developed during the summer. Her pale-pink nipples were just barely visible pushing up against her shirt. Whenever the slightest breeze brushed against them, I imagined I could hear them tighten up, making the sound of bacon sizzling in a pan.

And the portulacas bloomed. The day after I got back from Asakusa, I rushed out to buy some. For only 298 yen, I bought a pot filled with lush green. I put them in the sun, and the tissue-paper-like flowers began to bloom one after the next. They bloomed and wilted. Bloomed and wilted. The red flowers bloomed and wilted. That evening, my daughters went out to the riverbank to play with fireworks. The tiny red and blue sparks burned, lighting up the vast darkness of the riverbank for a moment—just a moment—before fading from view.

NOTE FROM THE AUTHOR

I borrowed voices from the novelist Seiko Ito's book *My Own Style of Veranda Gardening*, the rakugo comedian Bunraku Katsura's classic story "Funatoku," the poem "Almost a woman, my daughter, now / I hear she's a wandering shrine-maiden / When she walks the salty shore at Tago Bay / the fishermen must pester her, / squabbling about her prophecies, finding fault with whatever she says / Her life, how painful!" from *Songs to Make the Dust Dance*, the medieval courtier Kamo no Chomei's *A Collection to Promote Religious Awakening*, and the poet Jukichi Yagi's "The Simple Koto."

Fishing with Cormorants, Ito Hears of the Merits of Coming and Going

LET ME BACK UP A little. A friend of mine wrote to me about a Noh play that was going to be performed by firelight in Suizenji Park late on the first Saturday in August. His letter contained a copy of the program, and he'd even made a copy of the relevant pages from *One Hundred Noh Plays in Manga*, published by Heibonsha a couple of decades ago. The play was called *Ukai*, or *The Cormorant Fisher*, as it's sometimes known in English.

The friend was someone I'd encountered from time to time at the literature museum. I'd heard he was studying Noh chanting. When I was little, every year at Hikawa Shrine near where I lived, they did Noh chanting—the same kind of thing my friend was studying now. I also recall my calligraphy teacher taught Noh chanting. A large pine tree was painted on the back wall of the hall where we practiced our calligraphy, indicating a Noh stage. I bought a three-volume collection of Noh plays a number of years ago, but I still haven't read it. I'd been thinking that I really ought to read it sometime, so when I heard about the performance by firelight, I decided to go, and I thought it might be a good experience for Aiko. Right before we were set to leave, I got a call from my husband, and I told him what we were about to see. He let out a hearty laugh and said, poor girl! When I asked him why, he told me that about a half-century before, when he came to Japan for the first time with his wife at the time (two wives before me), he went to a famous Noh theater, but it was boring, boring, boring, boring. He complained, I didn't understand a thing, it was pure torture, I (he put stress on the pronoun for emphasis) love Japanese culture, and I love you (What? He was saying this like a plain old greeting), but I just can't feel any affection for mountain potatoes (*yamaimo*, he meant) or *natto* (there's no real way to say this in English ... fermented beans?), and Noh, and that one other guy—What's his name? The film guy, the director ... no, not that one, I told you before, *that* guy, you know who I mean.

As my husband got older, he was getting more and more forgetful, so I jumped in.

You mean Ozu.

I'D PERSUADED AIKO TO COME by telling her that it'd be like a dance. As darkness fell, the old man at the parking lot warned me that the park was already closed so we had to walk along a narrow path to get there. All the shops were shuttered and silent. By the time we reached the ticket booth, the first fire had already been lit to begin the process of illuminating the stage.

A curtain had been suspended behind a grove of trees. People had gathered, and although they weren't talking, we could hear them stirring. There was an unusual tension in the air, as if the action had already started on stage. At long last, the cicadas quieted down, and the sun sank below the horizon. The *miko* shrine maidens who were milling about lit the fires around the stage.

Ukai. This was it.

I'd read the stuff my friend sent me, but seeing it onstage, I couldn't make heads or tails out of what was happening. It was hard to tell if there was even a story. I couldn't catch what they were saying at all. It was all in the Japanese of centuries ago. I thought maybe it would be more fun to experience Noh indoors, not outdoors like this. That would make it more like contemporary poetry. The people chanting and playing instruments seemed to be having a good time, but Aiko was scratching herself and beginning to whine.

Mommy, she whispered, this is super, super, super, super boring, do we have to stay and watch the whole thing? She whimpered like she was in pain.

No reason to suffer, I thought. I took Aiko by the hand and using the cover of darkness to follow some other people out, I led her away. We were walking around a lake toward the exit as I explained: There's a kind of heron called a striated heron that lives here, it's a bird but it also fishes. Aiko immediately perked up. Fishes? How? With a rod? We went as far up the slope of Tsukiyama as the road went, and as we turned, we found a vending machine with its lights on. The can rolled out with an extra-loud bang. Looking back, we saw that the hill, pond, dancers, spectators, and herons had all disappeared into darkness.

Back home, I fished out the collection of Noh plays buried deep in my bookshelves. Brushing the dust off, I began to read. This time, I grasped the meaning of the incomprehensible words. I understood the plot clearly. Weeks have passed since then, and I've reread *Ukai* many times—well, not exactly reread, I'm so distractible that it'd be more accurate to say I've opened the book and looked at it many times.

The story is about a fisherman who was killed for poaching in a place that was officially off limits. When the murdered fisherman comes on stage, this is what he says in medieval Japanese. (As I said, I only figured it out when I saw it written.)

When the fisher's torch is quenched
What lamp shall guide him on the dark road that lies ahead?

He was fishing where he shouldn't have been, and that's what got him killed, but since he had killed so many living beings during his life (he's referring to the fish), there was no help for him. When he says this passage, he is thinking, what will become of me in the next world?

I'd never killed a living thing except maybe some poisonous insects, and I didn't do that because I wanted to, but because I felt like I had to. As I told myself this, I had a sudden revelation. What was I thinking? I've eaten meat, in fact, I really enjoyed it. I've also miscarried and had abortions. A number of times. I didn't really have a choice.

I should be chanting along with the fisherman. What lamp shall guide me on the dark road that lies ahead?

Indeed. And there's the point. Truly, this is the merit of coming and going.

Use it as the ability to help others. The text repeats. Use it as the ability to help others.

The letter from my friend had been on my desk for what seemed like ages. In it, there was a quote from the end of the play. I'd read it once but then got lost in something else, so I looked for it now. Maybe I'd thrown it away? I tried to recall what he'd told me—or what he'd been trying to tell me—but I couldn't remember. There's a children's song called "Mr. Goat Gets Mail" about a goat who eats a letter without reading it, so his friend has to write him another. My situation wasn't entirely the same though—no way I could I admit to my friend I'd thrown his letter away.

Truly, this is the merit of coming and going
Use it as the ability to help others
Use it as the ability to help others

"Coming and going" can mean just what it sounds like—a perfect way to describe my life—but the phrase also describes the unsettled life of a monk who wanders from place to place. The footnote reads: "The meritorious work a monk or priest performs on his or her wanderings through the world helps others become enlightened buddhas by acting as an external guiding force." It also explained that the passage is talking about "altruistically calling upon external forces (Amida Buddha's vow to deliver all living beings to the far shore beyond suffering)." That means helping people we meet. People who pass us. People who walk by. People with whom we interact, even people we don't interact with.

I think the letter might have contained some story about the people I'd encountered in my comings and goings in the world, or maybe some of the people who met me, but I can't remember. No, it's not like "Mr. Goat Gets Mail." I couldn't possibly bring myself to ask my friend to repeat the final point in his letter.

NOTE FROM THE AUTHOR

I borrowed voices from the Noh play *Ukai* (*The Cormorant Fisher*), from the poem "Cursed is the fisher with cormorants / I kill turtles which should live / ten thousand years, my birds / I tie by the neck. So I live in this world; / what will become of me in the next?" in *Songs to Make the Dust Dance*, and a personal letter from Sumiharu Akiyama.

Oh, Ears! Listen to the Sound of Sadness Trickling in the Urinal

OF ALL THE STORIES DAD told me when I was a kid sitting in his lap, the one about marrying Mom was his masterpiece. I knew he was just telling a tall tale, but he repeated it so often I assumed it was true. Maybe that was silly of me. He would always recite it to me with the faintest traces of a tune.

Long, long ago, when I wanted a wife, I put an ad in the paper.
Lo and behold, three thousand responses arrived.
One by one, the women came and lined up in front of the house.
One by one, I interviewed them.
One by one, I asked after their interests.
One by one, I moved on to the next.
Then came your mother,
Number two thousand five hundred in line.

Sometimes from my perch in his lap I'd ask, did you choose her right away? It didn't matter how many times I'd heard the story, I still asked.

He told me, yes, I did. So I had to tell the next five hundred women I'd already made up my mind.

Then I asked, what was Mom's reaction?

I remember all this like it was yesterday.

I THINK WHAT'S MISSING FROM Mom and Dad's life now is faith, I said to my neighbor. We had taken a table outside a bookstore café in a shopping mall near our California home and were chatting as we sipped coffee from our paper cups. There aren't many places where you can smoke in public in California, but outdoor coffee shops are one of them, so my neighbor was there, puffing away on her cigarette.

I've mentioned her before. She's quite a bit older than me, but we're incredibly close friends, more like family. She grew up in a Jewish household and married a Jewish man, but she has no interest in keeping kosher. She'll eat pork, shrimp, shellfish, and even beef in cream sauce. I don't believe in anything, she'd insist, I can't stand the way faith shapes politics today, it's not just that I can't stand it, I think it's crazy, the only things I believe in are myself and democracy and capitalism, I'm like my husband that way.

At the coffee shop, my neighbor leaned back in her chair, puzzled. Faith? Faith in what? What kind of faith?

Well, I said, slightly embarrassed. I don't know, some kind of belief. It doesn't matter to me what they believe in. Spiders, maybe.

Spiders? My neighbor leaned back even further.

AS I MENTIONED EARLIER, MOM hated spiders. As soon as she saw one, she'd squash it. She couldn't help herself. Actually, it wasn't just spiders. She'd swat flies and mosquitoes, caterpillars, cockroaches, moths, and just about any other insect unlucky enough to cross her path, but the image that's really seared into my memory is of us sitting down as a family, having a good time, when she'd spot a spider. Every time, she'd leap up, rush around like crazy, and squash the poor thing. That's why I'd made this suggestion to her in her bed in the hospital.

Mom, you must've killed too many spiders. Maybe this is the curse of the spider spirits.

Curses and spiritual merit were familiar ideas to her, so she took me seriously at first. She whispered, spiders, you say? When I get out of the hospital, I'll have to perform some memorial rites to appease their spirits.

I had her going, but almost immediately, she came back to her senses and rejected the idea outright. Spiders . . . no way!

I knew it was a strange idea, but I was disappointed that she didn't accept it.

World War II had left my parents feeling betrayed. Like everyone else in the country, they were thrown into nothingness. Tokyo had burned to the ground, but they put their noses to the grindstone for years and somehow managed to get by. They had nothing to believe in. Maybe nothing at all was really important to them.

We didn't have a Buddhist altar at home. We didn't hold Buddhist memorial services when people died, and we didn't have a relationship with any temple. We did, however, have a small Shinto altar. Dad once told me that the spirit of someone who had died appeared to him in bed and asked him to perform some memorial rites, so that's why he got it. Mom gave rice offerings, and Dad clapped his hands to attract the spirits' attention. I suppose that in their own way, they felt they were paying proper respect to the various gods, buddhas, spirits, and souls floating around, but at some point, the Shinto altar disappeared too. That was probably before the period of rapid economic growth in Japan. Before the Tokyo Olympics. Before the streetcars disappeared and the subways were created.

No, they didn't seem to believe in anything. Nothing at all.

When I asked Mom what happened to all the old things, she gave me the usual—oh, I got rid of them. It doesn't make sense to hold onto old things forever, you can always buy new stuff.

What a completely nihilistic answer.

But strangely enough, Mom went to the Jizo temple sometimes. Why? What did she believe? What did she want out of the experience? When I think about her and the Thorn-Pulling Jizo, I run up against these same fundamental questions. Why turn to the Thorn Puller?

When I returned in the summer, I gave Mom one of the substitute amulets from the Jizo temple in Sugamo.

This was the same type of amulet I'd forgotten to give her earlier. You'll remember I gave Oguri-san the one I'd originally bought for her. Seeing how well it worked, I bought another the next time I was in Sugamo. I'd been carrying the thing around with me ever since, determined to give it to her.

Mom thanked me and asked me to put it under her pillow. She said, this really brings back memories, I bet Sugamo has really changed.

But she didn't seem to dwell on it. She didn't mention grinding it up and swallowing it like the old tradition suggests.

A few days later, the amulet was gone. I asked her about it. You told me to put it under your pillow, but it's not there. What happened?

I didn't want it to get lost or thrown away when they changed the sheets, so I put it in that cloth purse, and your dad took it home. My wallet's in there too.

Aren't you supposed to carry it around with you? I asked.

No reason to go to so much trouble for little things like that. She answered as though she was talking about something she had gotten rid of forty years before.

I TOLD MY NEIGHBOR, MY parents are lonely and unhappy. That weighs heavily on me.

Mother was completely bedridden by that point. She only changed position every twenty minutes when the nurse came in.

Dad was living at the apartment with the dog. I'd call him in the mornings, Japan time, which was evening for me. He insisted he was okay. He went to Mom's clinic around noon. If I called him in the middle of the night California time, he'd be back from the clinic and would tell me Mom was fine. He'd be eating dinner. The helpers came around four o'clock and finished making supper around four-thirty, so he ate right away. Around five, he'd tell me goodnight and hang up.

No one was with him. He talked to no one except Mom and the helpers. The few connections he had with people had ended long ago. All he had was the warmth of the dog and the samurai novels he read all day long. He read them so intensely that I began to wonder if something in the novels of Shuhei Fujisawa or Shotaro Ikenami might be serving as a substitute for religion for him, so I read them to find out, but I couldn't find a thing. There were, however, some elements that might have led to his addiction—charismatic protagonists, delicious food, evil villains, love, and sex that exploded like distant thunder. Plus, people died. That's always interesting.

He told me TV had become too noisy and tasteless, he couldn't stand watching it anymore. All he watched was baseball. When the Giants lost, he got sad. Sometimes, he'd watch samurai movies. That's how he spent his days. Always the same thing.

When there was a clap of thunder, Chunsuke jumped into his lap. He'd pet her, cooing, what's the matter, are you frightened? Poor thing, are you frightened? So sad. She showed her belly, and he rubbed it. Even sadder.

He'd become lonely in his old age. Yes, old age is lonely.

His daughter returned once every month or two. He hadn't forgotten that she had her own life and family—as he put it, I'd "gone and got hitched"—but he was really happy when I visited. Relieved, actually. He understood that I came every month or two without fail. When I returned to California, he would suddenly wither up and stop moving again. His primary-care doctor would comment, I see your usual problems are back. Dad answered, I can't help it, when my daughter goes back home, all the tension that keeps me going suddenly goes away.

It took him ten minutes to stand up. He told me that he'd fallen down the previous night and couldn't get up for two hours. I told him it didn't do any good to tell me after the fact, he should have called me on the spot, but no matter how many times I said things like that, he'd still fall, spend two hours trying to get back up, and then complain afterward. There was nothing I could do. It was painful. Sad. Dark. What should I do? Was there something I could do? It was hard. Sad. Painful. Dark. Hard. Sad. Painful. Dark.

I went round and round in circles thinking about it. Was it just my parents or did all people get that unhappy as they grew old? One of my acquaintances had a father who was ninety-two and a mother who was ninety. They were healthy and lived on their own, and the father even drove himself places. That's a good thing, I said, but haven't they lost most of the people around them?

I went round and round in circles. Do they feel sad or not? Mom couldn't move her hands or feet, couldn't turn herself over in bed, couldn't use the toilet on her own, couldn't cook, couldn't return home, couldn't read, couldn't see the dog or her younger sister or friends anymore.

I went round and round in circles. Was Mom unable to die, or was she trying to avoid death altogether? Not long ago when she had cardiac problems, she asked for help but was told that the doctors weren't there at night, so she got upset and raised her voice with the nurses, saying, you call yourself a hospital?

Does life still have that much value to her?

No, it doesn't. My neighbor's answer was crisp and clear.

I guess all people grow unhappy when they get old.

That's right, she said with a big nod. I'm thinking of killing myself.

I was startled.

Why? I don't know anyone who's as active and energetic as you. You've got a dinner party every five minutes, and every ten, you fly around the world to some different country.

She said, my life used to be—past tense—really active and fun, I'm happy about that, but I'll only be happy as long as I can move freely, go wherever I want, and meet tons of new people. I can still do those things, but I don't know what'll happen when I can't. All the active, creative poets, musicians, and artists I know have grown old. Last month so-and-so died, so-and-so got cancer, so-and-so started showing symptoms of Parkinson's even though he won't admit it, he also started showing signs of dementia, we talk about having poetry readings, but the plans don't come together. If this continues, and my husband dies, and all the young poets leave me behind—I interrupted her to protest, that's impossible, you're surrounded by so many people—then I'm going to kill myself. Actually, I've been thinking about how I'd do it—no jumping off something tall, no gas ovens, the best way is to stick a hose into a car and fill it with carbon monoxide. Oh, getting old is so boring! Oh, hee-ROH-mee, it just gets more and more tedious. I'm in my early seventies now, the late seventies are going to be even more tedious, and the early eighties are going to be that much more tedious still.

But doesn't this culture frown on killing yourself?

It does, she nodded.

In Japan, people sometimes do it for spiritual merit, I explained. They go out on ships and sink, set themselves on fire, stuff like that.

That's impossible in this culture, my neighbor remarked.

They say when you do it, you've got to have faith.

Oh, pooh! My neighbor made a sound like a woodwind instrument. In her heart, resistance. Ridicule. Sarcasm. Hatred.

Then she added, you don't need faith. It's not like you're George W. Bush or something.

We were facing west, and in Encinitas, that meant that we were facing the ocean. The tables at the coffee shop were placed so that you could see the water in the distance, beyond the roofs. My friend and I kept turning our eyes to the waves glittering silver and gold under the afternoon sun.

I WAS READING A BOOK. There was a lot I didn't understand, so I set out on a quest. A quest for faith, that is—a quest for whatever faith means. A quest for advice on the best way to die. I was hoping I'd find something. I knew it was a long shot. I was hoping that if I could figure it out in time, I could tell my parents and share with them the best way to ease their suffering and die well. I wanted to share that with them, with everyone who lives in a void with nothing to believe in, relying only on their own slowly disappearing selves, leaving them floating in midair, waiting for the end to come.

First, I started to read *The Tibetan Book of the Dead*, but it's about what happens to those who are already dead, not about the dying, so I quit reading partway through. Next, I tried *Essentials of Rebirth into the Pure Land*, written a thousand years ago by the Japanese monk Genshin. It started with this passage:

The first of these various hells is called the Place of Filth.
This hell is filled with hot dung and filth which is very bitter
in taste and full of insects with hard stingers. The sinners

are put into this hell and forced to eat hot dung while the
worms crawl all over them, chewing and piercing their skin,
gnawing their flesh and even sucking the marrow from
their bones. Those who have killed deer or birds fall into
this hell.

I was drawn to this passage and reread it multiple times. The
prospect of falling into such a state was horrific. Being stewed in a
hell of hot shit and mud seemed worse than any suffering I could
imagine. But I read that as long as I didn't kill any deer or birds, I'd
avoid this horrible fate. Fortunately, I'd never done those things.
I wondered if by chance I did happen to find myself on the verge
of killing something, would remembering the hell of shit and mud
stop me from following through? And if it did, would that mean
that the seeds of faith were there, sprouting up inside me? The text
continues:

As we examine our own bodies, we find muscles and veins
intertwined, moist and soft skin as a covering and the nine
orifices from which vile things like dung and urine are constantly flowing out. The human body is like a storehouse
enclosed in a bamboo fence. As within the storehouse we
find various kinds of grains, so in the body we find all sorts
of vile things. Try moving one's joints, and one will find
they are truly frail without any steadiness whatsoever. The
foolish wish to have sex and other things, but if one knows
what I am about to say, then one will immediately be aware
what will happen when one clings to such notions. Do you

see? We find such vile things in the body as tears, saliva, and sweat, which are constantly flowing out of it, plus the pus and blood that fill it. The skull is full of brains, and phlegm bubbles up in the chest. Stuffed in among these things are the viscera of life—heat, fat, membranes, and the entrails, along with stinking, inflamed impurities, which are found in the same place. How we should fear the sinful body! It's like a person who lives full of resentment, but those who are ignorant and greedy are so foolish that they take great care of their bodies, all in vain. The human body, which is composed of so many stinking, filthy things, is like a half-ruined old castle. Day and night, the stream of worldly passions beats against it. The bones form the castle walls and the blood and flesh form the mud that plasters those walls. This castle of flesh and bone, which is so deserving of our hatred, which we paint with hues of anger, greed, and foolishness, is dragged along by the flesh and blood. It leads us in wrong directions. It simmers us in a stew of pain, both inside and out. Oh, Nanda! [Here, Genshin is calling out to one of the disciples of the historical Buddha.] This is true, you must understand this. Train your mind ceaselessly, day and night, to reflect upon what I have told you. If you do not hold onto desire and wish with all your might to be freed from the confusion of this world, you will be able to pass easily through the ocean of life and death.

That's how the first part of the text ends. I was just about to start reading the next section when I got an emergency email from one of Dad's home helpers who had helped me many times in the past. The subject line simply read, "Hospitalization."

> I imagine that this sudden email will alarm you, but I want to let you know your father is going to be hospitalized. The decision to check him in was largely so he could undergo some tests, but he seems to be having trouble pronouncing words correctly and is having severe palpitations, so the doctor made the decision to send him to the big hospital in town. I realize this is sudden, but he'll be in the hospital starting tomorrow. He may be there for as long as two weeks. Please don't worry about little Chunsuke. I'm taking her to the kennel for boarding like we talked about the time before last. Do you have any plans to come back?

Plans to come back? I sighed, clicked reply, and wrote, No, I don't.

But then I realized that I might shock her by sounding unappreciative and rude, so I changed my wording: I didn't have any plans, but I'll get on the earliest flight I can. Until then, please know that I greatly appreciate your help. Please extend my appreciation to the other home helper as well.

Those were the early days of e-tickets. Now you could just go to the airport counter without bringing a paper ticket. Show your ID, and they give you a boarding pass. That meant I could buy a ticket that day and board a plane the next. There was no way to get to Kumamoto without going all the way across Tokyo, from Narita International Airport all the way across Tokyo to Haneda, where I'd catch the domestic southbound flight. Fortunately, my plane was scheduled to land at Narita at four in the afternoon, so if I hurried, I could reach Haneda in time for the last flight south. However, my position as a homemaker complicated matters significantly. I needed the cheapest possible ticket, and to get a reduced rate for the domestic leg of the trip, the airlines required a paper ticket. I bought the ticket that day, went to pick it up the following day, and the day after that I crossed the International Date Line. That meant I arrived in Narita two days later and reached Kumamoto late in the evening of the fourth day after getting the email from Dad's helper. The rental car office and the kennel were closed by the time I arrived in Kumamoto, so I'd have to go to those places on the morning of the fifth day. I was worn ragged by the time I reached my place in Kumamoto and opened the refrigerator.

Margarine, mayonnaise, and soy sauce.

A few cans of beer. A bottle of wine. Three or four little plastic cups of *konnyaku* jelly.

It was still summer. I had a couple of bottles of iced black tea and barley tea left. Last time I was there, I'd also bought some vegetable juice, which was still there, and in the freezer, I found a pack of frozen pasta and a few frozen slices of bread.

I woke up early the next morning, picked up my rental car, then got Chunsuke from the kennel. I took her for a walk before going to see Dad. He was in the same hospital on top of the cliff where Mom had been earlier in the summer. He seemed the same as usual, just sloppier and more covered in wrinkles. His voice was so hoarse it sounded like it was coming from far away, like a bad phone connection going in and out. Maybe that was one of his symptoms.

I promised I'd bring Chunsuke the next day.

Dad could see her, but we'd have to arrange it so he could meet us at the hospital entrance since dogs weren't allowed in.

I asked if there was anything he needed, and he told me, things are fine, the home helper (not the one who wrote me the email, but the other one to whom I'd extended my appreciation) had taken care of everything. Dad said, there's a place here where you can smoke, the smoking area is outside behind the vending machines, you can sit out there in a chair and smoke. Dad told me, much to my consternation, you don't need to worry about me, but go see Mom as soon as you can, she's no doubt worried, will you do me a favor and tell her I'll be getting out soon? I bet Chunsuke's sad too.

Dad said, something's been bothering me. I can't get to the bathroom on time, it's like there's no time between when I have to go and the time the pee actually comes out, I've already wet myself twice. I had the nurse bring me a bedpan, but these days I'm so shrunken down there that it's hard to find, and by the time I have to go, I'm still trying to find the damn thing.

Oh no, just telling you this has made me want to pee, here it comes, here it comes!

I had no choice. I stuck my hand out. Dad couldn't see his penis from above, but I could, so I grabbed it. It was smaller and droopier than any cock I'd ever handled. I feel bad even calling it a cock—it was a sex organ, yes, but it felt like a kid's word might be more appropriate, wee-wee perhaps.

Long, long ago, when I wanted a wife, I put an ad in the paper.

Lo and behold, three thousand responses arrived.

One by one, the women came and lined up in front of the
house.
One by one, I interviewed them.
One by one, I asked after their interests.
One by one, I moved on to the next.
Then came your mother,
Number two thousand five hundred in line.

Mom was now bedridden, unable to move her hands and legs,
but back in the old days when Dad told me this story, she was still an
overweight middle-aged woman with an unhappy expression eternally fixed on her face. She would glare at Dad as he told the story
and grunt, dismissing his tale. What nonsense, she'd say. Dad told
her, I love you. What rubbish, she responded. I saw exchanges like
this all the time. I love you. When I was a kid, I took it for granted
that husbands said things like this to their wives. But then, her
response.

I asked, what was Mom like back when you first met? Dad
answered, as pretty as Silvana Mangano. I'd never seen the actress
he referred to, but he said her name often enough for it to stick in
my memory. I imagined her to be some incredible, ravishing beauty
with an unhappy expression like Mom's on her face. Dad had chosen her, selecting her from among three thousand beautiful women
to become his unhappy beauty, but since then he had aged. Now,
his wee-wee was old, drooping, hissing, gurgling, splashing into the
urinal.

When I left the hospital where Dad was, I went to the clinic
where Mom was. There were some things I wanted to read to her.

I didn't bother preparing too much, I just quickly gathered all the books on top of my desk and shoved them into my bag as I left home in the States. I'd read one of them on the plane—a book of Buddhist sutras that folded out, accordion-style. I'd bought it a while back without much thought, and it sat untouched on my desk for some time. One of my friends would tease me, saying, what's so sad that you've got to read stuff like that on the plane? Most people read mysteries, adventure stories, stuff like that. I told her to lay off, that's what interests me.

It was a continuation of my search for faith. I thought that maybe the *Heart Sutra* might teach me something, so I got it out in the plane. At the very end of the book of sutras is a text called "Hymn to Jizo." Surprised to find Jizo mentioned there, I was overcome with a warm rush of old memories and started to read, but before I knew it I'd broken into tears and was sobbing. Summer was over, and fewer passengers were on the transpacific flight. I had the two seats next to the window to myself. Thank goodness. I pulled a blanket over me and wept quietly. I'm not sure exactly what brought the tears on. Jizo is the protector of children, so people often pray to him when children die or when they have miscarriages or abortions. I've never experienced the death of a child. I was no stranger to abortions, but that didn't really bother me. What shook me the most was probably this passage: "They spent their day in play, but when the sun began to set. . . ."

I've experienced sadness and the heartbreaking feeling of being alone as twilight falls. My children had experienced it too because of me. I can't remember how many times I'd lifted into my arms one of my daughters who was exhausted from so much crying, and apologized over and over for how badly Mommy had behaved by leaving her alone. Maybe that's why the line got to me.

All this was still on my mind as I sat by Mom's pillow in the clinic. We started talking as if I hadn't been away for weeks. Perhaps she hadn't even realized that I'd been gone.

I told her that when I was on the plane, I read something and for some reason started crying. I had felt like it was describing the sadness of all the children who were ever born. I started reading the passage to her, translating it into modern Japanese as I went.

This is not a tale of this world.

This is a tale of the Riverbank of Sai, located far, far down the mountain path that leads to death.

The more you hear of this tale, the more pity you will feel.

Children in their second, third, fourth, and fifth years, children who had not yet reached the age of ten, gathered on the Riverbank of Sai and wept, I miss my father, I miss my mother, I'm so lonely, so, so lonely. Their weeping voices were different from those of this world, they reverberated with such sadness that they pierced the flesh and bones of all who heard. Those children gathered the rocks from the riverbank and built towers for transferring karma—the first layer was for their fathers, the second layer for their mothers, the third layer for their hometowns, for their brothers and sisters, for themselves—they whispered these things as they built the towers.

In this way, they spent their day in play, but when the

sun began to set, a demon from hell appeared and spoke in a terrifying voice: "Say, what are you doing? The parents you've left in the mortal world haven't been holding memorial services or doing good deeds, all they do is spend all day and night lamenting your deaths—'How cruel! How sad! How unfortunate!' Your parents' lamenting is what will cause you so much torment in hell. Don't blame me! It's my job to swing my black iron rod to smash the towers you make each time you think about how sad you've made them."

It was then that the bodhisattva Jizo appeared in a shimmering haze and said with pity in his voice, "Oh, weeping children, the only reason you have traveled here to the netherworld alone is because your lives were so short. The mortal world and the netherworld are so far apart, from now on, you should think of me as your parent in the netherworld, I want you to rely upon me." And with this, he gathered the children in the hem of his monk's robe and began to care for them. How wonderful! He had toddlers who could only grab hold of his priestly walking stick. He held the children tightly against his own flesh and soothed them, caring for them—how wonderful!

As I interpreted the text, I could see the tears well up in Mom's eyes.

Oh, oh, she said, as if wringing out the words.

Anyone who has been a mother

Remembers deep in their bones

A thing or two about children—
The children they gave birth to
The children they didn't give birth to
The children they raised
The children they didn't raise
The children they lost
Shiromi too, me too, my mother too . . .

Mom's words trailed off. And that's when I realized, this is it. These are the emotions that were missing from *Essentials of Rebirth into the Pure Land* and *The Tibetan Book of the Dead*. Emotions on display right before me. They were full of kindness, sadness, nostalgia, and gratitude too—so full of these things that they could rock your world and make you burst into tears before you knew it, they could deplete you of all your energy yet somehow leave you feeling better because of it.

As Mom tried to wipe her eyes, her paralyzed hand bobbed up and down near her nose. I was reminded of the large cauldron full of burning incense just inside the entrance to the Sugamo Jizo temple. Her hand looked like it was waving in the smoke, trying to waft it toward her to take in its blessings.

NOTE FROM THE AUTHOR
I borrowed voices from the poet Mitsuharu Kaneko's poem "Sink," Chuya Nakahara's poem "Frenzy on an Autumn Day," Genshin's treatise *Essays on Rebirth into the Pure Land*, and the Buddhist prayer "Hymn to Jizo."

Smoke Rises from Urashima on a Clear Autumn Day

THE HEAT OF SUMMER CONTINUED into October. It was late enough in the year that people felt it necessary to fortify themselves with knit shirts and boots, but then they spent the day walking around sweating like crazy. I wished everyone would forget the seasons and just continue wearing summer clothes. That's what I'd been doing so that I didn't get overheated in the fall the way you do at the height of summer. That made things comfortable, so much so that I wished the summery warmth could continue, but nothing lasts forever. The season changed little by little—the green lingered in the pines, cherries, camphors, ginkgos, and sumacs, while the leaves of the laurels and other trees quickly developed autumn colors. The other trees didn't drop their leaves or change color, they just crouched down to fortify themselves. Eventually, the sweet osmanthus began to fade. There was a big osmanthus by the parking lot out back, and my neighbors on both sides had them in their gardens. The park a few blocks down the street was planted full of them, and their scent penetrated my nose and mouth, filling all my organs. The aroma was so thick that it was more like a haze than a mere fragrance.

More like a haze than a mere fragrance.

DAD LEFT THE HOSPITAL WITHOUT incident. He had returned to what you might call life as usual, but was it really possible to rewind time that far? I was resigned to fate. I'd been through this many times already. When old folks go into a new environment like a hospital, they experience all sorts of trauma, they begin to show signs of dementia, they develop delusions, their personalities change. I'm not sure if those things continue indefinitely or if they're only temporary, but I do know the old folks never completely go back to life as it was. Dad was only hospitalized for some tests, and the results were better than expected, but I had the impression that I'd opened a jeweled box and now smoke was pouring out.

I thought of the folk tale about a young fisherman named Urashima Taro who rescues a magic turtle and is rewarded with a trip to the Dragon Palace far beneath the sea. After several days there, he returns home, but first he is presented with a jeweled box and told he should never, ever open it. Back home, he discovers he has been away not just a few days, but an entire century. Distraught, he opens the box, smoke pours out, and he turns into an old man on the spot.

Smoke was pouring out.

I went home to sleep. The place was empty, the windows were big, there were few furnishings, and everything was quiet. When my family came here to stay, everyone complained there was only one toilet, but why should that be a problem? In any case, I went to sleep and got up in the morning. Going to see Mom and Dad was like commuting to work.

Dad called in the morning. Hey.

Oh, hey, I groaned.

Good morning.

It's so early, I complained.

Do you want to come have coffee? The other day, one of the helpers bought me some really yummy coffee beans. I went to the bathroom around six o'clock, but then I fell down and wet myself. It took me an hour to get up and change my clothes! At times like that, I wish someone was here, my daughter or my wife, but both of you are somewhere else.

Sometimes I dare to imagine I'm an independent woman.

It was Dad who helped me go out into the world on my own. Mom was always scolding him for being a pain-in-the-ass do-nothing, but as the head of our household, he was an independent, self-supporting man. Financial independence is difficult, but spiritual independence is even harder. I had a really hard time going out on my own. I don't even know how many times I left only to come running back home. Now I brave rough weather by planting both feet firmly on the ground. I don't need to rely on my parents or husband all that much, but when I come back to Japan, I'm plagued with doubt—what on earth did all that independence and self-reliance mean?

My parents never worried about their daughter abandoning her own family in California for weeks on end to spend time with them. But that's not all—they seemed just fine confessing their weaknesses to their daughter: I pissed myself, a little crap came out too. In the old days, the old man in front of me was my hero. He helped the weak and stood up to the strong. He'd bravely fight any bear, wolf, or evildoer that threatened me, but now I understood something. To be a hero in Japanese culture, a man needs to have a weak point, and when he reveals it, he becomes a frail, fragile, wretched man, unable to do anything himself. Heroes are entirely reliant on their heroines, and heroes have to be ugly enough that other women don't turn their way. If a man doesn't meet these qualifications, is he really a hero? If all that is true, then what does independence really mean? Do young people declare their independence simply so they can step away from their parents and have sex?

I left my parents, had lots of sex, and gave birth to my daughters. At some point I found I'd become independent. I was running a household, raising children, saving money, and doing all the things that my "good-for-nothing" father couldn't. I fought for my daughters, I ran to help my parents when they were in crisis. Both my parents and society at large expected me to care for them in their old age, and I intended to follow through.

Long ago, Dad told me something when I was sitting on his lap. Girls mustn't give in, girls can do anything they want. I believed him and went out into the world. There were lots of things I found I could do if I set my mind to them. But now Dad was talking like he'd done a 180-degree turn. Neither my daughter nor my wife is here—I'm not sure if this was sarcasm, dementia, or a joke, but the words pierced me like thorns. What he was saying was, I wish they were here, either my daughter (who I wish hadn't left to get married) or my wife (but I really mean my daughter, who I wish would come back and take care of me).

ONE CLEAR AUTUMN DAY, I was at the literary museum talking about the portulacas, how they resemble crepe paper, when Oguri-san told me that if I was interested in Mt. Potalaka, there was a place I ought to see. Everyone around here seemed to know all about Potalaka. He told me that since time immemorial, a ritual has been performed in the region that supposedly gives people the same karma as traveling to Potalaka in person.

The ritual used to take place in Tamana, just north of Kumamoto, but Oguri-san said he didn't like to do it there because Mt. Unzen is visible on the far side of the Ariake Sea. If we were going to do it, we should go to the westernmost extreme of Amakusa, the small chain of islands southwest of Kumamoto, connected by a series of bridges to the mainland.

So one day, we set out in his car. I was concerned about Dad, so I told Oguri-san I wanted to get back to town as soon as possible. We decided to leave early in the morning.

He spoke in a light, jocular tone as we crossed town. Today we're in a hurry, but when you do this for real, you need to take your time, all right? We went through Uto, and at Misumi, I looked left at the harbor to the west. I told him that every time I go by Misumi, I get excited at the sight of the small islands out there in the water. Then we crossed the first bridge to Amakusa.

Oguri-san told me that because there's only one road through the area, it takes seven hours to get there when everyone is traveling during the Obon or New Year's holidays.

We crossed the second, then the third bridge that connects the islands.

After crossing the fourth and fifth bridges, we reached a part of the islands ironically named Hondo, meaning "the mainland," then we passed through a tunnel to a road that runs along the seashore.

In California the ocean also spreads out to the west, but the sky is blue, the water is deep, the land and air are really dry, and there are swarms of surfers and dolphins everywhere, making it just about impossible to imagine that the Pure Land lies somewhere out there on the far side of the water. Ages ago, I visited the Aran Islands, in Ireland, and there the water also opens to the west, but the land drops off into the sea, forming steep cliff walls. It was wild and desolate. Standing below the cliffs made me profoundly uneasy. At twilight, when everything started growing hazy and indistinct, we climbed back up the cliffs before the sun disappeared completely. The friend I was with was wearing white pants, and as she climbed in front of me her bottom looked like the bobbing tail of a wild rabbit. As darkness fell, her white bottom and fluffy little tail looked eerily otherworldly.

So what did they look like? Oguri-san asked.

Spirits, I suppose, especially because of where we were.

From the top of a cliff in the westernmost extreme of Amakusa, we looked down on the gently stirring sea.

He apologized, usually there are more waves. It's the East China Sea, so it's totally different from the Ariake Sea, which is mostly surrounded by land. There are usually white waves crashing over there, by those rocks. When I was a boy, we used to go down by that rocky spot. We'd walk along the water's edge around where the rocks jut out, to a place where we could swim. I grew up down there.

The sun was shining. The sea was a vivid shade of green. A layer of mist hung over the water. Then the depths of the water filled with light as if someone had moved an invisible panel, letting brightness flow in. I heard the piercing cry of black kites soaring over the water. On the cliffs, the broadleaf evergreen bushes flourished, forming thick, dense thickets. Hiding in the shade of the trees was an unmanned lighthouse and a small temple dedicated to thirteen buddhas. When I turned back to the west, I could see the dead moving about in the light at the farthest reaches of the sea.

I could see them. They were stirring.

Did you see that? Oguri-san asked. Those are the souls of the dead, they're in constant motion, they never stop, even for a second.

THE CLEAR AUTUMN DAYS CONTINUED. One day after the next. When the time came for me to go home to California, it was yet another clear autumn day.

I was up late cleaning the night before. Each time I crossed the ocean, I had to go through everything and make piles: the clothes I'd wear, the items I'd take, the books I planned to read, the papers and documents I had to take care of—the things I'd take, the things I wouldn't take. Next, I had to dispose of everything I was getting rid of. I often made mistakes—for instance, I'd leave some half-consumed milk in the fridge and then have to ask the neighbor who had a key to do it for me. Dawn was breaking by the time I finally got it all done and lay down to rest, but at 6:00 a.m. my phone rang. I wasn't sure if I'd even fallen asleep or not.

Hey.

Oh, hey, I groaned.

So today's the day you're leaving, right?

Yeah, I moaned. As long as I leave by nine, I'll make it.

I thought it would be a good idea to wake you up early, you're always running around like crazy at the last minute, Dad said. I couldn't sleep last night after I realized today was the day you're going. If you stop by, I'll put some coffee on for you.

So I stopped by.

When are you coming back? In that moment he reminded me of a small child.

December, I think.

Well, will you help me send my end-of-year gifts?

Sure, I'll do that for you.

Will you give Chunsuke a bath too?

Sure, I'll do that for you.

It would be great to get the *kotatsu* out around that time.

Sure, I'll do that for you.

I'll be waiting, he said simply.

I swallowed the coffee he'd made, and left, leaving Dad behind.

I had to go.

I went from Kumamoto to Haneda, from Haneda to Narita, I got on and off different vehicles, I went up and down stairs, I walked along what seemed like endless hallways and tunnels, dragging my luggage behind me. Everywhere I went—the outskirts of Kumamoto, around Haneda Airport, along the tracks of the airport monorail and the Narita Express—I saw goldenrod and silver miscanthus swaying in the landscape, filling vacant lots and fields. The autumn plants let out a tremendous roar as they shook in the wind.

The autumn plants shook in the wind.

NOTE FROM THE AUTHOR

I borrowed a voice from the Noh play *Obasute* (The Abandoned Old Woman).

A Lump Is Removed, Ito Meets
a Demon and the Sparrow-Dog
Devotees

I WAS WORRIED ABOUT AIKO. She was still only ten, so it made sense I wanted her by my side. My husband alone couldn't keep up with her. On the phone, he'd complain, I'm exhausted, really exhausted, I couldn't get anything done today, not a single thing, my hands are full here, I'm all alone, all I do is drive the kids around and take care of meals. He was constantly complaining, but deep inside I laughed at him. You think that's suffering? Even so, I wanted to get home to stop his complaints and to be with Aiko. But being ten years old is totally different from being three or five. She had school, her friends, Daddy, and the dogs. I'm sure she missed Mommy, but she seemed fine even when I wasn't there.

Honestly, I worried more about our puppy than Aiko.

Last year when Aiko and I were in Japan for four months, my husband bought a dog, hoping to curry Aiko's affection. I had no intention whatsoever of breaking up with him at the time. I planned on returning to California as usual, but apparently my husband was consumed with anxiety that he might never see Aiko again.

Aiko had been pleading on the phone. *Daaaaady*—she pronounced the vowel in the nasal way that Americans do, as though trying to wring as much out of it as she possibly could—I want a dog. He heard her and said, fine, I'll get you one for Christmas, what kind do you want? Not even a second passed before she shot back, a sparrow-dog! Like Grandpa's got! Like Chunsuke!

My husband hates dogs. When we got our shepherd a few years earlier, it took tons of patient consensus building and persuasion before he got on board. This time, however, when we arrived home the day before Christmas, a sparrow-dog was already waiting at the house. For a while, I kept mistakenly calling it "Chunsuke," but eventually I got used to it. A while back, when I mentioned that a dog bit my nipple—well, this was the dog I was talking about.

You'll remember that the shepherd my oldest daughter had taken to college had a hard time adjusting to life in the city, so that dog came back to live with us, and one dog became two. Morning and night I found myself walking them, holding two leashes, one big, one small. I felt like a cormorant fisher with his cormorants waddling along on leashes.

The shepherd picked fights with just about every dog she perceived as a worthy opponent. My heart was warmed by the fact that she perceived the new puppy not as an invader but as a member of the family, and she interacted with him patiently. The puppy understood how to interact, he recognized the shepherd as the alpha dog and was willing to give up whatever was necessary. I was impressed.

The puppy got bigger and bigger, and within a few months, he hit adolescence. When dogs move from regular peeing to marking their territory, boy, do they smell like pee. The stench continued from when he grew his second set of teeth to when he was neutered. While I was away, sometimes I wanted a hug, but not from Aiko or from my husband. I missed his little puppy body—his warmth and his strange smell.

BY THE TIME I CROSSED the Pacific, the season had shifted in California too. The oleanders growing in the freeway medians were past their prime, and the fleabane was covered with hairy tufts of white. Pampas grass was sending up silvery white spikes in the wild land and on the roadsides.

A number of small lumps had grown on my husband's face. Before, he only had one on his right cheek, but now they were on both cheeks and even his forehead, where they looked like failed attempts to grow demonic horns.

When I asked him what was going on, he said, they just developed, like nothing was the matter at all.

But you didn't have them before?

He played innocent. It seems you can get them anywhere.

The old lump on his right cheek had grown larger, red, and shiny, and stuck out of his whiskers. It's apparently infected, he told me, I'm going to have it removed, the center's full of pus. We called the doctor and made an appointment.

Lumps. I've been meaning to write about his lumps for ages, but I let it slide until now.

Here's how it started. My husband got a lump on his back. It grew noticeably larger and shiny. It was too big to be a pimple, so we started calling it a "lump." There was a black dot on top, which I recognized as an opening. Remembering how nice it feels to pop a pimple, I couldn't keep still. I made him lie on his stomach, explaining that I was going to give him a massage. I rubbed the lump with my fingers, pinched it with my fingernails, and squeezed like I was trying to pop a ground cherry out of its papery husk. Suddenly the stuff inside began to come out. It was thicker than pus and softer than what you'd find in a pimple. It kept coming and coming, as though his entire body was filled with it. What's more, it stank. I'm not sure how to describe it. Maybe like a concentrated animal smell? Maybe like the gamey wild animals Europeans ate so many generations ago? Maybe like the dregs of fermented milk?

Before long, the lump grew red, feverish, and swollen. In the end, my husband went to a doctor, who cut it open and cleaned it out. My husband complained that the reason it got so bad was because I'd been fiddling around with it.

Popping a pimple is a lot like having sex. It's also like rubbing someone's shoulders or masturbating. You use your body to fool around and forget yourself completely. And while we're on the subject of sex, let me just say how pathetic it is when people think that repeatedly sticking a penis in a vagina and pulling it out is all there is to it. One of my partners complained to me once, saying that was what he believed—I just remember thinking how little he knew.

But back to my husband's lump. It came back. I didn't touch it this time, but it festered, became swollen, and began to hurt. He went back to the doctor and had it cut open again. I don't remember how many times he repeated this. Then one day, a lump appeared on his cheek.

As his cheek grew round and puffy, there was something about my husband's appearance that brought back memories. I felt like I'd seen a similar face when I was a child. Like I was remembering someone I'd encountered before. When I thought about it, I realized I was remembering the folk tale about the old man who had a lump removed from his cheek. I felt like I'd been sucked into the old story.

This is how the folk tale goes. There was an old man who had a lump on the right side of his face. One day, he went into the woods and encountered a group of demons having a party, drinking, dancing, and carrying on. The old man joined in and danced around the bonfire so well that the demons insisted he return the following day. To ensure that he would return, they decided to take something valuable from him, and not knowing the ways of the world, they chose the growth on his face. When the lump was removed, the old man felt no pain at all. Back at home, he and his wife were overjoyed. It just so happened that his next-door neighbor also had a lump on his face. When he heard the old man's story, the neighbor decided to go find the demons so they could do the same for him. Unfortunately, he was a bad dancer, and so to get rid of him, the disappointed demons slapped the lump they had removed from the other man onto the neighbor's healthy cheek, leaving the poor man with growths on both sides of his face.

Like the wife of the lump-faced old man in the folk tale, I was with my husband all day long. I didn't set out to observe his lump, but I couldn't help noticing it. My husband was no good at dancing. He was more like the neighbor—a crappy lump-faced dancer who lived nearby. In fact, when I consider my husband's personality, I'd have to say, yes, he was more like the neighbor. He was the kind of guy who would run into a demon, miss his chance to have the lump removed, and end up coming home with another. And sure enough, when I got back from Japan, I discovered he had more shiny red lumps on his face.

HE RETURNED FROM THE DOCTOR wearing an extremely grumpy expression. As soon as he was in the door he started ranting, as if foisting his dissatisfaction onto me might improve the situation. What the hell was that? That man calls himself a doctor but can't take care of something this simple in a single visit? The medical system in this country is rotten—rotten to the core. He continued to shout and curse, so much that I don't entirely remember everything he said.

After he finished his tirade, I said, berating me isn't going to change anything.

He snapped at me, I'm not berating, I'm expressing myself. In my culture, this is how we talk in situations like this. It's okay for you to point out cultural differences, but not okay for me?

I quickly changed the subject. So, is the doctor going to operate?

He told me, it's right in the middle of my face, it's not something we should trust to an ordinary surgeon, I ought to go to a specialist to have it removed—a plastic surgeon could do it without causing nerve damage. But the doctor predicts that even if it's removed, it'll likely come back again. He referred me to a plastic surgeon. If I contact the surgeon now, maybe I'll be able to get an appointment in two weeks, but there's no way he'll operate the same day he sees me, that'll probably take another two weeks, or if I'm unlucky, three or four. So much goddamn waiting just to remove a tiny lump. I could tell that he was trying hard to show he wasn't attacking me—he was attacking the American medical establishment.

Just like the old man with the lump in the folk tale, my husband had a wife by his side. I'd had the vague sense that I'd have to live with him and his lumps for good, but I suppose there comes a time to say goodbye to everything.

I looked it up on the net. He had what is called a trichilemmal cyst. Inside is a little packet of grimy stuff. While I was poking around online, I happened across a video on some dermatologist's site. The lump was disinfected and cut open, revealing a flesh-colored packet inside. Using a fine pair of tweezers, the doctor pulled it out—(sigh). The flesh-colored packet was a little bloody as he slid it out—(sigh)—and laid it on its side. The doctor cut it open with a sharp scalpel and pulled out a butter-like blob of keratin from inside—(yet another sigh)—to show the camera. Watching the procedure, I felt a jolt of joy that left me trembling, so I added the site to my favorites. Since then, I've visited the site often to rewatch the video. Ever since I heard the old folk tale as a kid, I'd been imagining what lump removal might be like—I imagined the demons twisting and wrenching the lump off the man's cheek and sticking it back on, like they were screwing it on and off. In reality, however, it involves cutting it open and sliding the slimy center out. (Sigh, sigh, the joy of accomplishment.)

AROUND THAT TIME IS WHEN I first heard about a club for sparrow-dogs.

Back when it was only me and the shepherd taking walks, I had to pay careful attention that other dogs didn't come near. If a dog came near us, she'd try to protect me. She'd attack other dogs on my behalf, sometimes wounding them. Several times I had to pay vet bills that amounted to hundreds of dollars each. But sparrow-dogs were different. They were happy, curious, and eager to get along.

Through the sparrow-dog, I met a number of new people. There was a housewife I often encountered in the park walking her sparrow-dog. We exchanged greetings and stopped, recognizing that our dogs wanted to play. I'd order the shepherd to lie down, then let the sparrow-dogs play while we humans chatted. The housewife was exactly like her dog—happy, straightforward, eager to get along, and full of curiosity. She frequently invited us to a sparrow-dog club. Apparently, all the sparrow-dog owners in our area got together to walk their dogs in a botanical park owned by the local university.

I wasn't the least bit interested. Why interact with other dogs? Was I that pathetic? Both my husband and I would have been perfectly happy living out in the boonies like hermits or exiles, cut off from all human interaction. However, Aiko wasn't a hermit or exile, just a regular elementary school student, so she started whining about going to the club. Pronouncing her vowels like melted sugar, she implored him, *Daaaaaaady, pleeeeeeeeeeeeeaze!* Using her newly developing adolescent body to sidle up to him, she quickly won him over.

The club gathered in the park under the pure blue skies of California. In the shadows, the shade-loving vines leafed out, crawled, and dangled from high above, while in the sun, small flowers from the chrysanthemum family bloomed profusely in different colors. Pumpkins swelled between them, becoming ridiculously large at the end of their withered vines, punctuating the field with bright orange spots. *Here we are! Here we are!* Sure enough, there were lots of women with their sparrow-dogs. The only males present were the husband of the woman in charge of the park and my husband, whose face was covered with gauze after the removal of his lump. He looked like he'd been through tons of pain.

To my surprise, many of the women there had various physical challenges. In fact, several had dogs tethered to their electric wheelchairs. There were some extremely old women too. No, now that I think about it, it wasn't surprising at all. Before picking out Chunsuke, I looked into many different kinds of dogs before settling on a sparrow-dog. They're quiet, good-natured, pleasant, loyal, and straightforward. Even elderly people with physical ailments could take care of them. The owners were like their dogs too—quiet, good-natured, pleasant, and straightforward. They extended their hands without hesitation to anyone in trouble, just as they extended their hands lovingly to their dogs.

A woman in her early seventies, who appeared to be one of the leaders, smiled and asked the three of us, do you have any questions as a new owner?

Covering for my husband, who was cramping up from giving so many forced smiles, I said, we're having trouble housetraining him. It was easy with our other dogs, but this time, we're having a tough time. Do you have any good ideas?

The leader turned to a tiny withdrawn lady who looked to be in her late eighties and abruptly passed the conversation to her. What do you think?

The lady in her eighties was slow getting on board. You know, sparrow-dogs are wonderful, don't you think? They're wise, loving, loyal, and blessed with an independent spirit—did you know they live long too? These little babies live for twenty years, unlike larger dogs who die when they are only eight or nine! Your problem is that you chose a puppy. If you wanted a housetrained dog, you should have chosen an older one. One that is five years old or so.

A woman in her early sixties and a woman in her fifties agreed. That's right, that's right, they're too smart. That's why they don't always do what people tell them.

The crowd of fifty sparrow-dogs and fifty women were attracting attention. Someone walking by asked, is this some new cult? My husband's cheeks grew more cramped from his forced smiles. The gauze covering his cheek stood out, white against his skin.

How can I describe how badly he fit in? The group was dedicated to the love of sparrow-dogs, but he was filled with anxiety, standing there in the middle of it. I imagined he was feeling the same kind of anxiety as the old man who couldn't dance must have felt when he realized the demons weren't going to take away his lump but punish him instead. It was the kind of anxiety a non-believer might feel at the prospect of having his body being ripped apart. It was the kind of anxiety that people with no faith might feel when they are unable to die, like my friend who wanted to commit suicide, my mother who was bedridden in the clinic, or my father who was bored out of his skull. That kind of anxiety.

I decided to rescue him. I summoned up my courage and said to the leader, my daughter Aiko here wants to go on a walk with all of you, but if you don't mind my husband and I have to take care of some business at the university now. There's someone we've got to see today, we'll be back and pick her up once we're done.

In unison, the women assured me, oh, of course, that's no problem at all.

Sometimes a white lie isn't all bad. We left the group and rushed back as fast as we could. There's an expression in Japanese that goes, "piss in a frog's face." It means not complaining or flinching, even when all sorts of weird things happen. (They say that a frog won't complain even if someone urinates on it, but I don't know. I've never tried.) In any case, we didn't flinch in the face of all their weirdness. My husband and I got out of there unscathed, and we were none the worse for it.

We'd no sooner reached the car, still panting, when my husband said in a loud voice, they're absolutely loony!

And he laughed. He did it with an expression completely different from the forced smile he'd displayed earlier—the laughter burst forth from the bottom of his belly. Instinctively, I looked back at the group. For a second, I got caught up imagining what might happen if the loonies heard what he'd said, decided to take revenge, and rushed my husband as nimbly as their dogs, baring their teeth and attacking.

What a crazy notion! Such good-natured, pleasant, quiet dogs. The women too. The only thing casting a pall over my mood, however, was my anxiety about whether Aiko, whom they had led off into the bush, might ever escape their clutches.

NOTE FROM THE AUTHOR
I borrowed from *Madison's World Dog Encyclopedia.*

Ito Again Finds Herself in a Real Pinch and Dashes through Darkness for Her Child

THIS IS NO LONGER JUST a story about aging. I also need to talk about the crisis that befell my daughter.

The suffering of a child is unbearable.

The most unbearable of all the suffering that rains down upon us.

Trapped in cruel darkness, rolling around in agony all alone, we still find our way out eventually.

Then there's the suffering of death that befalls our parents.

All we can do is accept that, solemnly and silently.

But the suffering of our children is different.

We clearly recall their innocent, smiling faces.

When our children cried, we gave them our milk to fatten them, to comfort them long enough to stop their tears.

We help our children learn to laugh again.

We constantly want to help.

Our suffering children.

If we could look away, we probably would.

But we can't.

Our children call to us, look at me, look at me, help me, help me!

We help them even when it means sacrificing ourselves.

There are things we can't ignore once we've seen them.

Others might not look, but a mother with drooping breasts will open her eyes and see.

See the suffering of her grown children.

Her pain is so deep she won't shed tears.

I've shown this kind of pain to my parents more times than I care to remember.

In my mid-twenties, my exhausted mother once said, I wonder what karma has made this child suffer so much at the hands of men. I raised her so, so carefully, hoping, praying she'd be spared.

I WENT TO SEQUOIA NATIONAL PARK during the spring several years ago, and ever since then, I'd wanted to return for another visit. I decided to take Aiko in the fall during her autumn break from school. It would take seven hours each way, but I'd drive us, we'd see it and get back in time. It's in the mountains, so no doubt it would be chilly. But we'd be visiting off-season, so there wouldn't be many people or bears, and it would be easy enough to get a reservation at the park lodge. Once you cross Los Angeles and go over the mountains, there are lots of vineyards. Pass through them, and you reach oil fields. Oil pumps bob up and down like old-fashioned bird toys dipping their beaks in water. Pass them, and you reach orange orchards. Beekeepers bring their bees to the orchards to produce honey from the winter flowers. Honeybees slam against the windshield and bumper, smearing them with sticky goo. Past that, you reach the forest and enter the national park. Driving up the mountain roads through the park, you notice the trees in the forest getting bigger, then one giant tree after another appears then disappears back into the forest, and finally, the giant millennium-old sequoias appear before your eyes. I was looking forward to the trip and had run the simulation over and over in my head, but something happened that put all the plans on hold.

Yokiko was having a hard time in college. She was sinking little by little. I could see the changes from day to day.

At first I thought it was just one side of her personality expressing itself.

But at some point, I could no longer make that excuse.

She stopped laughing when we spoke on the phone.

She started calling me in tears, she started calling more and more often.

Her complaints escalated into wailing.

I can't eat, I can't sleep, I can't remember anything I study, I don't know what to do.

A cut to the hand will bleed, an ulcer in the intestine will make a man faint, but wounds to the heart can't be seen.

That's when it's time for a parent to get involved.

But something else happened first.

One day, in her physics class, her professor suddenly stopped the lecture and said, I can't stand this anymore.

Then, ignoring the two hundred astonished students, he walked out of the room, went somewhere, and killed himself.

Classes were canceled for a week.

About a week later, a university employee came and talked to the students.

An email was sent to inform them there were no plans to resume class.

Another email was sent to urge anyone who was shaken up to get counseling.

Are you shaken up? I asked.

Not really, she answered. I know that other people might be though.

That's when I made up my mind. The sequoias will be there for decades or centuries, so instead of a trip to see them with Aiko, I would use autumn break to go to Yokiko's school to see her. And if I could bring her back home, I would.

So I put my husband and Aiko in the car.

I switched our destination from the north-northeast where the sequoias are to the north-northwest where Yokiko's college is, and we set off.

Just a couple of weeks before, my husband had had cataract surgery.

Still, he kept grumbling, harrumph, it's not like I can't drive.

I asked him if he could or couldn't.

He grumbled some more, harrumph, things are out of focus, strong lights blind me, I can't see the road at night.

Definitely not a good idea to put him behind the wheel.

I resigned myself to driving the whole way.

So I did.

It wasn't an adrenaline rush or the superhuman strength you sometimes see in emergencies that supported me through the long drive. It was just the ridiculous energy of a worried mother.

Instead of taking the mind-numbingly bleak inland highway, we took the highway that runs along the coast.

It was a long drive.

The expressway through Los Angeles kept backing up, then

traffic would flow smoothly for a while before jamming up again.

As soon as we broke free, we merged onto the highway along the Pacific. The water spread across the horizon.

My husband and I shouted.

The sea! The sea! How beautiful! Look, no surfers, nothing at all. Just the ocean as far as you can see!

Aiko chimed in too, repeating the same emotion in both languages. *Waaaa, sugoi!* Wow, amazing!

But meanwhile, she was stretched out in the backseat, playing a video game that she'd finally managed to cajole us into buying over the summer.

That meant a constant stream of beeps, blips, and other electronic sounds.

When she got bored, she pulled out a recorder and started to blow.

That meant the constant, high-pitched screech of the recorder.

And her playing was way, way out of tune.

We passed by several of the old Spanish mission churches along the coast.

We went through a town, passing a power plant.

We went through another town and by some more mission churches.

Bell-shaped markers along the road indicated we were approaching Historic El Camino Real.

The missions had been built along the Royal Road.

As they extended north, they subjugated the indigenous population.

A long line of colonial ruins stretched along the blood-soaked road.

The west-facing sea stretched the whole way down the road.

There wasn't a soul anywhere along the coast.

The mountains dropped into the sea.

The sun dropped into the sea too.

It grew dark.

Thinking there might be a town around the next headland, I drove round only to find nothing but the headland itself.

The sky grew black, the sea as well.

The forest and cliffs too.

From time to time we saw lights moving.

We were so far from anything that there was no cellphone signal.

I kept driving and driving.

However, it felt like we were going around in circles. What should I do?

Were we really moving forward?

The headlands seemed to go forever. Was there really just one?

Did people live here? I wondered if the local population had been magically transformed into something else.

I began to get anxious.

Suddenly, the road began to climb, and we entered some woods.

Lights shone in the darkness, creating unmoving specks of brightness in the dark.

As the lights grew in number, they opened into a glittering town.

I pulled into a motel and parked the car.

I'd driven nine hours.

If we'd taken the inland route, we would've reached the university in eight hours, even with traffic.

But we'd chosen the coastal route on purpose.

We spent a night.

We got back on the road the next morning.

We don't live far from the ocean.

Wherever we go, we drive by the beach and see surfers out at sea.

The sea at home and the sea here are the same body of water. Both coasts face due west.

Imagine a boat sailing straight out to sea.

It would reach Hawaii, Guam, Saipan, Pohnpei, or maybe even Cape Inubosaki on the east coast of Honshu, near Tokyo.

However, go even further west, and that's where the Pure Land lies.

YOKIKO WAS STANDING QUIETLY AT the entrance to the university. When I hugged her, she wasn't the daughter I knew, she was nothing but bones—a backbone, ribs, and two scapulas. When I took her hand, it didn't belong to my daughter—her fingers felt like a bundle of burdock roots I'd just pulled from the refrigerator. She hadn't been eating, she didn't even open her mouth when she talked. She just looked at the ground without smiling. She seemed nothing like the girl I knew. I kept thinking that the girl before me wasn't her, but that was an illusion—she and my daughter were one and the same. I had to convince myself of that. I've been a mother for many years—when I see one of my daughters cry, my natural inclination is to put my hand on her back, ask what happened, and comfort her. When I took Yokiko in my arms like I used to so long ago, she wilted completely and melted into me. Though she's much taller than I am, she seemed to weigh much less. I'm not sure how to express how strange she felt. As I hugged her, it didn't feel like her, she seemed not even human, more like a rock or some object, maybe like the evil spirit in folklore that appears in the form of a child and begs people to pick it up so that it can take their lives, maybe like a changeling that threatens its parents and eats them because of karma from a previous life. Who knows? Maybe she was possessed by a fox spirit, maybe she was the crane-wife from the famous old folk tale. Things like that kept popping into my head. She didn't seem like my daughter, she didn't even seem human, more like a Japanese ghost. A spirit. A fox, a *tanuki*, or some other cruel, magical creature. Something else, but not her.

She was completely exhausted.

She wasn't tired for any of the usual reasons—she hadn't been working hard all day, she hadn't been out running. She was tired because life was difficult. As the mother who raised her, I knew life had been hard for her since infancy. From the beginning, she was a strange one—a fox, a *tanuki*, a magical creature, a ghost, maybe even an alien from outer space. If I'm honest, I should say that the same probably goes for all my family members. None of us lives an ordinary life, and even if we try, we inevitably develop secrets we'll carry to our graves. If we were to reveal our true selves, maybe we would all be ghosts, foxes, *tanuki*, or other mystical creatures. Yokiko had dealt with so much, she'd made so much effort, always hiding her real emotions behind a mask, but by the time she reached twenty, those protective masks no longer worked. The wear had started to show.

WE STAYED IN A HOTEL near her university. I'd reserved two rooms. I left my husband alone in one room. In the other, we left one bed free while Aiko and I climbed into the other to comfort Yokiko as she slept.

We spent the whole next day at a nearby lake. While the others played, I watched the energy drain from Yokiko right before my eyes. Aiko was as peppy as always. She spotted a boat rental and insisted we go out on the water. Yokiko didn't want to. Aiko did. Yokiko repeated she didn't. She said it was hard for her to keep up with me and Aiko since we were having so much fun. My husband said from the beginning that if he got into one of those little boats, he didn't think his back or knees would ever recover. What could I do? Caught in the middle, I rented a boat to take Aiko out, just the two of us.

When we got to the boat rental, I was surprised to see that they had canoes. Real ones. When he saw my shock, the man at the reception desk opened his mouth wide and laughed. He told me, I've only once ever seen a customer flip a canoe on the lake, and that was because he suddenly tried to stand up in it.

I chose to believe him. We paddled out with me in front and Aiko in back. The forecast was for clear skies but high waves. The lake water was salty. I don't know why. A cold wind blew over us in the middle of the lake. A flock of geese flew into the air right before us.

I shouted, I spy a shipwreck at two o'clock! When we paddled closer, we saw that the wreck was flying a flag with skull and cross-bones—the kind of decoration you'd put out at Halloween.

I shouted, I spy a pedal-boat at eleven o'clock! All men on

deck, try to avoid collision! Aiko shouted, to the right, to the right! Mommy, to the right! She wanted to use nautical terminology, but she didn't know the word "starboard" (and neither did I), so she settled on using extra-polite Japanese, which in the ordinary life of a child generally indicates something is special.

Aiko got excited and started calling out all sorts of things. I spy a flock of cormorants at two o'clock! A pelican is approaching from ten o'clock!

Captain, stop splashing.

Mommy, you've got to paddle!

I spy Yokiko at three o'clock! She's drinking coffee with Daddy.

Yokiko kept trying to avoid Aiko's gaze, but Aiko kept yelling out to her, so Yokiko gave in and turned to acknowledge us. She waved, but the movements of her hand were small, small, small, and weak.

My husband had left me to play with Aiko while he had coffee with Yokiko. He told me afterward, she wouldn't eat anything, but she's got no problem drinking as much coffee as she wants, when she's got time on her hands, she'll drink and drink and drink and drink, one gulp after the next, I kept buying her one refill after another, her belly must've been bloated with liquid, I thought she'd drown in coffee and in her own silence.

YOKIKO'S FACE HAD GROWN SO unsightly that I felt the urge to avert my eyes. But while I might not have wanted to look at her, everything about her was screaming look at me, look at me. I couldn't avoid her. When I did look right at her, she recoiled, saying in a clinging, babyish tone, don't look, don't look. I didn't think avoiding her was the right thing to do, so I kept my gaze fixed on her.

Yes, I saw her. Her cheeks were hollow and her face the color of a bruise. She was extremely gaunt, and I kept looking at the part of her mouth that never completely closed. The meat on her backside had shriveled up, and I kept looking at her thighs, which she tended to splay open. I couldn't help imagining that maybe her anus was wide open too. Much of her hair had fallen out, so much that she was well on her way to losing it all. I realized she looked like someone. I hated to think it, but she looked like an image I'd seen somewhere of Oiwa-san, the horrifying specter from the famous old ghost story *Yotsuya Kaidan*. Yokiko had none of the plumpness, bounciness, or liveliness you'd expect from a twenty-year-old.

It was time for a parent to get involved.

I was going to take her home.

But she insisted she couldn't go.

She explained, I want to go with you, Mom, but I can't, I can't go yet, I hate it here, I hate being alone, I hate that I spend my whole life feeling different from everyone else, right now I feel like a building that's only half-finished.

I remember seeing a half-finished building, I don't remember when.

All of it was exposed.

All the framework, all the steel girders, all the wiring.

Just like me, just like me, just like me, just like me, she shouted.

She was screaming to me that she was in pain, in pain, in pain, in pain.

But even so, she insisted, I can't go home yet, I can't go home yet.

She was at her wit's end.

I'd brought some manga we no longer needed back home to give her, volumes one through four of Naoki Urasawa's *20th Century Boys*. I'd considered a bunch of different things, but I brought these thinking she'd enjoy them most. It was the kind of manga you could read in a couple of hours, good enough you might read it multiple times before searching out the next volume to find out what happens next. In other words, it was the kind of manga that might make a person want to keep living. How could she resist?

She told me she didn't want them. She shouted, I don't have time to read manga, it'll eat up all my study time. If I start reading manga, I'll get caught up in them, and that'll wreck everything! Take the manga home, I don't want them.

She started crying, I keep thinking I'll study, but time just keeps slipping by, and I'm powerless to do a single thing.

Something was wrong with her, really wrong, and she needed therapy. Something had to be wrong. Not reading manga was a sure sign.

She sobbed, I can't go home yet, I can't go home yet.

So I took her to see some people at the university. We met with a counselor. I met the woman who was renting her a room. I set everything up so that she could come home any time she wanted. I worked out a plan so that if she ever found herself enveloped in chaos, I had a contact there who could lend a helping hand. I even tried to get her an appointment at the university health center so she could get a prescription, but the doctor was booked solid that week and the following one, so she'd have to go the week after that.

My goodness, I thought, so many burnt-out students. They were probably lined up at the health center, desperately waiting their turn.

And behind all those students were the mothers who raised them. No doubt they were worried about their desperate children, unable to do anything but watch.

Yokiko might not have had the time or inclination to read manga, but I was surprised to see she immediately started acting like an ordinary student around other people. I'd brought her to America when she was young, so her English pronunciation was excellent, and she was skilled at speaking politely in both English and Japanese, meaning she could maintain an appropriate degree of polite distance with people. However, when she spoke in Japanese with me, she immediately regressed and changed for the worse. Her language regressed, her way of walking regressed, her emotions regressed, everything regressed, regressed, regressed. She also forgot the polite style of speaking she'd learned in English, and before I knew it, she was speaking like an angry, upset child, stomping her feet, not knowing what to do with herself.

WE RETURNED HOME WITHOUT HER. On the way back, we sped along the bleak interior highway and arrived in just seven and a half hours. I couldn't get Yokiko out of my mind. Couldn't think about anything else. Couldn't think about anything else. Couldn't think about anything else. Then I realized, I'd forgotten something—my father. He'd been out of my thoughts for days, so I hurriedly picked up the phone to call him. He moaned, my leg hurts, I can't walk again, I had diarrhea again, I fell down in front of the toilet again, I had constipation again, and most importantly, I'm bored. I'm really bored, there's nothing to do all day.

I felt terrible.

I asked him, what about the plastic model I sent you the other day?

The parts were so small I couldn't see them.

What about the books I sent you the other day?

I finished them.

Did you give those adult coloring books a try?

I hate coloring books, I'm not like you. (When I was little, I was infatuated with *Kiichi's Coloring Books*, which were filled with pictures of cute little girls.) I'd rather draw my own pictures.

I sent you those colored pencils a little while back.

I don't feel like drawing.

When I write all this down now, it looks like a conversation between a spoiled child and his doting mother, but no, this conversation was between father and daughter. My eighty-four-year-old father's tone of voice told me he was confronting an emotion that could only be called despair.

But, but, but I'm bored, there's nothing to watch on TV, I'm not reading the papers, I've read most books (though all he read was dead samurai storytellers like Shotaro Ikenami and Shuhei Fujisawa), I'm just sitting here with Chunsuke staring blankly into space—is this what it's like to get old?

Despair is a quiet emotion. Clearly, that's what he was feeling.

WE WERE ENROLLED IN A cellphone plan that allowed us to make as many calls to family members as we wanted. Yokiko had been calling just about every day, but after our visit she started calling even more often. She'd call every two hours, every hour, sometimes every half-hour. She always sounded choked up, as if she was resisting the urge to burst into tears. She'd complain, I'm supposed to be studying for this or that but I haven't done it yet, I haven't done my homework for that one class yet, I haven't done my reading for that other class yet, I've only got two hours, but I don't even know where to begin, meanwhile the clock is ticking away.

In a teary voice, she'd say, I've got this thing to do and that thing to do, I've been sitting here for ages, but nothing comes into my head, I can't do a thing, I can't do a single thing I'm supposed to be doing.

I asked her, well, what's the first thing that needs to get done? She'd mumble her answer, then immediately start equivocating—but then this thing affects that thing, and that thing affects some other thing. . . .

I didn't have much choice. I sifted through her mumbled answers and helped her prioritize.

First, you should do this, second that, third this, fourth that . . .

She'd respond, oh, but then this has to do with that, and that has to do with this, and both of those have to do with this other thing.

Then, first you should do that, second this, third that, fourth this.

Yokiko would sniff over and over, trying to holding back the tears and snot beginning to drip from her nose.

I'd suggest, why don't you try doing them in that order?

Fine, she'd say through her tears.

It's okay not to do everything, it's okay to do things half-ass.

Fine, she'd repeat in a teary voice.

But before that, I told her, I want you to go to the cafeteria, buy a really big coffee, put lots of sugar in it, and get something to eat.

Fine, she'd repeat in her teary voice.

Yokiko's therapist was also worried about how thin she'd become—so worried, in fact, that she suggested sending her to a nutritionist before prescribing antidepressants. Everyone recognized she had an eating disorder. Even Yokiko herself. When she did eat, she'd think she'd eaten too much, then call me to complain about how much she'd eaten. But she loved sweet things. When we went to see her, I'd noticed that even though she refused everything else, she gobbled up every sweet thing she saw.

Say, it'd give me some peace of mind if you'd eat something sweet, maybe a muffin or a brownie, I want you to go get something warm and sweet, okay?

That made her burst into tears.

In the background, the dogs pricked up their ears, listening to every movement I made, every word I uttered. The shepherd was at my feet, and the sparrow-dog was curled up, lying in his basket in the corner of the room. He was lying down, not yet asleep. When I hung up with Yokiko, I let out a big sigh that got them both up, and they started pacing restlessly. In a strained voice, the shepherd started howling *woooooo, woooooo, woooooo* (meaning walk, walk, walk), as she wagged her tail. Meanwhile, the sparrow-dog started running around and barking in his high-pitched voice *ruff, ruff, ruff* (walk, walk, walk). He snapped at the shepherd, sometimes actually biting him, then the shepherd would take revenge. My god, shut up! I raised my voice to scold them, but they weren't listening.

The phone rang again. This time it was my oldest daughter. This was the daughter who was always traveling the world—the one I'd always have to ask, where are you now? She only called when she had a reason, and if we called her, she probably wouldn't pick up.

She was worried about Yokiko, and recently she'd been calling often to check up on her, but this time it seemed like something else was going on. She seemed reluctant to hang up, so I asked her directly. What's up? Did something happen?

When she was little and I asked her what had happened, she'd be quick to grumble, something hurt me, something hurt me. I listened carefully, aware that she was likely to spill the beans. She hesitated so much that the words came out little by little. Well, um . . . How shall I put it? I broke up with my partner a little while back . . . That doesn't matter much but . . . There's something wrong . . . with the way I'm eating . . . I'm having trouble relating to people and . . . And she began to cry. She sounded just like Yokiko. I just keep eating . . . I can't stop! And she began to wail.

My parents saw me like that many times when I was young. I had tons of trouble during my mid-twenties, so much so that I wore out my poor mother. That's why she said to me, I wonder what karma has made this child suffer so much at the hands of men, I raised her so, so carefully, hoping, praying she'd be spared.

Dad saw my troubles too. Even before I started having man problems. When I was Yokiko's age, I found life just too painful to bear. I was writhing in pain, unable to bear sitting still or being alone, so I'd go to Dad's workplace. At the time, he was working in a small printing shop. Dad would stop whatever he was doing. He'd stop the machines, turn to face me, move his chair to sit with me, and light a cigarette to make it clear that he was on break. He was determined to listen to me as much as I needed. He was sincere.

That's what a father—my father—would do, and so I tried my

best to be a good mother. I listened carefully. When I hung up, I realized how quickly the time had gone by—we'd been on the phone for an hour and a half. I sighed, and immediately the shepherd leapt up and started howling walk, walk, walk. The sparrow-dog leapt from his basket and started yapping walk, walk, walk too. I shut my eyes to block them out for a moment when the phone rang again. I picked it up to hear Yokiko bawling on the other end of the line. I spoke with her for a while, and when I eventually hung up, the dogs started up again. Right then, the door slammed shut, and Aiko bounded into the room with an energetic *Hiiiiii!* I realized that it was time for my regular call to Japan to see if my father was still awake and alive. In his hoarse elderly voice, Dad complained in the special way that only he could complain, last night I fell down again, I had diarrhea again, I had diarrhea, fell down, and couldn't get back up, I was all alone. I let out a big sigh as I hung up the phone, and right away my husband, who had been cooped up in his studio for a whole half-day, suddenly appeared and suggested we take a tea break together.

A humorous tanka poem occurred to me. The word *haha* means "mother" now, but in classical Japanese it had an additional meaning—an oak tree. Plus, the word sounds like laughter.

Tarachine mo,
Haha soba mo,
Haha, ha ha ha ha ha
Hachimen roppi no
Shiku hakku kamo

Though breasts may sag
An oak's leaves too
Are mothers, ha-ha-ha-ha-ha
Perhaps this is the four types of suffering and eight types of
bitterness
Of having eight faces and six arms

BECAUSE SOME BUDDHIST STATUES HAVE many faces and arms,
people sometimes think of them as doing all sorts of different
things at once. By trying to be everything for everyone, maybe I
was bringing on myself all the different kinds of suffering that exist
in this world.

For a moment, just a split second, an image flashed through my
brain. It was twilight, and I was gazing at the sea spreading out to
the west, listening to nothing but the waves. I was squatting over
a portable clay cooking stove in front of a thatched hut as a trail of
smoke snaked up into the sky. I was grilling a long, silver fish—a
sanma, which has bitter meat. I was going to eat it all myself. The
image of the chargrilled fish was so vivid, I could practically taste its
bitterness. And it was all mine, no one else's.

There's a Japanese expression "a bee sting on a crying face,"
which we use when someone is having a bunch of problems and
something happens to make the situation even worse. I was having
such a difficult time that day that I felt whoever coined that expression must have had me in mind. The fact that I was thinking about
the bitterness of a kind of fish I don't even like was an indication of
how wrong everything was going.

I found my eyeglass case completely chewed up. The sparrow-dog had obviously got to it while I was on the phone. A good friend had given it to me several years before. It was green and made in Germany, with a cartoon printed on the outside. Over the years, many people had told me how cute it was. I carried it around like a talisman, thinking of my friend every time I saw it. When I saw the ruined case, I inhaled sharply. The sound of my breath was enough to set the shepherd barking. She probably thought someone had come to the door. In her mind, all people who came to the house were robbers, and all dogs were wolves. With my rat-trapping speed, I grabbed the sparrow-dog by the scruff, and he pulled his tongue back in. I tossed him in the backyard, and he ran off, hiding his tail between his legs.

The case was important to me, but I had to be reasonable. It was just an old eyeglass case after all, and I'd practically worn it out over the years. Plus, my dogs had done in more eyeglasses than I could count. They'd chewed up brand-new ones I'd just had made. They'd gnawed on every pair of glasses and sunglasses I owned, so that whenever I put them on or took them off, the ragged parts would catch my hair and pull. They gnawed on everything—shoes, nipples, earphones, toothbrushes, even maxi pads dug out of the trash. If it had my scent on it, they'd search it out and chew it up. Maybe that was because they loved me, I don't know. Most of the time when they ruined my glasses or my shoes, I figured they were just being dogs and didn't really care, but when I saw the remains of the eyeglass case, the tears started to pour forth. I couldn't stop crying. As always, the shepherd came up to sniff me. My husband and Aiko just looked at me blankly. My voice grew louder as I wept. The more I cried, the more I could feel the hot waves of tears welling up. They melted away the stiffness in my shoulders.

Oh, I'm so frightened, so frightened.

I tried saying it out loud.

Oh, I'm so frightened, so frightened.

I may be a mother with drooping breasts, but I'm flesh and blood.

Long ago, I was a little girl.

When I was frightened, I cried.

I hoped Dad, Mom, my future husband, or the princes I heard about in fairy tales would come rescue me.

They did rescue me, over and over again. More times than I can count.

Dad, Mom, my husbands, the princes. All of them.

But now, there was no one to help.

Dad was old and on his deathbed.

Mom was dying and bedridden.

I couldn't rely on my husband or the princes anymore.

My breasts were sagging with age, and I was shaking from the roots, shaking back and forth, *yuaaan yuyooooooon*.

I had planted my feet firmly, I had gritted my teeth.

I had pretended not to be scared.

And I had faced suffering, suffering, suffering,

Suffering and even more suffering,

But yes, I was terribly frightened the whole time.

NOTE FROM THE AUTHOR

I borrowed voices from Yumiko Oshima's manga *Freud-shiki Ranmaru*, Chuya Nakahara's poem "Memories from When I Was Three," the nineteenth-century novelist Lafcadio Hearn, the eighth-century Buddhist monk Kyokai, the eighth-century poet Otomo no Yakamochi, the lyricist Ryuha Hayashi, the novelist Haruo Sato, the literary scholar Yaichi Haga, and the Meiji-period naval officer Saneyuki Akiyama.

Driven by Despair, the Female Followers of the Thorn Puller Attack Ito's Husband

ONE OF MY OLD SCHOOLMATES sent me an email, and in it was a line that struck me: "A few days before my father died, he whispered, I wonder if I'm going to be able to die well."

The email was from a high-school *senpai*—one of the older students. Until this year, I hadn't seen her since we graduated. She was a poet too, and when we were introduced, she announced that she'd gone to the same school a few years before me. We started exchanging emails.

When I was a first-year student and she a third-year student, we might have attended the same school assemblies or gathered around the same bonfires in the schoolyard. No doubt I passed the older girls as I ran down dark staircases while carrying on loudly with my friends. Who knows? One of them might have been her. When I met her earlier this year, it was at a gathering of poets in Tokyo—not much different from passing someone on a staircase, and in fact, I'd already half-forgotten what she looked like.

Our high school was toward the top of a sloping street in Bunkyo Ward. It was just a plain old public school, but to my surprise, years later I realized lots of poets, including me, got their start there.

There was a subway stop at the bottom of the hill. Because the school was high up, you could go to the roof and look over the entire Kanto Plain. Back then, there weren't many skyscrapers in Shinjuku. There were only two or three in Shinjuku, one in Nakano, and one in Ikebukuro. The rest of Tokyo was smoky, smoggy, dirty, flat, and close to the ground. Sometimes you could see Mt. Fuji or the Chichibu Mountains. During my three years there, I went up to the roof all the time and gazed into the distance. There was one especially high spot I loved to climb to. They say that only idiots and smoke climb to the highest places. I suppose that makes me an idiot.

It was nice to find another girl who'd gone to the same school and shared the same surroundings. In an email, I told her I'd been in the Biology Club, I joined thinking I'd like to watch weeds grow, but all we ended up doing was raising mice for students to dissect. She wrote back that during the summer after her first year of high school, she started going to the library all the time and reading poetry. Even though we were only two years apart, our experiences were totally different. She saw the student protests of the late 1960s and early '70s, but they'd died down by my time. She told me she didn't participate in any clubs at all.

We corresponded like that for a while. That's when she shared her father's lament.

I wonder if I'm going to be able to die well.

These words echoed in my mind.

A thought struck me. When we get pregnant and have babies, we buy books with titles like *Pregnancy and Birth for First-Timers* to teach us how to have children. Death is sort of like that. Everyone is doing it for the first time, but where were the books?

I found out my former schoolmate was living with her mother in Sugamo.

I TOOK MY HUSBAND TO Sugamo. It was December 24.

It was a Sunday, and the place was dizzying with all the feverish activity of the year end. There were so many old ladies packing the streets that I was reminded of tiny fish pressed up against one another, boiling in soy sauce. My husband stood in the middle of them, completely stuck, unable to move forward or retreat. Being raised in the West, he wasn't used to bumping against people while walking. He just stood there in the boiling crowd of old ladies, the top half of his body towering over them.

He's a huge man, much taller and much heavier. Plus, he's so old that when I asked him about the British air raids during World War II, he had his own memories to share. He once told me that he lived next to some band—Pink Floyd or T. Rex, maybe—and he just put up with the noise and swore, damn it, youngsters are so loud these days. That gives away his age right there. In short, he wasn't so far away in years from the old ladies jostling around him. He was wrinkly and bald, and what hair he had left was totally gray. From the point of view of the old ladies, he was just an old foreigner—nothing else. But it's strange. Because he was my husband, he seemed younger to me than my father. He had just enough energy to get in my way. In that regard, he was like the other, younger men I'd been involved with before him.

He'd been to Japan numerous times before we met. He was a foreigner and did all the things foreigners did—he'd gone on tours of AsaKUUUUsa and AkihaBAAAAra. (He pronounced these names with such a strong accent that I am compelled to write them this way.) He shopped at the kinds of places where hardcore shoppers go, like ITOOOOOya, the stationery store, and Kappa-bashi-DOOOOri, the restaurant supply street. He'd even walked through the gourmet food stalls in the basement of MitsuKOOOshi, sampling as he went.

But now that he was with a real live Japanese person, I wanted him to see a deeper side of Tokyo. I'd be his native informant. We'd walk through the area, taste some salted Daifuku mochi (one of the local specialties), visit Jizo at the temple, chow down on some lamprey (another local specialty), and buy some peppery *shichimi* spices as a souvenir. I even hoped to pick up a yukata for him at one of the stores in Sugamo that cater to an elderly clientele. A yukata would be perfect for when he got out of the bathtub in the evening.

Did I have any ulterior motive? Yes, I'll admit I did. I wanted Jizo to remove the thorns of our suffering.

I imagined that if I took him to the Thorn-Pulling Jizo and forced him to walk through the jostling crowds of old ladies, his outer layer might peel off, revealing the monster inside. I imagined his hide peeled back, skin flayed, and hair falling out. I knew he wouldn't understand Sugamo. His bald head would be filled with the usual disbelief and arrogance. His usual obstinacy. His usual pushiness. His usual lustiness. I imagined the ladies, all of whom were firm believers, getting angry at him and his disbelief. I imagined they had spent most of their lives despairing over badly behaved men. Would they attack him? I imagined the raspy sounds of their dried-up vaginas as they assaulted him. I imagined that this time, I wouldn't be the one attacking him—they'd do the job for me. They'd eat him up, tear him apart, and trample him underfoot. Meanwhile, I'd stomp my foot and shout, serves you right!

Things went badly from the start. The store at the beginning of the temple road that sells the salted Daifuku mochi was so crowded that we gave up and decided to try again on the way home. I told him it would've been better to come on a regular day, one that wasn't a special pilgrimage day, because it'd be less crowded. Even though I was irritated with him, it bothered me that people were staring at him. In our day and age, it isn't unusual to see foreigners in Tokyo, but in every direction, the old women looked up at him like they were gazing into the heavens. They pointed and whispered. I even saw some of them cover their mouths and laugh. Then that person would turn to someone else and whisper to someone else.

I pricked up my ears. Santa-san. They were calling him Santa Claus.

December 24 wasn't just a special day for Jizo. It was a special day for Santa too.

Look, it's Santa-san! Whisper, whisper. Santa-san! Whisper, whisper. Santa-san! Look, it's Santa-san! Murmur, murmur. Santa-san, Santa-san. Look, it's Santa-san! Mutter, mutter. Santa-san, Santa-san. Rustle, rustle. Look, it's Santa-san, Santa-san! Whisper, whisper. Santa-san, Santa-san. Murmur, murmur. Look, Santa-san, Santa-san, Santa-san, Santa-san. Whisper, whisper. Whisper, whisper. Santa-san, Santa-san, Santa-san.

Murmur, murmur. Whisper, whisper. The whispers rushed through the crowd.

When I told him what they were saying, the polite smile disappeared from his face, and he exploded.

You mean I look like him? That guy with the snow-white hair and belly like a bowlful of jelly?

You're a dead ringer, I thought, but I held my tongue.

His anger spilled forth, directed not just at the elderly pilgrims but at me too.

This is just like it was with the sparrow-dog club in California. I guess there are blind believers everywhere. You remember that time when you came to Japan and took Aiko to go worship some idol in a temple? She'd just learned to walk. You know, that really pissed me off, I thought my wife was agnostic like me, but I found out she had a secret faith, and to make matters worse, she was giving my daughter a religious education, my daughter, mind you, without my permission. But the problem's not just you—it's your friends too! When you go by a shrine, you toss in a coin and put your hands together, then you go by another temple and do it again. I ask who you're praying to, and you tell me to anyone who'll listen. What the hell? You've got no principles at all. What's up with that? Who are all these old ladies praying to anyway?

That's when I realized. I wanted to take him to "see" Jizo, but the main deity at the temple is never on display. Had I ever even seen it with my own eyes? No, I hadn't.

He pointed at the main building of the temple. What's inside?

I answered honestly. Probably a statue of Jizo sitting there in the dark. But I've never seen it.

It's an idol. Someone made it.

You're right. An idol.

How much did you throw in?

Five yen.

That's less than a dime.

But you know, in Japanese, *go-en*, the word for "five yen," is a homonym that means "a karmic connection." If you throw one in, it creates a relationship with the god and the place.

He turned his eyes to the sky and gestured in silent despair. What can you do with such stupidity?

Over there, you threw some incense into the gigantic cauldron, but here, you threw in a coin. Why do you have to throw things?

When you throw something, it carries your wishes.

What are you wishing for?

For our thorns to be pulled out.

By who?

I didn't know how to answer.

What about that statue over there? He pointed toward the famous statue of Kannon in front of the temple. A line of people were waiting to wash it.

People make wishes when they scrub it. The original one got scrubbed so many millions of times that it wore down and became just a plain old rock. That statue is a replacement. My parents used to wash it, but I've never done it, I never want to wait in line.

I thought about the things we'd done in Sugamo that day. We walked from the station. I bought incense (while thinking of the faces of each and every person I was praying for—one pack per person). I threw the lit incense into the cauldron (while thinking of each person and their suffering). I used my hands to fan the smoke toward me (while praying). I tossed a five-yen coin in the collection box. I prayed to the darkness.

Suddenly, it was all clear to me.

It's the smoke, not the idol. It's the smoke that I believe in, it rises into the air and disappears.

Smoke? He gave a derisive chuckle, then dismissed the whole conversation by saying, what kind of dumb religion is that?

For a moment, I was disgusted. If I was going to lash out, now was the right time. But I didn't.

LET ME TALK ABOUT THAT ulterior motive I mentioned a little while back.

I'd been imagining how my husband's hide would peel off to reveal the monster inside. His skin would peel. Peel back completely. It would flay and come right off. All his bad behaviors would manifest—like how he wouldn't help with housework, how he'd be super-arrogant while explaining things, how he'd swagger around proudly. And for what? I imagined the angry old ladies with their dried-up vaginas—lots and lots of vaginas—coming and trampling his shredded flesh. A scene right out of hell. And I'd be there stomping my foot, shouting, serves you right! I'd imagined the scene countless times. I'd hoped that maybe if we came on the special pilgrimage day, I'd find the strength and courage to confront him and his arrogance, buoyed by all the outspoken old women surrounding us on the way to the temple. I didn't have to ask the women about their lives to know. They'd no doubt experienced despair too.

So I brought him. I was angry. There'd be no one to get in the way. (Aiko, I mean.) I wanted to tear into him. I wanted to vent my long-standing frustrations. Now was the time, but I found myself hesitating.

He'd brought back several old photos from his recent European odyssey. He held them out proudly and announced, this is me as a young man. A bearded man in his late thirties stared out from the photograph, slightly embarrassed as he winked at the camera. It was obvious at a single glance that it wasn't a spontaneous snapshot—it had been taken by a professional.

I don't dislike it when men go bald. I think that creases around the eyes are sexy. I love beards, too. The balding, bearded young man with the creases around his eyes in the picture was winking in a way that was completely charming—if we were both in our thirties, I'd have immediately hopped into bed with him. But fifty years later, that bewitchingly sexy guy had aged and was now covered with wrinkles, turning into the old man right there with me.

Nothing stays the same. Everything is impermanent.

I remembered something. Aiko had been sweating. When I'd teased her, telling her, you stink, you stink, she told me, my armpits stink even worse—here, take a whiff. When I leaned in close, her body odor was enough to curl your nose, but there was something in her scent that brought forth fond feelings—I couldn't help myself, I took a deep breath. It's hard to explain, but there's a special sexy sweetness in some people's scent that can make a person horny. And when I think about sex, I think of my husband. But when had he grown so old? When had he lost his pleasant, natural scent? He'd lost his smell. Nothing stays the same.

There was an age gap between us, so I was always completely aware he'd turn into an old man one day, but when it actually happened, there were times I found myself recoiling. Sometimes I'd wake up at dawn and find myself sleeping next to a super-old man, so gray and wrinkled that he hardly seemed human. It was like I was living inside the puff of smoke from Urashima Taro's box that turned everything old. Of course, I'm fifty, with spots on my skin, silver hair, and a spreading waistline—I hate everything that begins with the letter S. That includes "Shiromi."

But compared to my husband, who was drowning in the deepest depths of old age, I still had time. I didn't deny death, but I wasn't staring it directly in the face, either. If anything, I was a wandering wife, never in one place for long. I merely sat and watched the smoke of old age envelop my husband.

I asked, what were you like in those days?

He said, you probably can't imagine what a self-centered, arrogant male chauvinist I was, I'm much more likeable now, some things get better with age.

I thought, you're still all those things now, but I held my tongue.

Arrogant and obstinate for sure, but he hadn't done anything bad enough to be torn to shreds while I shouted, serves you right! The Jizo at the temple might not be visible, but the smoke was. Even if I placed more faith in it than in Jizo, even if all the buddhas hated me, I still wanted to come here.

And dare I think it? I even hoped the pilgrimage might help my husband too.

EVERYONE KEPT COMPLAINING, IT'S COLD, it's cold, but the winters are getting warmer—nothing can stop that. Even though it was December, I thought a thin coat over a summer tank top was enough for me, but maybe that was just because I was approaching menopause.

The old women milling around us on the path to the temple were long past menopause. Judging from their appearance, none of them had hot flashes anymore. They were wearing pants and jackets, hats pulled down so far that their eyes were hardly visible, and they wore backpacks as if they were setting out on a hike. Their clothes were much thicker than those Grandma wore when she took my hand and led me to the temple all those years ago.

I remembered the thin kimono she wore, it must have been summer—I can't recall her in winter at all. She wore her kimono so loosely that you could see her breasts now and then. I recalled her walking along at a leisurely pace, as if she had no real destination in mind. Her eyebrows were plucked neatly, and her back straight as an arrow.

Once when Mom got sick, Grandma Toyoko came to stay with me. During the day she played with the dog, and at night, she took care of me.

Grandma and Grandpa always had cats and dogs in the house. I had a dog back then too, and when I came home from school, Grandma was sitting by the front door, holding it. Oh, come now, she'd whisper as the dog licked her on the mouth.

I never saw Grandma possessed by a spirit, but I did see her wake up just about every night in bed. If there was a sound in the night, she'd sit up, fold her legs beneath her, and start scolding me in a deep, husky voice that sounded like a man's as she stared at me. I couldn't understand her, so I'd get flustered and call out, Grandma, Grandma, but she wouldn't hear me. She'd shout a little while, suddenly slump over, then go back to sleep. Dad knew about this, he just calmly explained that's her habit—it's what she does when she wakes up in the middle of the night. Once I was no longer afraid of her "habit," I got used to it. She woke up every night on her own, but I figured if she was going to wake up anyway, I might as well wake her up on my own terms, right? Her shouts obviously weren't meant for me—she was talking to someone else, maybe someone who wasn't of this world. The proof was that I wasn't the only one she scolded. She'd stare and scold the sliding doors, the dresser, and everything else nearby. She was obviously giving voice to some despair deep within.

IT WAS TOO LATE. THINGS were already in motion. The old ladies' despair had reached the saturation point.

Some of the old ladies approached us, whispering and mumbling, Santa-san, Santa-san, from behind their covered mouths. Suddenly, I heard a deep husky voice like Grandma's when she woke in the night.

Teach this non-believer a lesson!
This is the pilgrimage path to Lord Jizo.
This is a special day dedicated to him.
How dare this Santa Claus come wandering here!
Teach this non-believer a lesson!

For a moment, the air grew quiet, even the deepest rustling of the forests and valleys fell still—not a creature was stirring. At first the old women looked confused, they looked around wide-eyed, but then, the voice boomed again. Teach the non-believer a lesson! This time the old women understood exactly what it was telling them to do, and they rushed toward us all at once, swooping down as quickly as a flock of pigeons. Possessed, they bounded over rocks and rivulets. Catching sight of him, they scurried up large boulders and began throwing stones and fir branches at him. The merciless old witches swung at him, slicing the air with their fir switches, but none struck him.

Once again, the voice sounded out. Be sure to teach this non-believer a lesson!

The crones flew at us. My husband started wailing, but no one understood English, plus his words were drowned out by their jeering anyway. Someone grabbed him by the elbow, planted her feet on his flanks, and kicked hard at him, jerking his arm off at the socket. Another old hag tore at his flesh on the other side. Before long, everyone was attacking. My husband's screams mixed with the old ladies' jeering to form a single voice that reverberated through the crowd. Some of the women grabbed his arms while others held onto his shoes and feet. His ribs jutted out from his torn flesh. The old hags started to play, using their bloody hands to toss pieces of his body back and forth. Before I knew it, I had joined in and was stomping on his ripped-up flesh with both feet. I laughed and jeered. How do you like that? Serves you right!

No, I was getting carried away in my daydream. I had to stop. A mob wouldn't solve anything. The Thorn Puller grants his blessings to everyone, even to lousy husbands—he'd protect my husband, he'd accept him into his fold. Yet even so, the murderous old witches continued to press against us, their faces smeared from long years of despair.

ONCE AGAIN, ITO FOUND HERSELF in a real pinch. I was at my wit's end, I wanted to give in, but I couldn't. I had to act. I had to walk, run, or do something—anything. So I grabbed my husband's hand

and began running, dragging him back toward Sugamo Station. When I'm faced with a crisis, I'm as tough as they come. Small things don't wear me out. I won't cry. I'm persistent and won't give up. I'm flexible enough to deal with whatever happens. Fate has made me strong. Even so, I don't know what would have happened to us if my high school *senpai* hadn't appeared out of thin air at that very moment. We were right beside the entrance to the pilgrimage route, near the temple with the grave of the poet I spoke about earlier, and suddenly there she was, standing with no apparent purpose. I'd had troubling recalling what she looked like after our short meeting, but as soon as I saw her here, I recognized her immediately. I began to think back—so many teenage memories of our school on the hill, of those days, of my worries, of my loneliness, of my impatience to get the hell out of there. I even remembered our school song—or parts of it anyway. "(Something, something, something) in the sky of tomorrow (something, something), our voices raised, (something, something) oh, school, my high school!" Well, maybe I didn't remember that much after all.

I could tell it was her, not just some random middle-aged woman. We might never have officially met in school, but we spent our adolescences in the same circles.

I called out to her. *Senpaiiiiiiiiiiii!* She looked at me, rushed over, and took my hand in hers.

We were around the same height. In the 1970s, we were probably about average height, but compared to people now, we'd both be small. She immediately knew something was wrong. She grabbed me and my husband, who had just barely managed to make it out of the mob alive, and started dragging us across Hakusan-dori, the big avenue by the station. There wasn't a crosswalk, only a pedestrian bridge with tons of stairs that seemed expressly designed to torture elderly pilgrims. Ignoring the pedestrian bridge, she dragged us into the street, stopping cars one after another. The drivers laid on their horns, but she boldly pulled us across the street as if it was her god-given right to be there. She was calm but forceful, and before we knew it, we'd reached safety on the other side. She raised one hand to thank the confused drivers as she urged us to cross. We supported my husband, who was so weak that you would have thought he'd really been torn to shreds, leaving bones and not much else. We walked down a narrow street, went through a gate into a highrise, passed some potted plants, got into an elevator, and walked to a door.

Another little old lady came out of the darkness.

I was surprised to find someone home. My husband glared at me, wondering what we were getting into.

My goodness, you left without telling me, the old lady said. No greeting or anything. It was like she was picking up a conversation from earlier.

This is my mother, my *senpai* explained.

Mother or not, she was just like the old ladies who had just come at us so fiercely by the temple. My schoolmate had saved us a few moments ago, but now here we were again. Was that the dastardly plan all along? We weren't going to be able to get away from the old witches, were we? We'd have to deal with them, even the attacking ones.

But after leading us to refuge in her home, my *senpai* immediately went to the kitchen to get us something to eat and drink.

Senpai, are you sure we're not bothering you?

In the kitchen, she turned to me, smiled, and said, of course not.

The old lady turned to us and said, welcome, my daughter didn't say anything about you coming before she left. . . .

The pronunciation of her consonants and vowels brought back memories, and so did seeing her relationship with her daughter. Long ago, Mom and I were close, we used to talk like that, but Mom was a big lady, and her voice was deeper. Grandma, however, was small in stature, so she sounded like that, but because she was of a different generation, her vocabulary was different from ours. If anything, the old lady reminded me of one of my aunts who used to live right there in Sugamo. That aunt had a similar build, had a similar voice, and spoke in a similar way. She lived in secret with her lover in a small apartment in Sengoku, at the far end of the neighborhood. I knew because Mom took me there once on the way back from the Jizo temple. We walked for a long time down small streets to get there. She was much younger than Mom and wore pretty kimonos. She always made a fuss over me, and on my birthday she'd take me to Fujiya, the cake store in front of the station, and buy me an entire strawberry-covered cake. She doesn't remember my birthday now, but every year I still call her on hers. For the last few years, she's said the same thing each time—oh my goodness, Shiromi, you remembered! And each year, in the same tone of voice, she tells me to be sure to take care of Mom.

I asked my schoolmate's mother where she was born. Her answer was crisp and concise. Shiba, then we moved to Koishikawa. Her speech jolted me, it resounded deep inside of me, and without thinking, I turned to my husband and said, listen to her. But he didn't have the energy for even that. He'd already collapsed into a chair, exhausted.

I thought to myself, I've found it.

What? you might ask.

My *gakiami*.

Several chapters ago, you might remember me mentioning the old story of Oguri Hangan. He was murdered, and after his body rotted, the King of Hell brought him back to life in the form of a sickly, distorted, grotesque creature called a *gakiami*. Unable to do anything for himself, he had to rely on other people to drag him to a hot spring to finally be healed.

Men are all *gakiami*—they might pretend to be heroes, but they're weak and useless on their own. Of course, I'm being flippant as I say this, but I've never met another man as *gakiami*-esque as my husband. The young, sexy man in the photos would have been lots of fun, but maybe my worn-out old husband was what I'd needed all along in a man—even if he was just a scentless shadow of his former self, unable to walk or bend easily or get it up.

I had wanted to be with him, I went to such lengths just for us to be together, and now, I had him.

My *senpai* had led me there, and with the help of her mother and the good graces of the Thorn Puller, I'd arrived at an epiphany.

I crouched down, brought my cheek close to his, took his face between my hands. The words came out slow and clear.

Listen, this is the language of my *senpai*, of her mother, of my aunt, of my grandmother, of my mother. This is our language. When I grow to be an old lady, this is how I want to speak, I want to use my language as our language.

I'm not sure if my *gakiami* understood, but he seemed to be listening with eyes shut.

My schoolmate asked, Shiromi-san, did you hear? They've built a new hot spring right here in Sugamo.

NOTE FROM THE AUTHOR

I borrowed voices from Euripides' *The Bacchae* (in the Japanese translation by Chiaki Matsudaira) and the *sekkyo-bushi* narrative *Oguri Hangan*. I've also borrowed voices from the poets Hinako Abe, Arthur Rimbaud, and Chuya Nakahara. The hot spring mentioned at the end is Somei Hot Springs, and every minute, it produces 500 liters of 48°C hot water, which has strong traces of sodium and monochloride. It takes eight minutes to walk from the station, but there's a free shuttle from the northern exit to the spring. It operates from 10:00 a.m. to 11:00 p.m. and the entrance fee is 1,260 yen. Check it out.

Good and Bad Ways of Dying, a Poet Stares Death in the Face

THERE'S A POET WHO LIVES in Kumamoto. For the sake of this book, let me call her Tasogare-san.

She had made a career of listening to the voices of the dead and incorporating them into her work. I read her for the first time soon after moving to Kumamoto, when my daughters were still nursing. I was used to Kumamoto dialect by then. She wrote in dialect, but still, there was something different about the way she used the language. It was like her voice had congealed directly on the page—I'd feel her voice go right through me, sinking into my flesh. In her poetry, the living and dead intermingled, you might think someone is alive but they're dead, and people who ought to be dead are alive—meanwhile, everyone eats, sleeps, defecates, has children, falls sick, and the seasons go by.

Some time passed before we ever spoke on the phone. In the middle of our first conversation, she said something that surprised me. Excuse me, I hope you don't mind me saying this, but you look a lot like me.

I remembered her saying this when I visited her home, meeting her for the first time. She greeted me at the door with messy hair and a wild expression, as though she had just trapped and eaten a bloody little animal. She wasn't young, but I still was. I thought we looked nothing alike at first, but later, catching a glimpse of myself in a mirror near her front door, I couldn't believe my eyes. It was like she'd suddenly turned into a young woman. I gasped and stared. Did I have any relatives in Kumamoto? Could we be related? I knew we weren't, but that's how much alike we looked.

I wish I had a dollar for every time someone has pointed out our resemblance. As a matter of fact, it happened just the other day in Tokyo with someone I was meeting for the first time.

One day at the literary museum, Oguri-san told me he had something to show me. He riffled through a cardboard box of old photos from the 1950s and 1960s that some photographer had donated.

Pointing to a couple of pictures, he asked, who do you think this is?

I was smiling. Wait, it definitely looked like me, but if that was me in the pictures, then who am I—the person who's looking at them? The resemblance was so strong that for a moment I was bewildered. Who am I? Where am I from again?

Over the next few years as I shuttled back and forth from Kumamoto to California and California to Kumamoto, always on the run, the poet and I made time to get together. There was something in her voice, language, face, and figure that brought back floods of feelings from the past. I was so charmed by her that I felt as giddy as a child. When I grew up, I wanted to be just like her.

I'D THOUGHT OF DEATH AS the end of life so often, but it had never occurred to me that everyone who dies is experiencing it for the first time. There's not a single soul alive who has died and knows how to do it just right. For that matter, no one's ever died a bad death and lived to tell about it either. "I screwed up last time, but this time I'll get it right"—nope, that's not how it works.

Once upon a time, when I didn't know things, I'd buy study guides with titles like *The Idiot's Guide to Basic Math* or *How to Read the Classics*. When I got pregnant, I bought *Pregnancy and Birth for First-Timers* and *Lamaze Technique for Dummies*. I participated in workshops, learned about giving birth and breathing technique, I practiced breathing in and out—*hee-whooo, hi-hi-whoooo*—until I got it down. I studied how to be pregnant just as I'd always studied whenever I wanted to learn something.

First, I wanted to know how our bodies work.

Lamaze taught me that instead of using the term "labor pains," we should say "contractions." Pain is subjective, and willpower can help us to control it. We also shouldn't close our eyes during contractions. You should stare pain directly in the face—if you don't, the pain will be even stronger.

Okay, but what about death?

Is there some other, more objective word we can use to refer to it? What transformations take place in the body when someone dies? What do people feel at the critical moment?

Once your heart stops working properly, your body stops expelling liquid, and fluid builds up in your lungs, then breathing becomes difficult, and you experience shortness of breath, you feel pressure on your chest, you begin to experience fear, wondering if you're dying, and you begin to pant—*haa haa haa haa* (Am I going to die?) *haa haa haa haa* (Am I going to die?) *haa haa haa haa* (Am I going to die?).

But at the moment of death, are you aware or not?

If you are, do you experience suffering?

What can you do to ease suffering?

Breathing techniques won't work. To breathe that way, you need willpower, and people lack the mental capacity for that when their energy is draining away. So what else can you do?

Drugs, I suppose. But I didn't know about them either. What kind of drugs are there? How do they ease the suffering? What side effects do they have?

Those are the kinds of things I wanted to know.

I started reading books about death from both East and West. I studied how people understood death, how they've talked about death.

One reason was because I wanted to talk with Tasogare-san about her own feelings about death. She'd been aging rapidly for several years and was suffering from severe Parkinson's disease and diabetes. She'd become disabled, unable to stand on her own. I realize that saying this might invite misunderstanding—she wasn't on death's doorstep exactly. Things hadn't gone that far, but given her illness and infirmity, I doubt a single moment went by when she wasn't looking at the very real prospect of her own demise. In short, I wanted to talk about death with someone who was facing it straight on.

Honestly, I wished I could've talked about death with Mom and Dad. But I couldn't. It was by trying to *avoid* looking at death square in the eye that Mom and Dad had survived so long. They avoided the subject, leaving them simply waiting, suspended in midair. I had the feeling that if I asked them about their real thoughts, they'd fall apart. That would be a terrible thing to do, cruel even.

So I decided to talk to Tasogare-san instead. She wouldn't beat around the bush. For decades, she'd been communing with the dead, interacting with them through poetry. I also suspected I might be the only person she could really tell what death's approach feels like—after all, we look alike, and I'm as persistent as she is. (Let me share a secret. Writing poetry is all about persistence, and nothing else.)

I devised a plan to talk with her. It might be hard, perhaps even embarrassing to have the conversation, but I wanted to speak frankly and hear her thoughts. Death, well, it's like this . . . I can't remember if it was toward the beginning of our conversations or the end, maybe even after we were all done, but at some point, she said something that really struck me: You'll never know about death until you try it.

SHE EMERGED SHAKILY FROM THE darkness at the back of her house. The scene looked vaguely familiar, then I realized I was remembering how the main character in *Ukai* shuffled onto the stage. Her posture, movements, and expression all reflected her obvious illness, but there was something of her in them too. Her head was shaking as she entered the living room, sat down, and turned on the electric heater behind her chair to warm the room.

We started with small talk of course. Tell me about those clothes you're wearing. You know that shop over there? What's good there?

We began to home in on our main topic. I mentioned a story I'd read from the Edo period. A body was spotted in a canal, and when it floated to one side, the people there prayed that the deceased would be reborn as a buddha before pushing the body back into the water. When it reached the other side, the people there pulled it out of the water and examined it. I had been surprised at how different the attitudes were on opposite sides of the same river. The poet explained, it takes incredible strength to lift a drowned body, plus, it was dangerous to drag a body onto the shore—it might spread disease and kill people.

We talked about a woman who spent all her energy trying to help her dying husband when the poet mentioned something remarkable. The dying man had said, it's lonely to die all by yourself, so I'm taking my partner along.

Taking his partner along? He didn't mean it in a bad way, did he?

No, nothing sinister. It's just that dying's so lonely.

Is loneliness the most distinctive characteristic of death?

To answer, she told me a story.

There's that famous passage in a Chikamatsu Monzaemon play in which a character laments, "what is left behind in this world, what is left behind in the night." But maybe a better way to describe that loneliness would be like this. When I went to visit my granny in the Goto Islands, she and the other old relatives used to see me off by saying, "It's sad to part with what's left behind." This was their way of saying, "I hate to see you go." Usually when you leave a place, you thank them for everything and tell them that you'll be back, but my granny and the other old ladies would tear up and say, "It's sad to part with what's left behind." What they really meant was "next time you come, we won't be around anymore."

I SAID, YOU'RE SEVENTY-EIGHT NOW. Do you think about your own death?

Every day, she answered.

In what way?

I want to die quickly.

Wow, really? (I got excited, we were coming to the heart of the matter.)

Yes.

But aren't you scared? It's not as if you've ever done it before.

I'm not scared.

What about pain and suffering?

I just don't want to experience pain.

What about sadness?

You mean about passing away? I'm not sad about dying at all.

Don't you want to hold on?

I've already lived long enough.

Really? You've spent enough time with your family?

Sure, I'm not scared. I could go at any time.

You think about it every day? When?

Every day. When I get up in the mornings, I think, I'm still alive.

What do you mean?

Hmmm, how should I put it? By living, I'm inconveniencing a lot of people. Me staying alive puts other people out.

You're not depressed though, right? You're happy, right?

Maybe I am depressed.

You think so?

Yeah, I do.

Really?

I've been depressed ever since I was little.

Since you were little? Has it gotten worse in the last several years? Or have you been in this same state your whole life?

Things get worse, little by little, little by little.

I see. Do you want to get better?

Well, that's not going to happen.

So this state is normal for you? You've wanted to die quickly ever since you were little?

Right.

If everyone was like you, we'd all be ready to look death in the face, no matter how old we are! (I laughed, trying to lighten the mood.) It wouldn't be at all frightening to take that last step.

Right. I just don't want any pain or suffering, but those aren't things you can really choose.

Suppose you felt really terrible. What would you do?

I'd want to end it quickly.

So I should tell your doctors then. I should tell them Tasogare-san wants to end it quickly. (I gave another laugh.)

I've already told them.

What did you say, specifically?

I don't want to keep on going when, for instance, I can't go to the toilet by myself anymore, or when there's no more real hope. I forbade them from putting me on life-support.

Where do you draw the line? When you can't go to the bathroom? When you're in a coma? When you can't eat anything anymore?

When I'm in a coma and can't go to the toilet.

But even if you were conscious, you might not be able to go to the toilet for whatever reason. What then? If you're conscious like right now and couldn't control yourself, you'd be ready to throw in the towel?

Right, I would.

But the law currently forbids doctor-assisted death.

That's true. I wonder if we can get a death-with-dignity law passed. I've been wanting to work with people to change the law.

Suppose someone can't go to the bathroom, it's still possible to live another thirty years if they're right in the head. Even without using the toilet.

I'd hate that.

Where do you draw the line? Twenty years? Ten years?

I draw the line at pain.

It's possible to live with pain, right?

I don't want that.

So the toilet is a big factor for you?

Yeah, I guess.

I suspect you'd get used to it though. About a year ago, my mother lost movement in both hands and legs, so she can't go to the bathroom or eat by herself anymore. But she's still conscious. Compared to the old days when she had a normal life, she's lost more than half her ability to follow what's going on around her. When she first became bedridden, she got depressed like you might expect. She lay there all day in a state of distraction. The look on her face said she wasn't feeling anything, she seemed to be wondering how she ended up that way, how things got that far, but after a while, her depression lifted. She told me that herself. Even so, she hasn't been able to go to the bathroom the whole time.

Back in the old days, folks used to say, I wish Buddha would come take me away soon, but you know, not everyone's life force is the same, sometimes life compels you to keep on living. I feel sorry for your mother, she must be suffering.

We don't have any choice, do we? We've got to keep on living until death comes for us, or until our life force peters out.

Right.

You're emotionally prepared for that?

Yeah, I am.

But I'm still not sure where to draw the line. You said if you can't go to the toilet, you don't want to be put on life-support. But what about right now? I imagine you're probably taking a bunch of pills every day for your illnesses. Would you stop taking them?

No way. I've got Parkinson's, right? It's really incapacitating to not be able to have full use of your arms and legs, so I take pills. I'm also taking diabetes meds too, but that's because the doctors tell me if I don't, I might have a stroke or something. That'd cause even more trouble for everyone around me, so I can't stop that either.

You wouldn't stop even if you couldn't go to the bathroom?

I'm not entirely sure. I guess I'd ask them not to feed me by artificial means. . . . Yeah, that's probably what I'd do.

Makes sense, provided you've sorted it all out clearly from the start.

Yeah, I don't want anyone to extend my life for no reason. I've told my doctors. It's not homicide if they stop providing assistance.

Do you think about suicide?

Yes, I do.

Have you ever thought about really doing it?

Countless times. I've tried countless times too.

I ASKED HER, DO YOU have a religion?

She responded, I don't really belong to any religion, certainly none of the typical ones from Europe or Asia, none of the usual Japanese sects, but I do think there's a life force in everything.

There are lots of Buddhist-like elements in your writing. Is that just a reflection of the beliefs where you were born and raised?

Yes, because Buddhism was what surrounded me.

You don't really use the language of Shinto.

I didn't have Shinto around me, so it didn't influence me—it's not that I dislike it, it's just that I don't have the language to talk about the world in Shinto terms.

What if you were born in a Christian environment?

In that case, my beliefs would probably be different. Christianity is monotheistic, so the down-to-earth kind of animism that I like so much wouldn't have been there to influence me.

The belief that Amida Buddha will take you away into the Pure Land is almost like a kind of monotheism.

During the early thirteenth century, when Shinran was around, he wanted to get rid of all the animistic elements in Japanese Buddhism.

So animism is what's really important to you, right? What's at the root of animism?

Life, the poet answered. And when I say life, I'm including all the plants and trees, all the life that fills the natural world. Starting with little things like small crabs—baby crabs, I mean—and microbes, all the way up. You know when the tide is out and you stand on the shallow shores, you can hear tons and tons of teeny, tiny voices coming from all kinds of living things around you? That's what I mean when I'm talking about life.

What do you feel toward them? Pity?

Pity? Harmony? I'm not sure what to say, but I feel like I'm just one of many small pieces of life. In one of his poems, Kenji Miyazawa says, "Body, scatter in the dust of the sky."

Kenji practiced Nichiren Buddhism. That's the kind of Buddhism your family practiced too, right?

Yeah, she nodded. But you know, I feel more like dust scattered on the seashore than dust scattered in the sky.

So what do death and dying mean to the dust itself?

Just becoming dust. Do the words "come back to life" appear anywhere in that poem? Does it say anything about what happens after scattering?

No, I told her. Kenji writes about cypress trees growing darker though.

I like the prospect of settling down and resting on a reed somewhere better than just scattering in the wind.

Is that what death means? Scattering? Finding a place to settle?

That's right. In the grass, stirred by the wind.

THAT BROUGHT US TO THE twelfth-century collection *Songs to Make the Dust Dance*. I knew that we were both fond of it, and I'd been hoping we could share our favorite poems with one another. As she put her glasses back on, the poet said, oh look! Your version is printed in such big letters, much easier to read than mine—mine's so small you need a magnifying glass. Bending over her tiny paperback edition, she cried, oh, look, look, here's the one.

Passing through this fleeting world
as I labor on the sea and mountains,
I am shunned by many buddhas—
what will become of me in the next life?

When I was young and wanted to die, I felt like I was being shunned by ten thousand buddhas—all the enlightened beings in the world, in other words. As a kid I often stuck up for people and argued on their behalf, but when I won, I'd feel bad. I'd criticize myself, thinking, you're such a know-it-all! My family were dedicated Buddhist practitioners. Every time something would happen, they'd start repeating *Namu Amida Butsu, Namu Amida Butsu*—All Praise to the Amida Buddha! So even when I was getting into arguments and doing something good, I was also misbehaving, acting like a brat. I did not yet understand what was meant by the old-fashioned expression "ten thousand buddhas," but I thought, if all the enlightened beings looked down at me, they'd think I was an awful human being. Winning made me feel like a jerk, and so I hated the entire world.

When you thought it, were you imagining just one buddha or many buddhas? What did they look like? Did you have an image of them in your mind?

It didn't matter which direction you looked,
There might be a buddha there before your eyes,
I suppose I imagined there were lots of them,

Lots of people who looked like beggars came to our house,
So my mother repeated to me again and again,
People like that go everywhere, you've got to treat them well,
They might be reincarnations of the great priest Kukai,
She told us giving them alms was the children's role,
She told us they'd hesitate to take from adults,
Most were Buddhist pilgrims, I suppose, but in any case,
We children would wrap money or rice in a lotus leaf,
Although I didn't know how to see the buddhahood in them,
We were taught to bow, nice and polite,
Because even a beggar could be an enlightened buddha.
Interesting, I answered. How did they tell you to bow?
The poet changed her posture and said, we slid our hands down as far as our knees, and then pressed our palms together in front of us.

And with that, she pressed her hands together in front of her, as if in prayer.

HANDS TOGETHER AS IF IN prayer. That was her answer.

Truly, this is the merit of coming and going.

Use it as the ability to help others.

Use it as the ability to help others.

I hadn't understood this passage from the end of *Ukai*. The footnotes had said, "The meritorious work a monk or priest performs on his or her wanderings through the world helps others become enlightened buddhas by acting as an external guiding force." Monks who passed by. Monks who passed through. I had thought receiving merit from Buddhist wanderers was something that didn't actually happen in the real world. The poet was the first to explain it to me. She showed me that people, places, and things are always connected to one another. What was important in her story was not the monks or even the coming and going, but the belief that no matter where you looked, there might be a buddha before your eyes. That's why it's important to continually do good deeds wherever you are.

I promise, I'll do them, I'll do them, I told myself.

IN THE COURSE OF OUR conversation, the poet read this poem from the same collection.

> Waking in the quiet at dawn,
> I wonder, my tears welling:
> having lived in this world of dreams,
> will I ever reach the Pure Land?

The poet commented, it sounds as if the speaker thinks it will happen, as if there's salvation even in the sadness of tears.

I wasn't entirely sure I agreed. I asked, doesn't that mean that the speaker might reach the Pure Land?

The "will I ever" sounds pretty hopeful, she said. "Will I" implies that it might happen.

I told her I'd read it more negatively. I'd thought it meant "I've lived such an irresponsible life until this point, how could I ever expect to reach the Pure Land?"

No, that's not right. Imagine, for instance, missing your parents or your ex-husband. Maybe the poem is talking about losing someone to death and never seeing them again, I'm not sure, but in any case, it's about being separated from your loved ones who will never return. Maybe you've lost a child, maybe destiny has dealt you a really bad hand. There're all sorts of possibilities. The line "I wonder, my tears welling" contains all those feelings. The poem mentions dawn because that's one of the chilliest moments of the day, right?

I nodded, it is.

The poet continued:

Spent in coldness and sadness,
My whole life has been fleeting like a dream,
Just as what lies before me, too, will soon be gone
I do not know whether I will become a buddha
Or whether a buddha will come to carry me away,
But all the sufferings of the present world will end,
And beyond that lies the Pure Land—
By thinking "will I ever reach the Pure Land?"
You may not be saved here and now,
But there is a path to salvation even so.

THAT LED ME TO A request I'd wanted to make.

There's a poem that you wrote in the form of a Buddhist sutra. When I read it, I felt like I got a sense of the world as you see it: there's this thing called "death" that's impossible to resist in the end, but there are more living things before us than dead things, there are tons of little living things all over the place, but the shadow of death always hangs over everything—that's what I took from it.

Since we're here now, will you read the poem for me? Would that be that okay?

She laughed, my goodness, I'm sure you could do it just as well, you're so good at reading. Still smiling, she started to recite the poem, which she'd written in classical Chinese. She had mentioned that long ago when she was young, she studied musical sutra recitation, so she'd set it to one of the melodies she remembered. Raised to the key of F, her voice stretched out, tough and thin, like mochi after a good firm pounding.

> Infinitely extending in ten directions
> Hundreds, thousands, millions, billions of generations
> Extending across incalculable measures of time
> So exceedingly deep and subtle
> In darkness without any light
> The plants and flowers flow on and on
> Blossoming far off in the distance—
> In a world of darkness, devoid of light
> An ocean of billions of lives not yet born

When she finished, she grew embarrassed and giggled. What an expression!

> The old woman with whom I'd spent those three hours
> Had inhabited a world separated by decades, perhaps even centuries from mine.
> She spent so much time trapping animals in the mountains and in the sea,

Scraping words together with bloodied hands and speaking,
Before falling infirm and sitting right before me.
However, as we sat facing one another in her room,
Her smiling face was so innocent that I was transported
To long ago, when my grandmother, my aunts, my mother
Led me by the hand to pray to Lord Jizo.
Transported, I was transformed into the dust of space and
time
And scattered to the winds before finally returning
To who I am now, here before you.
Up to this point, I have trapped animals in both mountains
and sea,
Scraped words together with bloodied hands and spoken
my mind,
And I will continue to do so from here on out.
One day, I too will grow old and infirm, and come here,
One step at a time, crossing a bridge to reach this side,
Where I too will sit with pen in trembling hand to sign my
work.

Because of my Parkinson's, my hand trembles so much that it's
hard to write.

How limiting, I said.

Yeah, it is. The poet said, there's so much I want to write that it's
piled up neck high.

As she said this, she signed my book in her trembling hand:

To Shiromi, from Tasogare Yukiko, "She who goes into twilight," late 2006.

NOTE FROM THE AUTHOR

I borrowed voices from various poems in *Songs to Make the Dust Dance*, the Noh play *Ukai* (The Cormorant Fisher), Chikamatsu Monzaemon's play *The Love Suicides at Sonezaki*, Kosan Yanagiya's classic rakugo tale *The Row-House of Careless Folks*, Rohan Koda's novella *Mystifying Tales*, Kenji Miyazawa's poetry collection *Spring and Asura*, personal communication from Michihiko Oikawa, Michiko Ishimure's novel *Cat's Cradle*, and from the book of conversations *Thinking Death*, which I wrote together with Michiko Ishimure.

Ito Grows Ill, a Bird Transforms into a Blossom, and the Giant Trees Stay Unchanged

SO WHAT NEXT?

The new year slowly rolled around.

I stayed in Japan until the New Year. Dad's helpers took three days off for the holiday.

My husband returned to California. That day in Sugamo when he was almost ripped to shreds, we went to Somei Hot Springs, and he soaked in the hot water, which brought him back to life. Thank goodness hot springs in Japan don't shut down around the Christmas holidays. My former *senpai* and her mother really turned things around for us. I flew back to Kumamoto with Aiko. Tons of things popped up to occupy me at the end of the year, but I rang in the New Year with Dad, Aiko, and Mom in the rehab clinic. After the helpers returned to work, I went back to California on the fifth.

How long would life go on like that? The time between my transpacific flights back and forth was gradually narrowing.

Time is a problem. Time is a huge problem. The time between my flights back and forth was growing shorter and shorter.

In the clinic, it appeared that nothing was changing for Mom, but really, she was quickly coming undone, and there was nothing much we could do.

The doctor said her kidneys were shutting down. He told us that after ringing out the old year. There's not a lot we can do to treat her, other than giving her an IV, and she doesn't want that at all.

I told the doctor I'd try to persuade her, but when I did, she immediately said she was afraid of needles, but a few moments later she admitted, it doesn't matter anymore, if things are hopeless, so be it.

I wanted to say, Mom, you might not care, but you'll be leaving Dad behind, and what will that mean for me? But I stopped myself. I thought, it is what it is, and I can't do anything about it. We need to let the dying die—if death was coming for her, then she should just go. I had to be okay with that.

I've put up with so much for so long. I don't need to go on anymore.

When Mom said that to me, what could I say?

Meanwhile, Dad was growing older and older too. No way to stop that, either.

Dad had given up smoking sometime around autumn. I'd kept my mouth shut about his smoking, as I knew it was hard. He'd been smoking for seventy years. When I asked him why he quit, he said, I did it as a sacrifice so my prayers would come true. When I asked what he'd prayed for, I immediately realized how stupid and insensitive the question was.

The time you spend in planes grows more and more unbearable the longer the flight is. You feel miserable, half-asleep, forced into unnatural positions, you want to move around, but there's no room. It's hell, and the worst part is you can't do a damn thing about it. All that time in a zombie-like state just makes it harder to recover from jetlag. Days go by, and it's still impossible to fall asleep and get a good rest.

The bone-dry, overly blue skies over my dazed head only made me feel smothered. I felt as though every bit of moisture was being sucked right out of my body. I began to feel incredibly hostile toward the air, sky, and sun—I'd only ever felt that sort of enmity toward another human being, and only on rare occasions. And to make matters worse, I underwent surgery.

YES, OCCASIONALLY I HAVE SURGERY too. Usually, I was the one taking care of my husband since he is twenty-eight years older, but he didn't have a monopoly on surgery. Maybe I should say I had a "procedure" instead of "surgery." It wasn't anything big. An unusual growth in my uterus. A precancerous growth caught at the very earliest stages. The doctor went in to remove it.

Two years earlier, my doctor had detected an abnormality while doing a routine exam for uterine cancer. Back when I was young, when I menstruated, I didn't just produce the normal amount of blood—it gushed out with so much force you'd think I was trying to drown someone. I sometimes joked that when I die, it'd be my uterus that killed me, so when an abnormality was discovered before my fiftieth birthday, I wasn't all that surprised. Here we go, I thought, it's coming.

The problem was that I was in California. The doctor gave me the diagnosis in English. On the phone. Using medical terms. When I asked him to say it again, he spoke in English. On the phone. Using medical terms. We weren't getting anywhere. The only words I understood were abnormal, HPV, and wart.

It was déjà vu.

A few years earlier, I had a urinary tract infection.

The doctor had used super-stiff medical terminology to give me the diagnosis that time too. The whole time he was talking, he was sitting across from me speaking English, but it didn't feel like I was interacting with a real live human being. His word choice left me completely in the dark. "After intercourse, after cleansing the region or urinating, or after defecating, one must cleanse from the anterior to the posterior." I told him to hold on, then tried to say what I thought he meant, substituting the vocabulary I was used to hearing. You're saying that after fucking, after washing or peeing, or after pooping, I should wipe from front to back? I fumed. That totally goes without saying—even a kindergartener knows that!

So two years ago, after hearing the alarming news from my gynecologist, I started looking around on the net, starting with the English terms "HPV" and "wart." In the process, I learned all sorts of new things.

Cancer of the cervix is a sexually transmitted disease. People who are sexually active are more likely to contract it. HPV is the same virus that causes genital warts.

This shook me up. I was as shaken up as if I'd had an unwanted pregnancy.

If I were to have uterine cancer, then it would be at the earliest stages. I'd heal. But genital warts? I didn't care if it was just a sexually transmitted disease or whatever. Yuck! No way I wanted that. I'm speaking as a woman here.

When women approach fifty, we slowly distance ourselves from dubious things like the pleasures of the floating world with its earthy pleasures, as well as the other passions that trouble the human heart. We still have those things, of course, but we stay quiet. We all have one or two secrets we can't share with our husbands.

I don't want to tell him mine. Nope, not come hell or high water.

But what about warts? The genital kind? They say it takes years for the virus to turn into a wart and grow cancerous. I considered all sorts of possibilities, but I couldn't come up with a way to talk to my husband about warts without hurting his feelings.

One of my female friends in Japan suggested I see a doctor next time I was in the country. Someone else suggested that a Japanese doctor might give me a different opinion. A third friend pointed out that if I got treated in Japan, my husband would never find out. These friends were warriors who had fought their way through life, knocking down every rogue problem that sprang up in their path.

So when I was in Kumamoto, I tried going to the small obstetric clinic where my second daughter was born, but I found it'd gone out of business. Everything's impermanent. When I went to a different clinic in my neighborhood and got checked out, the doctor said something even more terrifying: Since a doctor told you something seems abnormal in there, we probably should do a complete hysterectomy. As he probed me, I spoke to him from the opposite side of the curtain. Doctor, look, what I'm worried about right now is warts, do you see any? I felt around and pointed to the place where I thought something might be. We went back and forth like this for a while before he told me he couldn't find anything. I felt proud of myself for being so assertive. You can't speak openly to your gynecologist unless you've experienced dozens of internal examinations.

If there were no warts, then I wasn't going to worry. After all, HPV is a virus, and you can't tell who gave it to you, where you got it, or when. My husband and I were both on our third marriage, so we were well aware we each had plenty of experience before getting together. I decided if he ever doubted me and we got into an argument about sexually transmitted diseases, I'd just yell at him and call him a tight-assed, narrow-minded prude. And once I made that decision, it's funny how my worries disappeared completely.

There were no warts, but the cancer-causing virus was there, so I kept getting checked out over the next couple of years. Sometimes the doctor thought he sensed a bump, sometimes it seemed to have retreated. My primary caregiver in California was a patient man, but after a while, my requests for repeated examinations wore his patience thin. This could go on forever, he said, and then he suggested I have the problem spot removed. I made an appointment for the start of the new year. When the day came, I was so jetlagged I hardly knew if I was alive or dead. Just a few days earlier, Yokiko had postponed her return to college in the Bay Area and come back home to Southern California to be with us. I didn't have the time to fuss over my uterus, so I rushed off, had them scrape away at me, then immediately came back home.

Actually, the procedure was a lot like getting an abortion. You know, the old-fashioned way with curettage.

When I was young, getting my uterine walls scraped was no big deal. One time, after I came out of the anesthesia, I went into town, did a poetry reading, and even managed to grab a drink before heading home. But it's not that easy when you get to my age. Just getting a tiny little spot on my uterine wall scraped off left me dead tired. No, there wasn't any pain. No blood either, but I walk a ton, and getting up and down after that was no fun.

I was lamenting how decrepit I was becoming when, wouldn't you know it, my period appeared out of nowhere.

I can talk on and on about menstruation—it seems I always have more to say.

When I was a young woman, I thought of my periods as just a pain in the ass. When I became anorexic, they stopped altogether. Somewhere deep down, I felt they were intimately connected with me becoming a woman. That's why I hated them so much. But later, when I had my first daughter, I realized menstruation is linked to childbirth. I lost my annoyance and began to be grateful for my monthly visitor. Like I said before, my period came out in a big gush—a ferocious ball of energy taking the form of blood. I had a feeling deep inside that our uteruses aren't just for giving birth, but they also consume things, and one day mine might just gobble me right up.

When you reach this age, however, all the wise old ladies you rely on for advice are at different stages: some still have periods, some don't, and some are way beyond the whole thing altogether. Everyone told me, you had a child when you were older, so your uterus must be functioning just fine. You're still fresh as raw fish down there.

But my periods slowed down and started to lose their old ferocity. Everything was different from when they were at their most extreme—the flow, the space between cycles, the scent, and even the way they came on. In the old days, when I let myself go and had lots of sex between cycles, I was overcome with anxiety. I waited on pins and needles until I saw with my own eyes that my time of the month had returned. But there hadn't been anything for a while. So when my period returned after nothing for so long, I stood in front of the toilet and began to cackle out loud. *Whoo, ha, ha, ha, ha!* You can't even get past having to worry about getting pregnant? I laughed as if I was expelling a thousand years of pent-up resentment. Now, when did that happen again?

Let me see. Yes, when did that happen?

MY PERIOD CAME. IT OOZED slowly in a tired-out fashion, just like it had for the last few years. That was in the morning, five days after the scraping.

My husband was up and getting dressed sluggishly. I was still groggy in bed. Right then, the period suddenly sped up and came on with a vengeance, much like it had in the past. Feeling the liquid welling up, I sprang out of bed, ran to the bathroom, and straddled the toilet. Fresh blood spilled out, followed quickly by some bloody lumps.

I thought of a haiku by Soseki Natsume.

Quietly, tranquilly
Like a sea cucumber,
You gave birth

What had I given birth to? What on earth was going on?
I plunged my hand into the toilet to pull the lumps out. Shapeless

chicken liver. That's what they were like, but there were no chicken livers there—nor any human livers for that matter, other than the one inside me. The formless reddish-black clumps trembled on my palm.

Two lumps had come out with the blood. When I stood up, I could feel more inside sliding down toward my vaginal opening, and as I squatted again, they spilled out. This continued from nine o'clock until past noon. The blood came in fits and starts, and with it, lumps big enough to hold in my hand.

By the time the fourth or fifth one came out, I'd already realized something was seriously wrong. We got in touch with my doctor's clinic, but the receptionist just said she'd pass along the information to the doctor, and we didn't hear a thing. I'd often heard my husband grumble that the medical system in this country was rotten—rotten to the core, he'd say—and he was right. Before long, I was dizzy, nauseous, and covered in cold sweat, while the lower part of my body was drenched in so much blood you'd have thought I'd given birth. I called the clinic again, this time with a more urgent tone, and they told me to come in immediately. Goddamn it, they could have told me that the first time, I thought, but by then, I had no energy to complain. I collapsed right there on the floor.

My husband had been watching anxiously. I knew he needed to pick me up and take me to the emergency room, but he didn't have enough muscle despite his massive size. Twenty years ago, he could have picked up a bear, but now he was an old man. We didn't say it out loud, but we both knew that even if he tried to support me, there was no way he could get me up.

Incessant waves of nausea and dizziness washed over me. I tried to stand but couldn't, I tried to walk but couldn't. I threw myself toward the wall in front of me, and when I crashed into it, I stopped. I leaned on the wall with all my weight, then threw myself forward again toward the table a few steps away, and when I crashed into that, I stopped again. Using this method, I inched closer, step by step, toward the car outside.

My husband was upset of course, and when he's upset, he's a positive terror behind the wheel. He once told me he used to drive racecars—Jaguars and Mercedes (used ones, of course)—but I'd never seen him act like a racecar driver until that day. He might have driven used Jaguars and Mercedes back in the old days, but while I knew him, he'd had a steady stream of practical Japanese cars. Now that his wife was in crisis, however, he hopped into his Nissan Pathfinder and put the pedal to the metal. Just like the old days. Pathfinder—what a perfect name. Within moments, it found us a path to the ER.

My strength vanished as I tried to get out. I couldn't even take a step. I ordered my panicked husband to go inside and bring back a wheelchair. I stretched out my arms and legs and lay down in the parking lot.

A hot wind blew in from the desert just then, drying and heating up the whole world.

The sky was pure blue. The parking lot asphalt was on fire.

No doubt, a wildfire was burning somewhere.

The sunlight mercilessly pierced my flesh. I could hear its rays spearing me like skewers.

With much more of this, I'll end up dried up like beef jerky, I thought. The dizziness and nausea weren't letting up. One, two,

three, four Americans walked by. They pretended they weren't looking, but I cursed them as they passed. Shit. Damn. Take a good look.
Where do you find a homeless woman wearing pajamas and woolly
socks, clutching a Coach bag? You shitheads, you ought to be helping.
I heaped scorn on them, but I got the picture. I must've looked like
some old alcoholic Asian. They saw me and just walked on.

Eventually, some hospital employees ran over. They lifted me
into a wheelchair and rushed me into the ER. As three of them
worked to get me situated, I began to shake so hard my bones rattled.
Calm down, calm down, the doctor told me. I told him, I'm trying,
what should I do? Take a deep breath, he said. But that didn't stop
the shaking or the blood oozing from my vagina. I was losing feeling
in my fingers, my toes were getting cold, and my whole body was
shaking uncontrollably, even though it wasn't cold at all.

I thought of all the things I needed to do.

Make Yokiko happy.

Make Aiko happy.

Watch over Mom and Dad to the end, then stay with my husband to help him.

Yes, but what did I need to do right then?

Take Aiko to piano lessons at three o'clock.

Finish what I was writing and send it off by the deadline
tomorrow.

That's all? Just piano lessons and deadline?

Piano lessons and a deadline. Not a big deal. I'm lucky, I thought.
I was glad I didn't need to get on a transpacific flight anytime soon.
Really lucky. If I could just get through this, it didn't matter what
came next. But I had to deal with the bleeding first. I had to do that

on my own. I had to. I was the only one who could save myself. Me alone. Just me.

THE JAPANESE EXPRESSION "A DEMON succumbing to sunstroke" is used to describe a person with an iron constitution who falls prey to some small illness. The expression fit perfectly. I was a sunbaked demon all right, but of course, no one around me would have understood if I said that. I lay unconscious in bed for days. Afterward, I slept a lot, only occasionally crawling out of bed.

In the middle of my slow recovery, two misfortunes befell us.

The sparrow-dog was hit by a car and our cockatiel drowned in a cup of water. Poor Yokiko was there to witness both events. Even under the best circumstances, she was easily upset, but now she was so shaken that she sobbed out loud until she was hoarse and raspy.

Here's what happened to the sparrow-dog.

The front door was open. The door had never really shut properly. There were lots of times when one of us thought it was shut, but it wasn't really closed. This was one of those times. The sparrow-dog ran outside. Unfortunately, Yokiko happened to be out there on the other side of the road. It wasn't a place you'd ordinarily expect to find her, but that's where she was right then. Above, the sky was blue. The dog saw Yokiko and bounded into the road just as a car happened by. The car screeched, Yokiko screeched. By the time I rushed out, Yokiko was covered in the dog's blood, and she was sobbing. Her voice drowned out the dog whimpering in her arms. We sped off to the vet. One of his legs had been smashed to smithereens, and his flesh was badly torn. Even so, the vet managed to save him.

I was presented with a bill that left me dumbfounded, but solemnly and silently, I paid. What else could I do?

Afterward, the dog was forced to wear a collar that made him look like some Elizabethan gentleman. His shattered leg was wrapped around and around with bandages, leaving him with only three paws to hop around on. Our other dog, the shepherd, seemed to feel some responsibility for the disaster that had transpired under her watch, and she skulked in the corner. Yokiko got so caught up in nursing the sparrow-dog back to health that she began to forget her own troubles. Meanwhile, I was suffering from a guilty conscience.

On my most recent pilgrimage to Lord Jizo, I had prayed to the smoke. I prayed for Yokiko, I prayed for Aiko, I prayed for my oldest daughter who was off god-knows-where, I prayed for my father, I prayed for my mother, and, yes, I even prayed for my husband. However, it hadn't even occurred to me that I might need Jizo's help for my dogs too. Maybe that was why the disaster had occurred. I swore the next time I went, I'd be sure to buy two more bundles of incense, throw them into the rising smoke, and pray for the health and well-being of my dogs too.

But to tell the truth, there was a part of me that felt the sparrow-dog had acted as a substitute for Yokiko. Perhaps it was Lord Jizo, perhaps it was the smoke—in any case, whatever it was had remembered the sparrow-dog, even though I hadn't included him. It had decided that it was okay to hurt the poor dog if that would alleviate Yokiko's suffering.

I had given Yokiko the substitute amulet I bought on that trip, and she had been carrying it ever since. I imagine that if I unfolded it and looked at the little image of Jizo inside, I would find him completely transformed: covered in blood, leg smashed to smithereens, and flesh badly torn. Still, I couldn't bring myself to check.

The sight of the sparrow-dog limping around the house was a constant accusation: I served as a scapegoat—I was the substitute that took away your daughter's suffering. I wanted to put my hands together in supplication and pray to him, but I couldn't predict what my husband might say if he saw me do that. So I held back.

The sparrow-dog narrowly escaped death, but the cockatiel wasn't so lucky.

Cup, water, cockatiel. They were always together, but who knows why that day and that day alone, an accident took the bird's life. All I can say is that fate must have been working against the poor thing.

Yokiko discovered the dead bird and began sobbing again. Well, it would be more accurate to say she started whimpering, but by the time she ran into the living room to find us, the bird was already upside down in the cup, dead as a doornail. Its long tail feathers were sticking out. My husband pulled it out and put its limp body on a spread-out towel.

Yokiko sobbed so hard that her whole body shook. As I held her in my arms, I couldn't help feeling how ridiculous the situation was—it had happened so suddenly that I got angry at the bird. And then I realized, damn it, I hadn't thought to pray for it to Jizo either.

We'd lived together for years. When I'd come back into the house from outside, the bird would greet me with a long drawn-out whistle, and when we were eating, it would hop onto the table as if it wanted to eat with us. It would perch on our shoulders and lower its head, inviting us to stroke it, but when we reached out our fingers, it would open its eyes in anger, squawk with mouth open wide, and peck us. No, the dumb bird never accepted us as part of its family. Now, however, I found myself thinking only about the good memories—about how we took care of it and how cute it was—even though those memories were probably outnumbered by the times it pecked us.

Later, Aiko quietly told me that when we buried it, its body was stiff and sort of cold.

When we had showed Aiko the bundle and told her the bird had died, she didn't cry at first. She only started to cry when she took its dead body in her hands. As I was digging the hole to bury it, Yokiko and Aiko were in constant tears. Where was all their sadness coming from? Meanwhile, their fifty-year-old mother didn't shed a tear.

I'll tell you an embarrassing secret. I can't stand touching dead things.

I may be a whiz at catching live animals, and I can touch any living creature without getting creeped out, but strangely, when a body dies and stops moving, I get spooked and can't bring myself to touch it.

Corpses frighten me. They're scary. Just getting near them wigs me out.

I'm not even sure what I'm frightened of. I got away with never touching the dead cockatiel at all. I watched my two daughters hold and stroke it as they cried. I watched them bury it in the ground, weeping. I wondered, when Mom or Dad finally dies, will I be able to touch them? If I couldn't bring myself to do it, I'd be in trouble.

We planted a clump of euryops on top of the bird's grave. Euryops adapt and spread like weeds where we live. It grew like a little bush and produced a continual string of blossoms the same color as the cockatiel beneath it. I thought, the shit's going to hit the fan. My husband was watching our little group and looked completely fed up. Death, according to him, is nothingness. It's not possible for a dead bird to come back as a flower, but for Yokiko, Aiko, and me, birds could transform into blossoms. We had no trouble whatsoever accepting that idea.

I had seen plants slowly die more times than I could count, but the bird died suddenly. What about people, then? A poem by Chuya Nakahara starts like this: "The child who in the cold wind of midday took the sparrow in its hand to love, come nighttime, suddenly passed away." In the poem, it's not the bird that suddenly dies but a child. These days, however, people all die slowly like plants.

After the bird's funeral, when I was left alone, I washed the cockatiel's cage. As penance for not touching the dead bird, I gave the cage a good scrubbing, washing away all the shit and downy feathers stuck to it. I spread the remaining bird food in the garden as an offering, but before the wild birds that are always flying around our garden arrived to eat it, our big shepherd bounded outside and gobbled it all down.

Mom's suffering, Dad's suffering, my husband's suffering.
Yokiko's suffering, my suffering.
Unable to withstand the continuous suffering of our family,
Both the sparrow-dog and the cockatiel
Offered themselves up as substitutes.
When I said this, Yokiko nodded vigorously.
Yokiko, me, the dog, and the bird—

Four of us fell on hard times, but only one of us died,
Leaving the other three of us still alive.

When I said this, Yokiko nodded vigorously again.

EVENTUALLY, A CALL CAME from Dad.

I was overdue for a trip to Japan. I was thinking I ought to go back again soon, but I couldn't motivate myself after everything that had happened with Yokiko and me. But I had been worried about Dad. I had noticed the tone of his voice had been sinking. His voice had sunk so far that it seemed thick and stagnant at the bottom of the telephone receiver. I summoned up as much enthusiasm as I could muster and spoke in a bright voice to show him he could count on me for support.

What are you up to?

I know this is another way of asking how he was doing, but it was what I'd settled on when starting a conversation with him. I thought this was better than "What's happened?" which didn't quite capture the right nuance for a telephone call that had no real objective other than to check in. So I started all three of my calls to him each day this way, even though I knew Dad wasn't up to anything at all.

Dad's voice was slow. *Your mo-ther . . .*

She says she wants to come home, I spoke to the doctor today, I said her legs aren't going to get any better, so he should just let her come home, I was thinking we could have one of the home helpers help us out, she's got insurance, they have her down as bedridden so insurance ought to help, but if she doesn't come home, she'll be there for the rest of her life. Dad spoke slowly in a long, deliberate run-on sentence like an old-time storyteller, but his voice sounded deflated.

But Dad, it's a huge burden to care for someone you live with—that'll be incredibly hard on you.

I gave a detailed description of all the tribulations I predicted he might face.

If that's all there is to it, I'll be fine, I've just got to do it, right? Dad spoke as if he was fantasizing about some city of the future.

But Dad, I've heard all these stories about a husband or wife who gets exhausted caring for their aging spouse—sometimes they even end up killing their partner and themselves.

I gave a detailed description of a couple of different recent cases where that very thing had happened. They had caused quite the sensation.

I'll be fine, I've just got to do it, right? As if from his distant futuristic city, Dad spoke robotically.

Dad seemed, at least on the surface, to understand everything that had been going on all along, but it wasn't until that day that he finally really understood Mom's legs were never going to heal. Mom's legs had changed color and shape so much they looked like dim sum chicken feet. Like they had been boiled. It was impossible to imagine the blood flowing through them again and suddenly bringing them back to life. How could someone look at them and still not understand? I'd known for over a year there was no hope for her legs. There was something else I understood too—Dad might have realized this just now, but before long, he probably would lose his grasp on the situation again. He would look at the same thing but not see it. He wouldn't understand. He wouldn't take things in.

His ability to think had diminished with age. Dementia was setting in.

The next time you come, talk to the doctor, I'll say that you'll talk to him next time you're here, you know, he keeps talking about a bed or something, all kinds of people talk about all sorts of things, but I can't really follow. Dad was obviously irritated. Then he fell silent for a few moments, and in a hushed voice, he made a confession.

You know, I've been thinking of taking up smoking again.

I sighed. On my end of the phone, I readjusted my sitting position. Even though you went to all the trouble to quit?

I think I'm depressed, when people talk to me, I can't even lend them a friendly ear, they tell me to talk to people and make a decision, then they go on and mumble something I don't understand, I don't know what kind of consulting I'm supposed to be doing, plus I don't know when you're coming home next, so there's nothing I can really do, I've got tons of reasons to be depressed.

There's not being able to smoke. There's your mother. There's me.

I know that smoking won't change anything,

But if I light up a cigarette, smoke will come out,

Maybe just watching the smoke rise will improve things somehow.

IN FEBRUARY, WHEN THE MOUNTAINS were at their coldest, my family did something we'd talked about for a long time. We finally went to Sequoia National Park.

This was the trip we had postponed during the autumn break in

October, but it was a different season now. There'd be no one else out there deep in the mountains, no one even coming out to enjoy the snow.

We crossed Los Angeles, went down a mountainside into the valley below, then cut across the valley. There were fields of grapevines that had just started coming back to life, almond orchards that would bloom profusely later in the spring, orange and lemon orchards that never seemed to change. We drove to the base of the Sierra Nevadas, and as soon as we entered the park, there was snow. We managed to get the snow chains we'd brought along onto the tires, and we began climbing the twisting and turning hills at the sluggish pace of ten or twenty miles per hour. The forest was covered in snow. There were deep valleys, rocks sticking out, and snowy hills in the distance. The color of the sky was so luxuriously rich, it took my breath away. We kept on driving and driving, still without reaching the giant trees.

Finally, not long before the sun was getting ready to set, we found ourselves in front of them. They were thousands of years old. Meanwhile, my husband and I were bundled up in old ski outfits that probably hadn't been used for forty years.

The giant trees stood before us.

There were fences around them to protect their roots. The enclosures continued through the forest of massive trees. The snow that had gathered on the ground had frozen over. Here and there, we saw saplings and young trees growing. Dead trees had fallen, leaving great gaping holes in the earth. There was even a tree that had split in two and died but remained standing. We found burn marks on the trunks of the giant trees. A thick coat of bright yellowish-green moss covered the trunks of some of the younger trees—although I say younger, they were probably centuries old too.

The giant trees survived. They lived right up to the moment of their death, and only then did they finally die.

I said to my husband, at times like this, a desire wells up inside me to wrap the trees in straw and white paper with sacred marks (I wanted to use the word *shimenawa* to describe the things that Shinto priests put around sacred trees, but that wouldn't mean anything to him, so I didn't even try), and I want to put my hands together and pray (I wanted to use a word that was more solemn, like worship, but I didn't know it in English).

I see you are an animist after all, he sighed. He was an atheist and proud of it, so it sounded like he was completely looking down on me. Maybe I was predisposed to hear it that way, but even so, he made it seem like he assumed atheists stood high above all other people, as if they were proudly overturning all of Judeo-Christian civilization. Hadn't he learned his lesson in Sugamo when he got mobbed by the throngs of old ladies who didn't share his views? I was fed up.

I wanted to harass him. Why do you say that? What do you think when you see these?

His answer was humble. I just think. I think about how teeny-tiny I am.

I teased him. People call that the beginning of religion. But my husband didn't believe, couldn't believe in anyone or anything, he only believed in himself and put his ego at the center of everything. He denied it vehemently, but I didn't want to lose.

I said to him, I recognize that

I'm just a small bit of dust in this world,
I believe in this great, gigantic existence,
I believe in the moss and the green,
I believe in the spirits that inhabit every single grain of rice,
I believe in the goodness of people and the goodness of dogs,
I believe in smoke,
I believe in substitutes that remove the thorns of suffering,
I believe, I know that
I will be one with this great, gigantic existence,
One small particle of dust scattered in this world.

AIKO DIDN'T SEEM TO CARE about the trees at all. She walked around saying, wow, super, wow, darn it's cold, but she didn't seem to be seeing or thinking anything. Let's go, I saw a sign over there, it said something about snow sports, let's go, snow sports over there, you bought this for me, I want to use it, use this! She was carrying a plastic sled we'd just bought. She dropped it and put her foot on it. Not knowing what else to do, we went to another part of the forest where there were frozen picnic tables. The only living things in sight were the clusters of giant trees. On the surrounding slopes, we could see tracks in the snow where other people had been sledding.

Aiko had to walk along slick, slippery paths to get to a good sledding slope. She didn't seem the least bit frightened. She climbed up the path over and over, then quickly slid right down to the bottom. There were giant trees there too. They weren't thousands of years old, they were still young—only a few centuries old—and were covered with moss. Rivulets of water flowed through gaps in the snow.

Small, crushed plants grew between the chunks of hardened snow. Here and there, we saw the stumps of cut trees.

There was a bump on the slope, piled high with snow and ice. Aiko's sled hit it, and she flew into the air. Whoa! she screamed, and as the sled slowed down, she ran into one of the stumps. Yokiko, who had been watching over her, swooped her up in her arms as the sled finally came to a halt.

That scream. That laughter.

I'm alive, I'm alive, I'm alive, I'm alive. That was what she was saying to me. No other way to interpret it. Aiko was saying that to me.

Just hearing it, I felt as if my whole being was being shaken violently awake.

I looked up. Ouch. A few minutes ago, I'd fallen and hurt my neck. It hurt. My creaky neck was throbbing. How unfair. I'd slipped and fallen, striking my shoulder, back, forearm, neck, and wrist hard on the snowy ground. Aiko and Yokiko were running about as fast as they could. Even my husband, who was shaky on the most ordinary roads, was trotting along happily like a bear, as if there was nothing there to fear at all.

I had a thought. Putting up with the pain in my throbbing neck, I looked up. I couldn't see the treetops, but I could see the green needles and moss. I tilted my head back further. I still couldn't see the tops of the trees, but I could see the blue sky above.

Yokiko called me. Aiko called me. I answered and turned around. Ouch. The pain in my neck called out to me too.

Right then, the two of them slid down the long, long slope, seated together on the sled. A high-pitched squeal. *Oh boy!* A shout of joy. *My gosh!* A groan. *No way!* Another shout of joy. *Oh my god!*

I felt myself shake again. I shook until I felt myself. *I exist. Here.* Meanwhile, they were shouting themselves hoarse. *I'm alive, I'm alive, I'm alive, I'm alive! I'm alive, I'm alive, I'm alive, I'm alive!*

NOTE FROM THE AUTHOR

I borrowed from a poem in *Songs to Make the Dust Dance*: "Was I born to play? / Was I born to frolic? / As I hear the children playing, / even my old body starts to sway." I've also borrowed voices from the novel *Two People Riding* by Toshiko Hirata, *What Did You Eat?* by the chef Nahomi Edamoto, *Memories and Other Things* by Soseki Natsume, the story "Drum of Flame" by rakugo raconteur Shinsho Kokontei, the poem "Memories of a Winter Day" by Chuya Nakahara, and *Spring and Asura* by poet Kenji Miyazawa.

Translator's Acknowledgments

HIROMI ITO AND I ARE deeply grateful to the judges at the University of Chicago who chose this book to receive the William F. Sibley Memorial Subvention Award for Japanese Translation. This grant helped make it possible for Stone Bridge Press to publish this book as the first volume in their new Monkey imprint, associated with the annual anthology *MONKEY New Writing from Japan*.

WHEREVER ITO "BORROWED VOICES" FROM the late twelfth-century collection *Ryojin hisho* (Songs to Make the Dust Dance), I have cited the translations by Yung-hee Kim in *Songs to Make the Dust Dance* (University of California Press, 1994), provided the poems had a translation in Kim's study. The translation of the passage from *Ukai (The Cormorant Fisher)* is cited from Arthur Waley, *The No Plays of Japan* (George Allen & Unwin, 1921). The passages written by Genshin are a slightly modified version of the translation by A.K. Reischauer published as "Genshin's Ojo Yoshu: Collected Essays on Birth into the Pure Land" in *Transactions of the Asiatic Society of Japan*, 2nd series, vol. 3 (December 1930). The translations of Chuya Nakahara come from my manuscript of Chuya translations, which I have undertaken with a generous 2020 grant from the National Endowment for the Arts. The short, in-line quotation from Franz Kafka comes from the Critical Edition of *The Metamorphosis*, translated by a translator I particularly admire, Susan Bernofsky (W.W. Norton & Company, 2014).

Only a couple of the other works that Ito has cited in this book, such as those of the poet and short-story author Kenji Miyazawa, have existing English translations. However, since the quotations were extremely short and less central to her text, I have not gone to those translations to locate and borrow specific language from them. Instead, I have translated Ito's "voices" directly from the Japanese.

FIRST AND FOREMOST, I'D LIKE to thank Peter Goodman, the visionary publisher at Stone Bridge Press in Berkeley. Many thanks to *MONKEY* editors Ted Goossen, Motoyuki Shibata, and Meg Taylor and copy editor Ruth Gaskill. Thanks as well to David Buuck from *Tripwire* and Gerald Maa and C.J. Bartunek from the *Georgia Review* for their passionate support of Ito's work. Earlier drafts of excerpts from this book were first published in *MONKEY, Monkey Business, Georgia Review,* and *Tripwire*. It was through their encouragement and support that I slowly worked through this long, complicated, but extremely rewarding book.

I also am grateful to the translator-scholar Irmela Hijiya-Kirschnereit, who produced the German translation of this same book, and to the Japanese literature scholars Reiko Abe Auestad and Tomoko Aoyama, who are both passionate fans of this work and provided helpful suggestions.

David Feaster was the first person to read this book in its entirety in English, and I thank him for his suggestions. I also thank the brilliant students at Western Michigan University who read the manuscript for this book in my Japanese literature seminar in spring 2021. Their thoughts, questions, reflections, and suggestions helped a great deal as I polished the manuscript.

This translation is dedicated to Ito herself, who read drafts of the chapters (despite her protestations that she cannot read English well) and encouraged me to find creative solutions, including ones that might depart somewhat from the original, to capture her distinctive humor. She also encouraged me to figure out ways to work into the text essential cultural information that might be unfamiliar to non-Japanese readers. She is not only a writer with a voice like no one else's, but also a dear friend and confidante who has played an important role in my own life.

ABOUT THE AUTHOR AND TRANSLATOR

HIROMI ITO came to national attention in Japan in the 1980s for her groundbreaking poetry about pregnancy, childbirth, and female sexuality. After relocating to the U.S. in the 1990s, she began to write about the immigrant experience and biculturalism. In recent years, she has focused on the ways that dying and death shape human experience. English translations include *Killing Kanoko* and *Wild Grass on the Riverbank*.

JEFFREY ANGLES is a writer and professor of Japanese language and literature at Western Michigan University. He is the first non-native poet writing in Japanese to win the Yomiuri Prize for Literature, a highly coveted prize for poetry. His translation of the modernist classic *The Book of the Dead* by Shinobu Orikuchi won both the Miyoshi Award and the Scaglione Prize for translation.